WHAT PEOPl

MW00795031

"As a panoramic portrait of Reagan's America seen through the eyes of Danny, an everyman factotum who's a precursor to the gig workcr, Shufflcrs is quietly incendiary and has never been more timely. ...Frank Haberle's novel in stories remind us how close we all are to falling through the rotting floorboards of the America we refuse to see."

—Leland Cheuk, author of *No Good Very Bad Asian*

"Frank Haberle is a storyteller's storyteller—down-to-earth, subtle, humble, but confident when it counts. In Shufflers he blends experience, craft, wisdom and wit to put forth a collection of tales that will move you emotionally when you read it—and mean even more to you after you read it."

—John McCaffrey, Author of *Book of Ash* and *Two-Syllable Men*

"I love Frank Haberle's stories and will dive into a new one any chance I can get—face first, off a cliff, without looking. ...Open this collection anywhere and become an instant fan."

— M. M. De Voe, author of *Book & Baby*

"I yearn for a world that embraces eccentrics and perhaps deems thcm prophets. Frank Haberle's skillfully rendered stories remind us to pay attention to damaged individuals, renew our capacities to have spontaneous experiences, and remember the what-the-hellishness of youth."

— Lori Kent , Hunter College, Founder of Code Vert Arts

SHUFFLERS

A novel in stories by
Frank Haberle

Flexible Press
Minneapolis, Minnesota 2021

Print ISBN: 978-1-7364033-2-7
eBook ISBN: 978-1-7364033-3-4

Flexible Press LLC
Editors William E Burleson
Vicki Adang, Mark My Words Editorial Services, LLC
Cover via Canva
Photos via Unsplash. Thank you to:
Cover: from a photo by Oziel Gómez
A Huge Mechanical Spider: Khachik Simonian
A Ripping, Puffing, Rattling Noise: Zhenyu Luo
That Box-Like Contraption: Alex Kristanas
Deep, Hydraulic Whispers: Tim Oun
A Green and Glacial Sea: Thomas Lardeau

THANK YOU

Thank you to my family—Joan, Eirnan, Alin, and Mariel—for your patience and presence.

Thank you to my brothers and sisters—Mary Patricia, Ernest John, Therese, Anne, Romey, Tom, and Sean—for your kindness and resilience.

Thank you to the storytellers of the Moving Pen for your kind ears and courageous voices.

And to you, you back there—you who let me crash on your couch or bought me a pack of smokes or picked me up in a bus station—thank you for sending me on my way.

CONTENTS

PART I

香港
男女理髮廳

A HUGE
MECHANICAL
SPIDER

STICKMAN

The old neon sign blinks "Billiards, Billiards, Billiards."

The sign hangs above twin steel doors that are dented from kicks, more from the inside than out. Inside the doors is a wide staircase with tintype walls. At the top of the stairs, when Danny turns the corner, he enters a huge parking lot of old pool tables with ripped, stained felt. Wire-strung woodchips keep score over each table. The cues, lined up in racks on the walls, are all warped. The balls are chipped and take weird rolls down the rutted surfaces. But when they fall into the leather pockets, the balls make a gentle "poof" sound, like they have been dropped into a soft leather mitt.

Sitting at a podium is a guy named Charlie. Charlie has a head like a cue ball and mismatched burnsides starting behind a huge pair of ears, which make him look funny, but he isn't. "Twenty-eight," he says when Danny walks in, handing him a tray of chipped balls, or "Twenty-nine." "Eight dollars," he says when Danny hands him the tray two hours later, or "Seven dollars." That's it from Charlie. Next to the podium is a coke machine. For fifty cents, if Danny pushes the Fanta Orange button, out pops a frosty can of Schlitz. "Here," Charlie says, handing Danny a small paper bag that he has to keep the Schlitz in, because drinking on the premises is forbidden. Smoking is not, and the place is filled with smoke, even when nobody is there.

*

Today Charlie puts Danny at table twenty-eight, next to a hissing radiator, right under a huge picture window. Danny picks a cue, racks, and breaks. The balls scatter across twenty-eight's dusty surface, finding ruts and creases and a slow hill down the right bank, and a ball falls. It's a stripe. Danny doesn't like stripes. This isn't going to go well, he thinks.

Danny looks up at the table thirty-one, and in the shadows, he sees Stickman, leaning on his cue, staring down at a guy on the street. Danny lights up a smoke and watches. The guy outside is wearing a "Frankie Says RELAX" T-shirt under a cheap leather jacket. He is angrily pulling the tape from a cassette out of a Walkman. He looks for a second at the handful of cassette tape in one hand and the Walkman in the other. He stuffs the brown tape into a pocket and throws the Walkman into a garbage pail. He waves down a taxi and disappears up Fourteenth Street toward Union Square. Stickman keeps staring at the place that was occupied by cassette-guy.

"Hey, man," Danny says. He never calls him Stickman, not in front of him. "What are you doing?"

"I'm having a face attack," Stickman says without looking up.

"Oh," Danny says. "Cool." He takes a slug of Schlitz and hits a bank shot. Then he walks the dog on the eleven. It's all looking up, Danny thinks, but then he gets stuck on a rail behind the three. Before he considers the consequences, he's got the eight ball dribbling into the side pocket for a scratch.

Danny drains his beer can and crumples it, bag and all, and puts it under the table. He looks over at the Coke machine, then at his neighbor.

"Hey, man. You want a Schlitz?"

"No," Stickman says, still staring down at the street, fixated. "No," he repeats in that skinny New Orleans voice of his. "Not now, man. I'm almost finished here."

"Suit yourself." Danny buys two more Schlitz from the machine. Without looking up, Charlie hands him two more bags. He racks again and breaks for solids, and this goes much better. In three rounds Danny runs the next-to-last ball into the side pocket. When it falls in the mitt—poof—Stickman walks over.

"Hey, man," he says. "Wow. You ever have yourself a face attack?"

"Now what exactly are you talking about," Danny asks. He banks the eight ball off the far rail—careful, because Stickman is watching, to tap the desired pocket beforehand with the tip of his cue—and the ball rolls submissively in. Poof.

"Well, it's like this," he continues. "A face attack is when you are walking around this here city all day, and you see all these faces, and your brain just can't process it, man, and then it's like all them people have plastic masks on, with long rubbery noses and eyes like coals and skin like dripping wax and stuff."

Stickman pulls a bottle of something out of his pocket and sucks on it mindlessly. When he stops, the whole pool hall smells like licorice. "That's what a face attack is," he says, looking over his shoulder at the picture window, the masses of bodies, the orange glow of river light bouncing off the face of the municipal building across the street. "Face attacks," he says, and he shudders. "Man. They give me the Jimmies."

They walk out together, Danny and Stickman, and go a few blocks east on the avenue. At a cross street, they start to part ways—Danny for a bar to sit alone in. Danny will pick a bar, pretend he's waiting for a friend, drink five or six drinks, pretend his friend never shows up, and head for the subway home.

"So I was wondering," Stickman says, "what you might be doing this evening."

"I'm doing nothing," Danny says.

"Well, it's like this," Stickman says. "I'm going over to visit my sister. You remember my sister?"

Danny met Stickman's sister once. He was walking one late summer night past some street vendors. Stickman, standing by a vendor, waved him over. He was talking to a girl who was selling jewelry. What Danny remembers about her was that she looked like a cat without whiskers. Her jewelry was made mostly of bones. She was Stickman's sister. She didn't speak to Danny or look at him when Stickman introduced him. She started railing into Stickman pretty hard, something about losing her keys or bringing her stuff back to his apartment or something. Danny stood there awkwardly for a few minutes, and then he left.

"Yeah," Danny says. "I remember your sister. Well, yeah, of course I remember her. Everybody remembers your sister."

They stop on the corner. Stickman tries to hitch up his pants, which is kind of ridiculous—he is little more than a skeleton and has nothing to hitch his pants to. He lights a cigarette, cupping his hands, then offers one to Danny. "Well, the thing is, I got this little old bookshelf I got to bring over to her house. You think you could give me a hand bringing it over there?"

"Huh," Danny says, taking a slow drag of the cigarette, its embers glowing warmly just under the tip of his cold nose. "A bookshelf, huh?"

"Oh, she'll feed us a big dinner if we go over there now. She cooks jambalaya every Sunday night, all shrimp and andouille sausage and stuff. Yes, sir. Ho, boy."

"Sure." Danny hasn't eaten all day. "Sure, I'll help you. Where does she live?"

"She's just over the river there, right over that there bridge."

"Bridge? What bridge?" But Stickman has already started walking, and Danny follows him.

Stickman stops in front of the steel fence of a city graveyard. He looks up at the unlit windows of an apartment building behind the graveyard, its back windows and fire escapes and laundry lines and pipes and wires all sticking out over the graves.

"Well, that there's my place," he says. "Give me a hand, will you?"

Danny helps him push a steel gate inward, revealing a little path between the gravestones that leads to a cellar door. Stickman pulls on the cellar door, and it swings open. They enter a pitch-black basement. Danny stumbles through darkness, his arms out in front of him. Stickman says "shush," and then "shush now." He pulls on a light cord; a rickety staircase appears. Danny follows Stickman up three flights. He jiggles a key into a door lock. The door pops open. They are standing in a bare room. Two windows. No curtains. No furniture, except for a big, empty bookcase maybe ten feet tall.

"There she be," Stickman says. "Now all we got to do is get her back down there, the way we came."

"Can't we just take it out through the front door?"

"Now don't be ridiculous," Stickman says. "If the landlord sees us walking out the front door, he's going to start asking questions."

"What questions?" Danny asks. But Stickman is already taking the bookcase down and resting one end on his shoulder. Danny picks up the other end. It's heavy, and he is not in the best of shape.

"There now," Stickman says, leading the bookcase and Danny back down the narrow staircase.

Back out on the street, Stickman makes a hard right on Avenue A. Barely dodging a cascade of traffic, they cross Houston Street and wind left and right through streets crowded with boxes of coats, sweaters, T-shirts. Stickman plunges down a subway station entrance, and Danny follows with his side of the bookcase.

"You can't take that thing on the train," the token booth clerk says without looking up from his paper.

They walk back up to the avenue, and Stickman tries to wave down a cab.

"You can't take that thing in a taxi," one driver slows down to yell at them.

They stand the bookcase up on the corner. Stickman offers Danny another cigarette.

"Well," Danny says, "we gave it our best shot."

"Well," Stickman says after a minute, flicking his cigarette into the avenue. "I guess we're just going to have to walk it there."

The blocks pass by, and the city and night part and streak around Danny. Faces float by, but they stare straight ahead, icy and emotionless. On long streets, kids in snorkel jackets run around them and under the bookshelf. "Come on, mister," they yell, "let me ride in it!" Along the way, Stickman tells Danny a very long story about growing up in a southern city— his father was a Romanian prince, or something, who escaped the Nazis, or something, and taught tennis to fat rich children at a private club while his own children went hungry—and Stickman and his sister were taken in by the poor family next door who fed them plates of jambalaya every Sunday and taught them how to catch crayfish. Or something. Danny fades in and out of the story. He is thirsty and thinking of his next beer more than he is thinking about jambalaya.

But then Danny starts thinking of the sister, the one who looks like a cat. Maybe she was just cranky that day. She has good reason to be hostile at first, Danny thinks, with a childhood like that. But she'll be so happy to get this bookshelf. She'll be so surprised that Stickman and his big friend carried it all the way to her house, all the way across the river. She'll invite Danny to stay for dinner, and as the three of them sit around her table, eating a big jambalaya dinner, she'll tell Danny all about their childhood and their father and the Nazis and the tennis and the poor crayfish family, and Danny will listen really closely to her. It will be the start of a new and different time in Danny's life, when he starts to hang out with real people. He will have real friends, like Stickman and his sister, and he won't be a shuffler anymore, and he won't hang out in bars alone pretending to wait for imaginary friends.

"Hold up here now a minute," Stickman says. They have reached the foot of a metal staircase climbing to a walkway over a bridge. He re-hitches up his pants. Again with the pants. He's starting to look crazy. He's breathing heavy. Danny knows that he is too—even in the March cold, he's sweated out all of the beer—but he's not giving up until Stickman does.

"So listen, man," Danny says to Stickman, while accepting another cigarette. "Tell me the truth now. Is this really your bookcase? Or did we just steal it?"

"Steal it? Now that's just plain crazy." He reaches into his pocket, pulls out the bottle, and fills the air with licorice. "This here is my bookcase. My bookcase. And I'm giving it to my sister. Come on now," he says.

They struggle up the bridge stairs. At the top, there's a broken chain-link fence. They pass through it, and the headlights of cars crossing the bridge stream below them. The walkway arcs gently above and between the roadways, surrounded by the skeletal steel ribs of the bridge, all streaked with graffiti. They walk across steel plates spot-welded onto the girders. The plates are warped and rock upward when they step on them, exposing cracks between the plates and the dark black river well below them. Danny starts thinking of the sister, the cat, again. He starts to daydream that she's asking him questions about his life. He tries anticipating what her questions will be and what his answers will be.

At the far end of the bridge, the walkway grows darker. The bookcase is cutting a divot into Danny's neck. Stickman is muttering curses ten feet behind him. At the landing before another set of steps, Danny can make out the silhouettes of four or five men lying on the steel sheets, their hooded heads nodded down onto their chests. One has his right pants leg rolled up and a needle stuck in his ankle, standing up like it fell out of the sky.

"Hey, man, is that a bookcase?" he asks.

"Yes," Danny says.

"Is that oak?"

"No, sir," Stickman says. "That's maple."

"Maple," he says. "Man. You can't beat maple."

An hour and thirty blocks later, they turn a corner to a row of little frame houses, neatly lit by streetlamps. Danny turns so Stickman can buzz the door. His sister, the cat, pulls it open. She is on the telephone, a long cord leading back into an unlit kitchen. It's a very nice little house, somebody else's. It does not smell like jambalaya.

"So this crazy thing happened where we couldn't get it on the subway, and we couldn't get us a cab," Stickman starts telling her. Her back is turned, and she is still talking. "So we just started walking with it, and before you know it—"

"Just put it over THERE," she turns and says. "No, not you," she says into the phone.

Danny helps Stickman put the bookshelf in place. Stickman shrugs at Danny, then turns to her. They both stand there for a minute, their hands in their pockets. She turns around and glares at both of them.

"Can't you see I'm busy here?" she says.

They walk out in silence. Stickman leads Danny to the subway and buys him a token. They ride the train together in silence. Stickman starts drinking that stuff again, really draining the bottle; the subway car fills with the licorice smell, but nobody looks up. At his stop, Stickman gets up, unfolding himself and pulling his pants up one last time.

"We must have walked that bookcase like six miles or something," he says.

Danny gets off at his stop and walks up the avenue until he finds a bar he hasn't frequented yet. He sits down on a stool, and sometime later he comes out. He stands in the street alone at three in the morning, looking out at the streaks of people coming and going. And then it happens—everybody who passes wears a plastic mask with a rubber nose and eyes like black coals, shaking, shaking. Face attack! Danny thinks. It's a face attack! He can't wait to tell Stickman. But when he goes back to the billiards hall a few days later, the steel doors are locked forever.

T-SHIRT LADY

The T-Shirt Lady needs a helper. Danny reads it in the free paper. He laughs when he sees it. She's the one who sells T-shirts on the street. She wears Jackie O sunglasses and a scarf. She wears an oversized T-shirt that reads "The T-Shirt Lady" in huge black letters. All her T-shirts say the same thing: "The T-Shirt Lady." Nobody ever buys them.

Danny laughs, but he starts to take notice. Each day on his rounds, he stops to watch her. He leans on a lamppost across from her for longer and longer each day. He watches her methodically fold and refold the white shirts in neat rows, small through extra-large. He watches her pull each shirt out, crease it tightly, and tuck it neatly back in place. He sees her reach into her little belt purse, pull out her Chapstick, and work her lips in front of the little mirror. The little mirror is for people trying on T-shirts, although no one ever does. No one ever tries one on, let alone buys one. Still. Danny shifts his weight on the lamppost, scratches his chest, and chuckles. Still, somehow, the T-Shirt Lady needs a helper.

Then, one silver afternoon, Danny's watching. And she collapses.

She looks up into the sky above Danny. Danny looks up too. A sheet of blue pigeons turns in formation above a cornice. When Danny looks back, she's lying on the sidewalk. At first nobody seems to notice her. Danny finds himself walking blindly through traffic to help. A cab skids to a halt, a truck blasts its horn inches from his ear. By the time Danny crosses the street, somebody's there, standing over her. A crowd forms but does nothing. The crowd becomes a large gray mass blocking the street, from the trees, from the sky.

Danny wants to help her, but when he gets to her, he freezes. The T-shirt Lady lays face up on the sidewalk, the Jackie O glasses folded neatly next to her face. Her eyes are open, but it looks like she's sleeping. Her T-Shirt Lady T-shirt drapes around her formless body like a blanket. The T-shirts she pulled down with her lay spread on the sidewalk like crumpled flowers.

The man who got there before Danny is old and thick and smells like hot onions. "Lady?" he asks in a booming voice. "Oh god. Lady?"

He bends his knees to get as close to her as he can, but his knees don't bend very far. Danny looks over his shoulder. The old man grabs Danny's sleeve between his thumb and forefinger and pulls him down. "Get her tongue. Look at it. Her tongue."

Danny kneels slowly beside her, resting his knees on one of the fallen shirts. Her skin is slate, ocean blue. Her mouth is closed peacefully. Danny puts his face close to hers, then pulls back. "She's breathing," he says. "She's breathing fine."

"Take this," the man yells. He pushes something against Danny's arm. It's his unfolded wallet. "Wait a minute." He pulls a wad of bills out of the wallet, tucks them in his breast pocket, and pushes it back at Danny. "Take it!" he yells. "Come on! The tongue!"

Some years ago, Danny remembers now, he was on an airplane. A stewardess reached over, smiling, to hand him a Coke. But he wouldn't take it because he was on an airplane, and he knew he was about to die.

A yellow taxi pulls beside the T-shirt stand. The crowd parts. A huge man with a long black beard and a turban walks up purposefully. He takes in each image with burning black eyes: the blue woman lying on her back, the two men leaning over her, the T-shirts.

"What is happening?" he demands.

"Nothing," the old man says.

"What have you done to this lady?"

"I didn't do nothing," the old man says, stepping back. His voice is a fraction of what it was. He pulls his wallet from Danny's hand. "I didn't do nothing to her. She just fell down."

Then the T-Shirt lady sits up. She blinks at Danny. She's younger than he thought. Her cheeks flush with little pink blotches. "Did you see it?" she whispers.

"It's gone now," Danny says. "Whatever it is. Or was."

"Oh." When Danny looks up again, the turbaned man and the old man have faded into the crowd, which itself melts away, leaving an empty sidewalk littered with T-Shirt Lady T-shirts. She rubs her neck and looks up into the sky. The pigeons circle again, fifty or one hundred of them, making the same sharp turn in unison. From this side of the street, the T-Shirt Lady's side, the afternoon sun flashes against their cold white bellies. Danny is blinded for a second. The light disappears. When he turns back, the T-Shirt Lady is still blinking at him.

"I'm the T-Shirt Lady," she says, her voice deep and certain.

"I know you are," Danny says, offering her a hand. "Please let me help you."

SOMETHING TO SHOW YOU

Danny turns the corner onto Ninth Avenue, and there he is. Just like the lady on the phone said. A little bald man in a pink alligator shirt in front of a big yellow truck. He's slapping a clipboard and yelling at a smaller man in a dirty T-shirt.

"Hi," Danny says. "Are you Rusty?"

"You—you're fifteen minutes late! Please, come on!" Rusty throws his arms out. "People, come on! My people who work get paid. People don't work, I'm not paying them shit. When my people are late, they're not working. When they're not working, guess what?"

"They don't get paid?" Danny asks.

Rusty slaps his forehead hard. "Lou, show this big idiot downstairs. Show him quickly what he needs to do. I need this truck loaded and out of here by two o'clock."

Rusty climbs into a gold Mercedes and skids into traffic, leaving Danny with Lou. Lou's face is etched with thin white scars. He looks angry, like Danny just cost him twenty bucks.

Lou leads Danny through steel doors into a basement. Danny is wrapped in a warm, musty smell, like steamed dirt. Corridors of shelves are packed with silt-covered objects. Hundreds of Charlie McCarthy ventriloquist dolls. Dozens of water-stained erector sets. Rows of Korean police riot helmets. Two men clear whole shelves with fast sweeps of their arms, sending things crashing into boxes. Another wraps things delicately in newspaper.

"This here's the collection," Lou says.

"Collection of what?"

"Never mind what. Mister Rusty said it goes. So it goes. It's all gotta go by two. We pack it up fast, we load the truck fast, and we take it down to the auction site fast."

A row of Shirley Temple dolls stares down at Danny with crusted eyes. He picks one up and throws her headfirst into a dust-filled box.

"You mean like that?"

Lou's gold teeth glint in the darkness.

"I mean like that. Only faster."

At 2:45 the four men squeeze into the truck's cab. Lou says because Danny's the new guy, he has to ride in back. He climbs into the truck. Lou pulls the door down and locks it. In the heat and darkness, against the shifting mountain of boxes, Danny loses his senses. He starts to panic. He can't breathe. A horn blasts. Things crack in the boxes. The truck swerves. Danny hurtles through space, braced for a collision.

The truck stops. The door opens. Rusty stands in front of Danny on a loading dock, beating his clipboard against a steel pipe.

"I said two o'clock!" he yells at Lou.

"Yeah, Mister Rusty," Lou says, pointing at Danny. "What can I say. I'm breaking in a new guy."

A huge brick building with steel-shuttered windows soars above Danny. In its shadows he unloads boxes, crates, mannequins, carousel horses. Lou pushes a button. An elevator thumps down a shaft and opens. Hunched on a stool inside is an old man in yellow shoes and a checkered hat. He pulls the lattice gate closed, then presses a button. Danny rises ten stories to a vast showroom lined with empty tables. Black curtains hang from bare brick walls between huge windows. Danny drops the boxes by the tables, then returns to the elevator for another load.

On the fourth load up, Lou starts making fun of Mister Lee.

"Mister Lee," he says, "I smell apricot brandy. You been drinking apricot brandy?"

"I'll say this much, my friend. Nobody drinks nothing on this job. I worked in this building forty-four years. I know my job."

"Mister Lee, those are some shoes. Do you play golf in those shoes?"

Danny rides up and down eight more times, ten times, until the truck is empty. Rusty points to the delicate packer.

"Billy," he says, slapping his clipboard. "Billy and the big idiot. Get upstairs and start setting up. And the boxes better be unloaded and set up by the time we get back."

Upstairs on the showroom floor, Danny looks at the hundreds of boxes, stretches, yawns, and lights a smoke.

"Man," Danny says. "I never seen so much shit in my whole life."

Billy picks up a box.

"I really thought I was gonna suffocate in the back of that truck."

Billy turns away from Danny.

"Hey," Danny says. "You want a smoke?"

Billy starts walking across the room. "No," he says. He pulls open a box and starts carefully unwrapping antique tea sets, wiping each delicate piece, and placing them on trays in a row on a table.

Danny pulls back a curtain and opens one of the huge windows. He blows smoke out into the hot afternoon haze. He looks down onto five-story walk-ups laced with ornate fire escapes. The sun beats down on silver roofs.

Below Danny, on the top floor of one of the buildings, he can make out an open window. In it, an old woman is crying.

She presses her face with thick red hands. Her elbows rest on the ledge. Her huge bare arms shudder, like somebody's jiggling her from behind. She drops her hands and looks up at the sky.

She turns slowly toward Danny. Danny jumps back, waits, holds his breath. When he looks out again, the old woman's face is back in her hands.

Danny flicks his cigarette out the window. He opens one of the boxes. It's filled with little Victorian porcelain dolls in yellowed lace dresses, cracked and tangled. Arms and legs pop out in all directions. He closes the box back up. Another box is crammed with old copper medical equipment, now dented. Danny picks up a crate filled with surviving antique fire trucks. He walks it down to a table next to Billy. He starts to dump it on the table, then stops. He sets the box down and starts untangling the trucks. He spreads them out in a neat row, side by side, a fleet. Then he returns to the elevator landing for another box.

The truck horn blares repeatedly downstairs. "Let's go!" Rusty yells from the street.

Danny presses the elevator button. Mr. Lee pulls the gate open.

"How's it going," Danny says.

"I'm just fine, son," Mr. Lee says, clutching the throttle. "Thank you for asking."

Lights flicker on a console: nine, then eight, then seven.

"This is some building," Danny says.

"Been here forty-four years. I used to be floor manager. Down in the steam engine."

"Steam engine?"

"Sure. This whole building was a printing press. Biggest in the city. We ran a steam engine down in the basement. Two blocks long, block wide. I had twenty men working for me. We pumped steam up to ten floors of print rollers, running night and day, 365. They shut it all down twenty years ago."

"Really? What happened?"

"I don't know. Lectricity."

Mr. Lee shifts his hat higher onto his brow, mops his forehead with a handkerchief, and stops the elevator.

"Well, thanks for the lift."

"Later, son," Mr. Lee says. "Later on, maybe I got something to show you."

Danny works late into the night in silence, and increasingly carefully, unloading two more truckloads. Before Rusty lets everybody go at twelve, he glares at Danny.

"Everybody better be back here at eight a.m.," he says. "The key word here being 'eight.'"

It has rained, then stopped. Danny walks through packed canyon corridors, past shifting shrouded figures, uptown. Shattered umbrellas are everywhere. The streets and sidewalks hold pools of black water. Danny buys a rack of tallboys at the twenty-four-hour deli and climbs four flights to his rented room. In the living room the answering machine isn't blinking. He enters his tiny room off the kitchen, sits on his bed, and drinks the tallboys methodically, one by one, staring out the little window into the airshaft.

*

Danny wakes up, still sitting on his bed, at eight. He jogs downtown. He pushes the loading dock button, but the elevator is silent. He finds an open door and runs up the ten flights of stairs to the showroom.

The early-morning sun glares off the wide floor beams. Danny's soaked in sweat. Rusty's voice thunders through the showroom. Danny follows a row of old vaudeville posters to its source.

"Don't let one of these pissants touch nothing," Rusty's saying. "Not one goddamn thing. They ask to touch it, say no. They reach for it, bite their goddamned finger off."

Danny tries to sneak in behind the others, but they're all wearing identical black work suits, "Rusty's Auction House" emblazoned in pink letters across the back. Rusty catches Danny in the corner of his eye.

"What time is it?"

"I don't know," Danny says. "My watch stopped."

Rusty reaches out and grabs his wrist. He jerks Danny's forearm up to his face.

"You don't have a watch," Rusty says calmly, squeezing his wrist tighter.

"I, um, must have lost it."

Rusty releases Danny's arm. He throws him a jumpsuit. Danny climbs into it, but it's too tight; the legs only come to his knees, and the sleeves barely reach his elbows. Lou looks at him and breaks into another gold grin.

"Man," he says. "Now you look big and stupid."

"The showroom floor opens in five minutes," Rusty announces. "They have one day to look over what we've got. The auction starts this time tomorrow." He looks at Danny. "If you show up on time, some of you may still have a job tomorrow. If not, I can always find another set of idiots. And I don't have to pay people nothing. Not one red cent. So if I fire people, they're fired. If people finish the job, they get paid."

Rusty takes a deep breath. "All right. Get to stations. No smoke breaks. No bathroom breaks. No screwing off. Remember these are our customers. And don't let anybody break anything. They break anything, break their necks."

Danny turns to Lou. "What's my station?"

"Toys."

"Toys! Sounds great."

"No," Lou says. "Not great. Toys is the most stupid ass job. Everybody wants to touch them. Everybody wants to wind them up, see if the winder works. But nobody can touch nothing. Not one goddamned toy. Got that?"

"Got it."

"You gotta look like somebody's gonna get smacked."

"Okay."

Lou starts to walk away, then stops.

"But don't smack nobody."

"Okay."

"You need to smack somebody, you call me."

The toys line three rows of tables. Danny looks down at an ancient windup clown, with a maniacal face, pedaling a tricycle. Old paint flecks cling to fine brown rust. He can't stop himself from picking it up and turning the winder half a notch. Its legs start pedaling slowly, and its head rocks back and forth. Everything works, despite the many years in the basement, despite the truck ride.

Danny pictures himself showing it to the old lady across the street. He can just knock on her door, hold it out to her, and show her how it works.

"Look," Danny can say to her. "It still works."

The clown stops pedaling. Danny puts him down gently in the middle of the table. He picks him up again. Slowly, as if his arm is independent of his body, Danny tries to stuff the toy into the half-zipped jumpsuit, under his arm. Just to see. But the suit is too tight. Then the main elevator doors open. Hundreds of people enter the showroom. Fifty of them head straight for the toys. Danny sets the clown down. "Please don't handle the toys," he says, walking up and down the aisle. "Please leave the toys on the table."

"Oh! I'm sorry," an elderly man with sunglasses says, dropping a doll.

A pair of miniature men stand shoulder to shoulder, their backs turned to Danny. They wear tweed jackets despite the heat and thick glasses perched on their noses. They're handling an old coin bank, testing its various parts.

"Please don't handle the toys," Danny says.

They turn to Danny and look him up and down.

"It's a bank," one giggles.

"Please put it down."

The elevator doors open again. More collectors file out onto the floor. They rush across the room and swarm around tables, touching everything.

A thunderous noise echoes through the showroom; one of the tea sets has been knocked over. Through the crowd Danny sees Billy fall to the floor and try to gather a few surviving pieces among the smashed shards of china. A woman stands over him, laughing. "Oh, come on! It's all insured," she shrieks. "Isn't it?"

The crowd closes around Billy. Danny takes a few steps toward him. Maybe he can help. Then he remembers the toys. He turns back to his tables, now more crowded than ever. The two miniature men have found his clown. They are twisting his legs to make him pedal faster.

"Put him down," Danny says. They turn away from him.

"I said put him down!"

They see Danny coming at them. Their mouths drop open, and they step back. Danny takes the toy from their hands. They shrink away from him. Danny takes another step. Lou grabs his arm from behind.

"Whoa, now. Mister Rusty wants to have a word."

Lou leads Danny through the crowd to the loading dock elevator doors where Rusty stands, glaring at him.

"I saw that. Think I didn't see that?"

"Yeah."

"They are our customers. They are very important customers. And you're nothing to me. You hear me?"

"Yeah."

Danny wants to grab Rusty by the ears. He wants to twist and rip his head off.

"*Nothing*. Now get out of my suit and get out of here."

Danny wants to twist and rip his head off, but he doesn't. He takes off the suit and walks to the service elevator. Mr. Lee pulls the door open and nods. When the door shuts, Danny really does smell it—apricots, turpentine, wet cardboard.

"Man," he says. "I could really use a drink."

Mr. Lee says nothing. They ride down in silence—six, then five, then four. At three he says, "So now you want to see something?"

"Sure."

The elevator keeps going past the loading dock floor to the basement. Mr. Lee climbs from his stool. He's permanently bent, a walking question mark. He leads Danny down a long, dark cement hallway to a steel fire door. He pulls the door open and flips a switch.

"Here it is," he says.

A huge red machine spreads in all directions. Rows of polished brass pistons squat, waiting to pounce, or fire. Boilers and steam valves and pipes twist in reds and greens and blues, golds and coppers and silvers. Every square inch of the machine and the room is swept, scrubbed, and polished. Danny's heart surges. It looks like a battleship engine. It looks like a pregnant mechanical spider.

"Does it still work?"

"Oh, yes," Mr. Lee says. "You better believe it still works."

HEADLESS IGNATZ

Danny sits down on a stoop on Twenty-First Street in a shady spot next to the 13th Precinct. He pulls the lid from the coffee cup. He looks down into a pool of stale cream. He takes a big slurp. He burns his upper lip, his tongue, his gums. He blows and slurps. He burns himself again.

Across the street, an old man slumps in a folding chair. A floppy tennis hat is pulled down over his eyes. Three items sit beside him on a ledge: an old dust broom, a small red rug, and a plaster mouse body, a foot tall, holding a brick and missing its head.

Danny knows that body. He knows that brick. It's that comic mouse. It's Ignatz from *Krazy Kat*. It's got to be fifty years old. It's got to be worth something.

Danny crosses the street. Above him there's an ancient brick building. Red and green paint flakes spray gently on the old man's shoulders. His eyes pressed shut. His mouth wide open.

"Hello," Danny says.

The old man sucks his tongue into his mouth.

"Hello yourself."

"This stuff. What's it, for sale or something?"

"What? This stuff? It's for sale."

Ignatz's neck is snapped clean. With the head he's a collectible. You glue the head on, you fix him up, you've got a hundred bucks.

"How much for Ignatz?" Danny asks.

"Ig what?"

"The mouse with the brick. How much?"

"Oh! The mouse. Five dollars."

"Five dollars? Oh. Does he have a head?"

"Sure, I got a head. I got it in the back somewhere." The old man points toward a wooden door behind him. "I got a house full of stuff."

"Oh!" Danny rubs the bumpy tip of his tongue against the back of his teeth.

"I'll tell you what. I'll find the head. For free. You come back later for the head. Only you got to take the body now. I ain't dragging the body back up the stairs. I got a hernia."

"Okay then." Danny fishes the change from his pocket. "I'll take him."

Danny's back in his small rented room, his door open into the small foyer that connects to the front door, the bathroom, and the living room. He's lying on his cot, his arms folded behind his head. He licks his upper lip, still blistered from the coffee. He's staring at the headless Ignatz. He tries to remember the face. He remembers grainy old cartoons. Ignatz has a crush on Krazy Kat and chases him, or her, with a brick. It was all very confusing. Danny thinks of the old man. What if there is no head? What if he can't find it? What if he breaks it?

Keys rattle the apartment's front door bolt. Before Danny can kick the door shut, Gina the Hairdresser, his roommate's girlfriend, is standing at the door.

"You're here?" she asks.

"Who, me? Yeah. I'm here."

"What a day," Gina says. She drops her bags and slumps against the wall outside Danny's door. Her hair, huge untamed curls, spills across her face.

"I had this guy come into the salon today?" Gina says, straightening one of the tangles with her fingers. "This guy wants his bangs cut, and I say, 'How much,' and he says, 'I don't know, this much,' and he says it with all this attitude, and I say, 'Okay,' and I'm cutting his bangs, and he's yelling across the room at Cody about this girl he's screwing, and he's married, you know, and he's giving all the details, and Cody's not listening, and I roll my eyes, and then I unroll them, and I look at the floor. And I realize I just chopped off this huge chunk of the guy's hair."

"Huh," Danny says.

"So the guy starts bitching at me, and I say, 'What's your problem,' and he calls me a stupid bitch, and Cody says, 'I can't take this anymore,' and he storms out of the place, and it's *his* place. And I'm alone with this guy with a huge gash in his hair."

"Great," Danny says. He reaches for his boots on top of his dirty laundry.

"So I look at the guy, and the guy looks at me. And he pulls forty bucks out of his pocket, and he puts it on my chair, and he runs off after Cody."

Gina gives up on the tangle, pulls her hair back, then pulls the huge strands around her head. She wraps until she's completely hidden, a big ball of hair sitting on a leather jacket.

"I don't get people," she says.

Danny gets up and steps toward the front door. Gina drops her hands, emerging from the hair. She looks at him.

"Where you going?" she asks.

"I gotta go out."

"I need a drink," Gina says. "You want to go get a drink?"

"I can't," Danny says. "I gotta meet somebody."

"Oh. Did Dave talk to you about the rent?"

"Oh, yeah," Danny says.

"Cuz it's the seventh, you know."

"Seventh! Yeah," Danny says, pulling the apartment door closed behind him.

Night shadows blanket the front of the old man's battered building. Danny sits on the same stoop, drinking a tallboy from a paper bag. A breeze blows down the street, sending paper tatters down the sidewalk. A lone yellow bulb glows above the old man's door. A hundred bucks easy, Danny thinks. Maybe one-fifty. One-fifty and he's bought a ticket to Boston. He knows where to take it, who to talk to. These streets are filled with treasure, collectibles, artifacts. People sell silver for pocket change. They throw gold into dumpsters.

One-fifty. Danny says it again, setting the price in his head. He tries to picture the old man rummaging through things, but he can't. He wants to hear boxes and bags dumped out on the floor, but the avenue drowns out everything. What if he isn't looking? What if he doesn't even live here? What if he just conned you out of five bucks? Danny finishes his beer, digs through his pockets, digs up another dollar in change, and returns to the bodega for another.

Back on the stoop, Danny pops open the cold can. He sucks the cool foam off the rim, lets it soak into the morning's burns. An Ignatz statue's gotta be pretty rare, he thinks. Now he remembers the comic strip a little better. Ignatz was in love with Krazy Kat and threw bricks at him, or her. Or Krazy Kat was in love with Ignatz, who fended him or her off with bricks. There was a third character, an Officer Grupp or Gup or Pup, who was in love with the one that loved the other one and threw the other one in jail. Danny can only scratch his head over that one. Scratch his head, yawn, and doze on the stoop until the early hours of morning.

Danny wakes up in his room. Dave's tapping gently on his door.

"Hey, dude," he asks. "You in there?"

Danny waits in silence for the tapping to stop. The front door closes. He waits ten minutes, laces his boots, and runs down the stairs.

Danny finds the old man dozing in his folded chair. The tennis hat has fallen to the ground. Strands of comb-over white hair jut wildly from a freckled head. His neck is twisted hideously, like his head is slowly wrenching itself from his shoulders. There are three new items on the stoop: an empty wood picture frame, a crumpled paisley shirt, and a smiling mouse head, squinting one large eye, taking aim.

"Hey there," Danny says. The old man looks up. His eyes focus. He squints at the morning sunlight. He looks to the statue head, then he looks back at the young man who bought the headless mouse the day before, and he smiles.

"There he is," the old man says to the head. "I knew he'd be back."

PALISADES

Big Brother tells Danny he should head back up to Boston, where they know people who know people. Big Brother is a part-time trumpet player and a full-time cook, passing through the city on his way out West. Danny has come up to Washington Heights this morning to find Big Brother, crashing on the floor of his ex-girlfriend Cassie's little floor-through. Cassie isn't there. They don't know what to make of this. They don't want to alert the super of their presence or of Cassie's absence. When they go out, they pull the door shut but not all the way shut. They don't know if Cassie took her keys.

Danny and Brother walk over to 181st Street. They enter a bodega and buy a buttered roll and a coffee for a buck. They stand on the corner, splitting the roll and the coffee. Happiness Candy, Mullers Meat Market, Rexall Drugs; boarded-up stores streak up the street and down the street. Some kids on the other corner start saying stuff. "Yo! Ossifer! Ossifer!" they chirp. The kids think Danny and Big Brother are cops staking them out. This makes Danny feel safe, at the same time it makes him feel unsafe. It is really, really hot. Big Brother sits down on his trumpet case—he carries that thing everywhere he goes—and stares off to the west.

"What do you say we walk over to Paramus?" Big Brother says.

Danny looks down the street and across the river at the Palisades, brittle strips of gray-red cliffs under a gray-red sky.

"Paramus?" Danny asks. "Why you want to go to Paramus?"

"I know a guy, a sax player," Brother says, draining the last lukewarm grains of coffee from the Styrofoam cup. "I used to play with him Sundays in Fort Tilden. He lives with his mom in Paramus. His mom's got a pool, I think."

Danny and Big Brother walk over to the bridge and up onto the rust-caked walkway. A steamy silver light splashes up at them from the Hudson far below. Heat shimmers from the concrete, the steel, the pavement. The cars and trucks all honk in unison, seemingly at them, because they are moving faster than the cars. The bridge ends; they cross a footbridge, and they are enveloped in stifling trees. They follow a footpath that disappears into the woods, along the top of the cliff's high ledges at first, then spiraling back into the deep woods. They walk on and on, and the sun beats down on the weedy trees, and every time they pop out above the river, Danny thinks they are going to get a breeze, but all they get is hot, evaporating Hudson River stink, like sour milk and minerals.

In Danny's eyes, Big Brother is a legendary walker who spends whole days strolling from East Harlem to Coney Island because he wants a hot dog, or from Hell's Kitchen to Flushing to go to a Mets game. But this heat today, this heat is starting to wither even Big Brother. He keeps switching his trumpet case from right to left to right, like it weighs a hundred pounds. The trail breaks out onto the roadway. They follow it for a spell. The passing traffic creates something like a hot, moving wind tunnel. They are just about to cut into the woods again when they hear a siren—pumped once—just behind them.

A Jersey state trooper climbs out of his patrol car.

"Are we doing something wrong, officer?" Big Brother asks. He has sweated through his brown V-neck T-shirt, and his long hair is sticking out in all directions.

"I'm going to need to see some identification," the trooper says, holding his holster with one hand and the soaked rim of his hat with the other.

"Identification? I didn't bring any identification. You bring any identification?"

"Me?" Danny asks. "No. I didn't bring any identification."

"You should always carry identification," the officer says. "Where are you headed?"

"Paramus," Danny says. "We're walking to Paramus."

"Paramus? Paramus isn't in this direction. It's in that direction," the officer says, nodding to the left. "About fifteen miles in that direction."

"Oh! Good to know. Thank you, sir," Big Brother says.

The officer climbs back into his car. "You're welcome," he says.

"Say, officer," Big Brother says, pressing his luck. "Do you know if there's a store up this way? We didn't bring any water or anything."

"There's a gas station a couple miles up the road, but you can't walk on this road. Don't let me catch you walking on this road."

The officer speeds off.

"What do you think?" Big Brother asks.

"Let's follow the trail," Danny says. "It probably leads to the store."

The trail does not lead to the store. It takes a sharp right turn and leads straight to the edge of the cliff. Danny looks down over the lip. Piles of rock separate the bottom of the cliff from the brown, sludgy water.

"There's a park down there, I bet," Big Brother says. "I bet they have a snack bar or a soda machine or something."

Big Brother throws the trumpet case over the edge. Clatter, clatter, splash. "What'd you do that for?" Danny asks. Big

Brother grabs a vine, tests it, and swings down from this ledge to the next.

"It's the Hudson River," he yells up to Danny. "There's just got to be a park down there." He jumps off that ledge and disappears.

Later, Danny couldn't remember how they got to the bottom of that cliff. He could only remember the feeling of the soft red rock sliding across his face—big, smooth-faced stone that burned his skin. He remembered gripping vines with sweaty hands and sliding down a rock scrabble on his pants. At one place, a tree clinging to the cliff was a ladder; at another spot, somebody had tied off a frayed rope.

Somehow Danny finds himself at the bottom next to Big Brother, who is retrieving the trumpet case from the foaming brown river water, plastic bags and pieces of Styrofoam clinging to the rocks.

"Damn! Chocolate milk," Big Brother yells, bending down as if to drink it.

"Don't drink it!" Danny yells at him.

"I'm not going to drink it. What do you think I am? Stupid?"

It is hotter down by the water. Danny follows Big Brother down the river, climbing over rocks, back toward the glimmering bridge, seemingly miles away and not getting any closer. The city across the river looks like it is encased in smoke. In a bend at the bottom of the cliff, they come across a clump of trees.

Two surprisingly ugly men emerge from the trees, low to the ground, carrying fishing poles and a cooler. They look like something from a movie: tank-top undershirts, gold chains, baggy suit pants, five-o'clock shadows. Potatoes and Onions, Danny chuckles to himself. Potatoes pulls a revolver out of his pants and holds it by his side. Danny stops chuckling.

"How you doing?" Big Brother says, staring at the cooler.

"Not so bad," Potatoes says. "How *you* doing?"

"Oh, pretty good," Big Brother says. "A little thirsty though. Do you know how far it is back to the bridge?"

"Far enough," Onions says.

"I guess we'll get there soon enough," Big Brother says.

"Maybe you'll get there. Maybe you won't."

"Okay, then!" Big Brother says.

"Say, whaddaya got in that briefcase?" Potatoes asks.

"This? Oh, this is a trumpet," Big Brother says.

"Whaddaya think? Ya think there's a trumpet in there?" Potatoes asks Onions.

"I don't think so," Onions says.

"Here, I'll show you," Big Brother says. Danny thinks, is he going to hit Potatoes in the face with it? Does he know Potatoes has a gun?

Big Brother holds the trumpet loosely in his hand—just loosely enough, Danny thinks, that he might just be thinking about it.

"You think he knows how to play that thing?" Onions asks Potatoes.

"Go on. Play that thing," Potatoes says.

Big Brother holds the trumpet up to his cracked, parched lips, and he starts playing. The notes bounce off the hot cliffs; they climb up with the mist, right up the sides of the Palisades. It is strange—the music has a sweetness to it, like Danny never noticed before or never really appreciated. It is like each note has a color assigned to it, and each color shades another part of the cliff. Potatoes and Onions are looking at it too. They are looking at the cliffs, all raising up and around and behind them, hundreds of big red fingers reaching for the sky. Their hairy shoulders drop. Their mouths hang open.

Big Brother stops playing. He puts the trumpet back in the case and rubs his lips with his forearm.

"That was real sweet," Potatoes says. "What was that, Chet Baker?"

"No, sir, that was a Charlie Parker," Big Brother says.

Potatoes and Onions look at each other, turn around, and disappear back into the brush. Big Brother shrugs at Danny. "I wonder what he had in that cooler," Big Brother says when they set off again, back toward the bridge.

"Best not to think about it," Danny says.

Thirsty. Thirsty. They turn a corner, and they are in a parking lot of a little vista; there is a Coke machine by a kiosk, and the base of the bridge is just beyond that, and a road winds up the cliffs just beyond that. Big Brother has two dollars, and they each drink a Coke, icy cold, as slow as they can. Big Brother crumples his can and throws it ten feet, a perfect arc, into a wastebasket.

"You knew that guy had a gun, right?" Danny says.

"Yeah, I knew," Big Brother says. He wipes his dripping mop of hair back off his forehead and stares up at the bridge, still just barely visible in the haze above them.

"So what do you suppose happened to Cassie?" Big Brother asks as if it just occurred to him.

"I don't know, man," Danny says, looking at a road now, a two-lane road, rising from the parking lot and climbing up a cleft in the cliff. "I guess we better go find out."

BUCKY DENT

In Boston, Danny tracks down the friends-of-friends who live in a group house on Hooker Street. One of the friends-of-friends has a friend who knows a guy who needs a guy. Danny calls the guy who needs a guy; he has to get out to Jamaica Plain by bus in the morning and report to Bucky Dent.

Danny doesn't ask the guy, but on the bus over he keeps asking himself, could it be *the* Bucky Dent? He gets off the bus and walks through a river of dead trees, past piles of rusted, flattened cars, and then towers of bald tires and rows of bashed-up school buses, all wrapped up in razor wire and plywood fencing. Danny turns a corner, and the old factory looms above him. It was once a huge brewery, but it was abandoned some years before. Danny bangs on a steel-plated door, thinking, isn't this just like Bucky Dent? Isn't this the kind of place you end up six years after hitting the greatest home run of all time?

The door slides open. A huge bearded man in a sleeveless work shirt stares at Danny. He has welding goggles on top of his head.

"Looking for Bucky Dent," Danny says.

"Well, you found him."

Behind Bucky Dent, things clang and whirl and shoot out sparks. He waves Danny in and pulls the steel door shut. Inside, sunlight filters through the patched roof. A dozen hippie carpenters scramble around three massive, half-constructed golden arches. Bucky waves Danny over to a big table where one of the carpenters is rolling green contact cement onto a huge piece of plywood.

"Hey, man," the hippie carpenter says. "You got to do this here. You got to roll the glue out perfect. Then you got to roll that fabric"—he points to a massive roll of red velvet—"out onto the glued side, only you got to do it perfect, or there's gonna be bubbles, and we can't have bubbles."

The hippie carpenter runs off into the rafters to hang some giant sheet of something from the roof. Danny takes the roller and gets to work. He does the best he can. An hour later, he's rolled the sheet out, cut it perfect, and dried it with a giant blow dryer. Finished, he admires his work. Then it starts to bubble. Bubbles everywhere. The guy climbs down from the rafters. "Hey, man, that looks like crap. Flip it over and try again. And get it right this time. You got to dry it even."

At this moment, Danny remembers how, over pitchers at the Dugout, the friend-of-a-friend had told him that the brewery, after closing, had been repurposed as a scene shop for an opera company across the river, and they needed experienced scenic carpenters to help them build huge, rolling golden arch set-pieces like they would have in Troy. Danny also remembers convincing the friend-of-a-friend that he was an experienced scenic carpenter, although he hadn't painted a set since high school.

At the base of one of the arches, hidden in the shadows, is a small woman who is painting gold leaf onto the pillars. She looks up at Danny for a moment; is she waving with her brush? She looks really sad. There are splotches of gold on her face. At the time Danny notices her, he is screwing up the second panel even worse than the first.

"What is your name?" she whispers to Danny. He tells her.

"What is your name?" Danny whispers. She tells him.

Then they are silent again. Danny tries pressing the red velvet onto the glued surface, then smoothing it with the back of his hand.

Bubbles. Even more bubbles.

"I'm so sorry," she whispers.

"Oh, it's okay. I'll figure it out."

"Not for you, dip-ass—for the bird."

"What bird?"

"The bird on top of the arch," she whispers, pointing. Danny looks up. A white bird, like a seagull, but too big, like an owl, but too bird-like.

"He's been trapped in here for days," she says. "Everybody is too busy to let it out. It can't get out."

Danny looks down at the red velvet. The bubbles are bubbling. Little bubbles are forming on bigger bubbles. He is going to get fired.

"I'll get it," Danny says.

He turns and pulls a giant ladder over to the arch and starts climbing. Everyone stops what they are doing and watches him—the girl, the hippies, Bucky Dent somewhere in the shadows—but nobody says anything. So Danny climbs to the top of the ladder, certain that he will free the bird, but not sure how.

CHUCKTOWN

Birdman hangs out at the other end of the back alley, between the old tannery and the old fur storage plant. Birdman wears a white kitchen shirt that is always soaking wet, even when there's a cool evening breeze blowing off the canal and up the alley. He wears green dickie workpants and black clip-up galoshes, always unclipped. Birdman is always there, staring up at the wires that hang heavily between the heavy cinder block backs of the buildings. He holds a cigarette with two yellow-stained fingers up close to his long, lippy face. The cigarette is always lit, with a long orange ember, but Danny never, never sees him take a drag off that cigarette.

Danny sees Birdman only in twilight, when he gets sent to the back alley with the broken-down cardboard boxes and bags of Styrofoam packing materials. He takes the rubbish out only at night because the Chucktown Chamber of Commerce, who he is supposed to work with but has ended up working for, tells him to dump it in other people's dumpsters. He has to make three or four trips each night. He slides the big bags and stacks of cardboard into the dumpsters and then hurries back to the loading dock.

By the end of each day, the glue from the cardboard burns deep into the cuts in Danny's palms and fingers. On the way back from the dumpsters, he bends down and presses his hands, palms down, into a cold puddle. He waits until his hands are cold and wrinkled. Crouching there, bent over, Danny looks up sideways to see if Birdman is there. He is always there, someplace down the alley, staring up at the wires.

During the day, cars and trucks and taxis honk from an invisible trestle, behind the old tannery someplace, that rushes them through the sky so they never have to set their wheels down here in Chucktown. Later, just minutes before rush hour, the alley is draped in its own special, damp silence. Sunlight shifts from this wall to that, highlighting different red-and-green dumpsters, piles of rubbish, old, abandoned cars. A few hours later, the light drains from the thin strip of sky, and the bridge echoes its strange, eerie clanging noises. Then, when Danny comes out with the last stacks of cardboard and huge plastic bags stuffed with cracked packing foam and crumpled shrink wrap, he stands there for a little longer. He watches big drafts of steam float from the rooftops. He gazes at the floodlights and their little pools of light. Even in the dark, Birdman is still there.

One night Danny tries to say hi to Birdman. "Hi there!" he yells, waving down the alley. But Birdman doesn't look over at him. And he doesn't say hi back. He just stares up at the wires.

And this same night, when Danny re-enters the plant after his twilight dumpster run, the Chucktown Chamber of Commerce is already packing it up. Danny calls them the Chucktown Chamber of Commerce, but they really aren't the chamber of anything. Their names are Sis, Bobo, Lenny, and Squid. They are hash heads, which, Danny learned quickly, is a very different thing from a pothead. They are completely incapacitated from the hour they all shuffle in together to the hour they leave. They take turns going to the bathroom, or they sit on boxes, watching Danny do most of the work. The work involves moving huge cardboard crates around with palette jacks, unpacking the contents, and assembling them to the best of Danny's abilities. Some mornings he comes in and the things he assembled are gone and new crates have arrived. Danny never finds out what the things he assembles are for, and the job only lasts a few weeks, but he has a weird knack for putting them together.

"Well, numbnuts," Bobo says from his box when Danny comes back into the plant this night. "It's eight o'clock. We're punching out. You gonna lock up when you're done with the rubbish?" Bobo is missing all the teeth on one side of his mouth, making his face all crooked. An oversized "More Than a Feeling" Boston LIVE! sweatshirt dangles from his shoulders, and strings of matted orange hair stick out from his Red Sox cap.

Lennie, who Danny guesses is Bobo's brother, is staring at the zipper of his brown pleather coat, but he isn't pulling the zipper up.

"Nuther day, nuther dollar," he says. Then he turns to Danny. "Hey, numbnuts. Birdman still out there?"

"Yes," Danny says, pulling another massive plastic bag out of a box and collecting another pile of debris. "Birdman is still out there." Lennie asks him this every time he goes outside, and the answer is always the same.

"Hey," Danny says to them this time, the words bursting out of his mouth before he can catch them. "What do you think Birdman's doing out there?"

"Probl'y selling drugs," Lennie sniffles.

"Nah, he's watching something for somebody," Squid, who has spent the day laying spread-eagle on the floor, holding his stomach, and moaning about a pain in his insides, says. Now that it is time to go, he jumps up and is in his coat before the rest of them.

"I don't think so," Sis says. Sis is the only one who scares Danny. She looks like a person who killed and ate her family. She just has that look. The other three, Danny figured out pretty quickly, are scared of her too. "I think," Sis says, "he works for the Portuguese."

When she says that, they all stop their slow packing-up ritual for a moment, like they have all been thinking the same thing but never dared to utter those words.

"I think maybe, numbnuts," Bobo says, "you should just ask him what he's doing."

"Who, me?"

"Yeah, you, numbnuts." Lenny says. "He sees you every day. He's familiar."

"But what am I going to ask him? What am I supposed to say?"

Sis turns to stare at Danny, possibly for the first time in the three weeks he's worked there. Her eyes are glassy, sleepy, terrifying. Definitely killed them, Danny thinks. Probably ate them. "You need to go out there and ask Birdman what he's doing out there. You need to find out." Sis turns and dangles the keys to her Dodge Dart at the other three. They all walk obediently to the front door of the plant. "You need to find out, and you need to tell us. You need to tell us what Birdman's doing out there. You need to find out."

The steel door clangs shut, and Danny is left in the damp, dark warehouse chamber, surrounded by half-assembled machine parts, pneumatic staplers, air hammers, bags of nuts and bolts, and the never-ending pile of packing materials. In an hour, he has the whole place cleaned up and everything put away, the last of the refuse on the dock. He pulls open the steel gate to the loading dock and pulls the refuse out behind him. He pulls down and padlocks the steel gate. Then he turns to face the alley. It is darker than most nights; low rips of clouds catch in the shimmering lights of the city. It smells like rain is going to sweep in any minute.

Up at the end of the alley, Birdman's silhouette stares up at the wires, wrapped in a cloud of cigarette smoke. Then the smoke disappears, and there is another cloud, but Danny doesn't see him puff the cigarette. He drags the refuse to an overstuffed dumpster on the far end of the alley, stuffs it in further, and pushes the hatch down as far as he can. The puddles gather in patches of cracked pavement; Danny bends over and presses his swollen, aching hands into the water until it melts.

Then he stands up and walks down the alley toward Birdman, bracing himself for his answer.

IPSWICH

After a couple weeks, the Boston friends-of-friends make it clear that their couch visitor has overstayed his welcome. Danny gets in touch with Booch. Booch tells Danny he should come up the coast. Booch and this other guy Danny used to know are painting houses in Ipswich, and, Booch says, Danny can come up and work with them and make a few hundred dollars. They are living in the other guy's mom's house. Booch tells Danny he can crash there for as long as he wants. So Danny gets on a bus, and then he gets on a train, and he heads up to Ipswich.

Booch and the other guy meet Danny at the train station. They pack into the little cab of the pickup truck because the back is filled with paint cans and tarps. They are playing Steely Dan on the eight-track. The other guy hands Danny a pounder and a smoke. The hills roll toward the town.

Well, it is really lovely here, Danny thinks. I forgot how lovely it is. The pounder sloshes around in his hand. Little clapboard farmhouses with neat hedges wind and twist down to a harbor with little white boats. They stop at the other guy's house, and he goes inside to talk to his mom. Booch gives

Danny another smoke, and they lean on the back of the truck, waiting.

"You know," Booch says. "There's some people up here looking for you."

"Yeah, well, you know," Danny says. He tries to look like he doesn't care.

"No big deal. Just thought you'd want to know."

In Danny's book, Booch is all right; they played high school football together, and Booch was the big stud quarterback with the long hair and the white cleats who went out West to sit on a college bench for a season before he dropped out. Now Booch is back, and he still looks all sun-browned and shaggy, splattered with white paint.

The other guy comes out of the house, all hunched up.

"So my mom, sort of, said it's not cool," he says, not looking at Danny. "She, sort of, said you can't crash here."

The three of them load back into the cab of the truck. Booch hands Danny another pounder and another smoke. They put Little Feat on the eight-track, and they drop Danny off at the station.

It is getting dark, and Danny is hungry. At a pay phone under a spotlight humming with circling bugs, he digs through the scraps of paper in his wallet and finds Beano's number. "Hey, man! Wow. It's been a really long time," Beano says. "You should definitely crash here. We should definitely hang out."

Danny buys a rack of pounders at the packie next to the station—the fat man glares at him but doesn't card him—and he drinks all of them, one after the other, sitting on the concrete platform. A train appears, doors open, like it was there all along. Danny jumps on the train just as it pulls out.

Danny jumps off at the next station. He steps off the platform into the darkness of the parking lot. After a while, he sees Beano, passing under a streetlamp, walking toward him.

"Sorry, guy," Beano says. "Got my license suspended. I guess we'll have to walk it."

In the dim fluorescent light, Danny can barely recognize Beano. He is twice as wide as Danny remembered, in a wide-striped alligator shirt. He is another one from that high school football team, the center. Everybody Danny knows up here was on that football team. They all thought they were going to play together for the Pats. Now look at us, Danny thinks.

"Hey, man," Danny says to Beano. "You got a smoke?"

"No, me, no, I don't smoke anymore. It's really been a while, hasn't it. But you need me to buy some smokes? You need something to eat? You should really eat something. You look really bad. We're going right by a store."

After walking along the two-lane road—headlights and high beams bearing down on their faces—they come to a gas station with a snack bar. Beano buys Danny a turkey grinder, a microwave job, and a pack of smokes. He sits across from Danny in the plastic booth, staring out at a group of men in sleeveless T-shirts gathered around two headbanger cars at the pumps. Beano tells Danny about his job, about working for his dad, cleaning the used cars his dad sells. He asks Danny what he is doing.

"Nothing," Danny shrugs. "I guess I'm doing nothing."

"That's really pretty disappointing," Beano says. "You should really be doing something."

"What do you think I should be doing?"

"I don't know. I just don't think I've ever met anybody so busy doing nothing."

"Do they sell beer here?"

"No. They don't sell beer here."

"You want to go to a bar or something?"

"I sort of got to work tomorrow."

They don't talk after that. Danny blows his smoke away from Beano. Then they get up and start walking again. After what seems like forever, they turn onto a side street. Beano stops in front of a box house that looks like every other box house in the world. All the lights are on.

"You don't mind sleeping in the garage for a while? My dad isn't going to be cool with you being here. So can you just be quiet? Can you just sleep out there?"

In the garage there is a big boat with a tarp over it. There is a refrigerator filled with Ballantine's Ale. Danny finds a strip of carpet by a workbench and lays down on it, his head on the little backpack he's been dragging around, drinking a can. When he finishes it, he gets another. Danny's on his fourth can when the door to the garage opens and the light flickers on. Beano's dad looks down at him, the cans around his head, lying on the floor of his garage.

"What the hell are you doing?" he says.

"I'm watching your boat for you, sir."

Danny thought he'd remember him, but maybe he didn't.

"I'm going to get my gun," he says. "And if you're still here when I get back, I'm going to use it."

"No need, sir," Danny says. He gets up, collects the cans, and walks out into the darkness. He keeps walking, houses and houses, boxes and boxes, until he finds the train tracks. He walks down them for a long time. It starts to rain, a misty rain blowing off the sea and across the spread of pine scrubs around the elevated rail bed. Then Danny sees a set of goalposts and a single spotlight illuminating a scoreboard behind a school. He climbs a wire fence, scraping a nice, new bloody cut from the twisted wires across his forearm.

Danny stops at the ten-yard-line hashmark, looks around in the dim light, and drops into a three-point stance.

Booch is standing behind Beano, crouching, yelling a fake audible through his mouthpiece. "Blue Forty-Two! Blue Forty-Two!" Lapper pulls from the fullback slot and resets to Danny's right, a fireplug, standing. Two Redshirts follow Lapper, the primary target, up the line. Booch dusts the mud from his forearm, the signal: Danny the tight end is now the primary target. People are yelling in the shadows—he can hear his big brother, down from college for the game: "Come on, Danny!" One Redshirt is standing across from Danny, shivering his hands—a strange and effective distraction.

Beano's dad, the coach, runs down the sideline signaling timeout—but Booch doesn't hear him or doesn't want to hear him. "Hut! Hut!" Danny takes two steps, fakes right, cuts left, and looks back—Booch with fire in his eyes watching a brown ball with white stripes spin toward Danny's outstretched hands. There's a flash of light or lightning or a lone set of headlights. Danny keeps running to the sideline and up to the aluminum stands, ducking under just as the rain starts for real. He lies down on a hard wood bench and folds his arms around himself. He sleeps until the sun pops over the pine trees, just behind the far goalpost. Then he climbs back out to the tracks again, heading south, to try his luck with Lapper.

RED TIDE

Danny hitches up to Maine to find Lapper, who's moved up to Moose Harbor for the summer, and he ends up staying for a while. About a week into this visit, Lapper lets him know that if Danny needs to work for a couple of days—"If you need money for a bus back home or whatever, not that you have to leave or anything"—he may have landed something for him. He tells Danny this while he's pulling off his penny loafers at the kitchen table after going out drinking without him. Lapper has become a penny loafer man, a moustache man, a Ray-Ban man. Danny lies on his couch in his boxer shorts under a damp blanket, blowing big smoke rings up at the picture window.

"So, there's some lady," Lapper says. "I met her at that bar down there. I happened to tell her that I was looking for work. 'Work?' she asks me. 'In this town? Work went out of this town with the red tide. My husband had to dry dock the boat,' she tells me. 'He headed all the way up to Bath for a government job. Work, huh.' So I was about to check out, but then she starts swirling her drink around in her glass, which means she's thinking. 'I'll tell you what,' she says. 'My husband's boat is up on dry dock up the inlet. You want some work? Do you want to paint it? It's just a little thing. It looks like crap right now. Only, you got to scrape it first. There's some barnacles and stuff. Scrape it and paint it, and I'll give you fifty bucks, and I'll supply the paint. But you better show up and be ready to scrape at nine because I'm headed down to town at nine, and I won't be back until later.'"

Danny is now sitting up on Lapper's couch, looking out the picture window at the midnight inlet at low tide—a couple of old lobster boats lit up by a streetlamp on a dock, leaning up on the mud, caked in algae and a red film, the cold, dead portholes staring out, unblinking. And he says to Lapper, "But she offered *you* the job."

"But I don't *need* the job. *You* need the job."

"Yeah, but don't you think she'll notice that I'm not you?"

"No way, man. She was really lit."

"But I don't know how to scrape goddamned barnacles," Danny says, draining Lapper's last beer that he pulled from his refrigerator an hour before.

"Neither do I," Lapper says, getting up to go to bed. "And that better not be my last beer."

In the morning, Danny walks down the long, winding road that runs alongside the inlet. Her street number is neatly painted on the side of an empty mailbox that looks like a lobster trap. Danny walks down a short hill, following the driveway through a patch of short pine trees. A woman is sitting on a porch, drinking something from a large mug. She's wearing sunglasses. Danny points to a large lobster boat, a forty-footer with a cabin and tower, up on blocks on a lawn by a dock.

"That's the one," the woman says, waving a lit cigarette toward it. "Everything you need is in the shed. Right where he left it."

Danny walks to the boat. He puts his hand on the hull. The lower half of the boat is caked in barnacles. There are barnacles on top of the barnacles.

"This is going to take a while," he says.

She gets up from her chair and walks around the porch toward her car. "It'll take exactly fifty dollars, that's what it will take," she says. "I'll be back by five. If you're done by five, you'll have your fifty bucks."

Danny watches her drive up the driveway. He sits down on the lawn, looking at the boat. He smokes a cigarette. He gets up, walks to the shed, and looks into it—there are shelves of cobwebbed red paint cans, rollers, paint scrapers, sandpaper next to a pile of nets, traps, buoys. He walks back to the lawn, sits down, then lays down, staring up at the hazy silver sky. The whole place smells like dead fish. He considers falling asleep. Such a soft lawn.

Then he thinks of her face when she comes back and he's done. He thinks think of Lapper's face when he opens up the refrigerator and there's a new six pack in there. Danny gets up, returns to the shed, and pulls out a paint scraper. He gets to work.

A week later, Danny is still in Moose Harbor, walking up the other long road that loops around the harbor. It's like a big, sweaty arm dotted with little houses, separating the inlet from the ocean. At the end of the arm, there's a parking lot and then the pier. At the pier, little fishing boats come up in waves, and a crane offloads their catches into big bins that are rolled into water tanks, then into trucks. The trucks have to navigate the narrow road and the parking lot, which is also filled with waves of tourists who come to stare at the lighthouse off the coast, the boats, the pier, and the harbor.

Danny has tried all week to get a job on the pier, and they offer him a job in the Moose Harbor Clam Shack. The Clam Shack needs a fry cook. Teenagers work the Clam Shack, but they keep quitting. They start fights with the tourists, who complain about the burned and overpriced food. This is explained to Danny by an older woman who manages the pier from a little office above the seafood tanks. On the plywood walls around her tiny desk she scribbles weights and boat names and destinations and dollar signs.

"I don't have time to manage the Clam Shack. You," she says to Danny, "you will be a fry cook, but you really need to manage the shack. Managing the shack means managing the kids. Can you manage the kids?"

"Sure."

"Good. Have you ever operated a fryolator?"

She hurriedly takes Danny to the Clam Shack to show him how to operate the fryolator. As Danny follows her, he notices she has a pronounced limp. She could be a schoolteacher or something. "I can't tell you how much we appreciate you taking this on," she says nicely. "You know it doesn't pay like the job you applied for, but we just can't afford an extra hand on the pier right now, not with the red tide. There's just not a lot of work coming in. You'll really be helping us out. And if you make it to Labor Day, we'll throw in a hundred bucks."

The Clam Shack is four feet wide by eight feet long. It is built on stilts over rocks that are coated in seaweed, tacked onto the edge of the pier that has picnic tables and a view of the lighthouse. A sizzling noise comes from the interior;

smoke pours out a little window. A dozen tourists in white sneakers impatiently mill outside.

The lady pulls open a screen door. Three people are standing elbow to elbow. One is trying to cook fishcakes over a grill. He has a round red face, a downy moustache, and a sweat-soaked apron. Behind him is a young blond girl plopping tartar sauce onto a row of hamburger buns and scooping it off the spoon with a free finger. A third girl, older, stands leaning at a little sliding window, squinting at the elderly woman who's leaning in on the other side of the window, pointing at this and that.

"I'm sorry, ma'am," she says. "But we don't have that right now."

"But it says it right here on the sign that you do have it," the customer says, pointing up at the menu. "The seafood basket. I want the seafood basket."

"Hold on everyone," the lady says from the entrance, holding the door for Danny. "Here's the new fry cook."

"How's he going to even fit in here?" Tartar Sauce Girl asks.

"Fryolator's over there," Grill Cook says. "Have yourself a party."

Danny squeezes past them to the back of the shack where two fry baskets hang over a pool of bubbling orange oil. A breading drawer and sifter lay open next to it, the flour caked and dirty. Danny turns back, but the lady is gone, limping back to the pier, distracted by other things.

"Two seafood baskets," the girl at the window says, tacking two slips of paper above the fryolator. The papers are blotched with her oily fingerprints.

"Where's the seafood?" Danny says. A drop of sweat rolls off his nose and splashes into the oil, making a sizzling sound.

Grill Cook reaches behind him into a little refrigerator, its door hanging wide open, and pulls out a plastic container.

"Here you go, buddy," he says. "Four shrimp, three scallops, a fish stick, and three fried clams in each seafood box."

Danny opens the bin, and the smell of aging shellfish surrounds him; there's no way out.

"But how do I make it?" Danny asks.

"How would I know?" he answers, laughing, and the girls laugh too. "Nobody told us how to do anything."

"Just start frying stuff," Tartar Sauce Girl says, wiping off a bun she's dropped on the floor with her T-shirt. "You'll figure it out."

"Fry Cook!" the three start chanting in unison, giggling. "Fry Cook! Fry Cook!"

Danny never does figure it out. Another week goes by. Now it is five in the morning, and he is standing on the edge of the dock. It's still dark out, but there's a thin yellow line of light on the rim of the earth, between the ocean and a layer of black, angry clouds, and the thin yellow line is spreading out wider and wider and starts sparking up little orange and red whiffs under the clouds and then the world around him. There are warehouses behind him, rusted tin corrugated structures with no windows, with big steel cranes and winches and chains reaching out over the dock, piles with ropes and nets and Styrofoam crates. The seagulls are screaming, just screaming, and the whole place stinks of dead, dead fish. I can make a run for it, Danny thinks, and he turns toward the warehouses, but then Mickey's huge, hairy hand grabs him by the forearm.

"Where you going, buddy?" he says. "Cappy says it's cool, man, you're in, but you gotta hurry. Grab one of these coils and follow me."

Naturally low to the ground, Mickey slings a pile of thick rope onto his shoulder. Danny tries to do the same and stumbles backward. He steadies himself, but the rope uncoils and tangles around his legs, like it is attacking him.

"What are you doing, man?" Mickey says, having stopped to watch. "Don't mess around, man! Recoil that!"

Danny re-tangles the rope around himself. The rope seems more accepting, but it is very wet and heavy. He stumbles along, following Mickey, between rows and rows of boats with rigging clanging up above them, rocking in the swells—The Crusty Crab, The Stone Pony, The Lucky Lady. Mickey climbs over the back of one of them, and Danny climbs in behind him without falling in the water.

A huge bear of a man sits in a lounge chair, which appears to be welded to the deck, facing the back of the boat. Two huge fishing poles stick out of cup holders on either armrest. He's wearing rubber pants and a bloodstained T-shirt. "I'm with stupid," the T-shirt says. From where he's sitting, a hand beneath the slogan points out to sea.

The man watches Danny stumble onto the deck and runs a hand through his long beard. "You having a little trouble with that rope there?" the man says.

Danny looks back at the rope, trailing over the dock. "No, sir," he says, pulling at it. "I think I got it." He tries to create a new coil at his feet, but it falls apart in a heap. Dirty, leaky water fills his sneakers and swishes around his feet. "Sorry," he says. Cappy looks over at Mickey, who's already looped his coil over a hook.

"Is this your pal?" Cappy asks.

"Sort of," Mickey says. "Sorry."

Cappy turns to Danny. "Did Mickey tell you what we're doing today?"

"Um, fishing?"

"That is correct," Cappy says. "We're about to go fishing. We need to fill this boat with fish. We fill it, you get paid. We don't, you don't get paid. We just need to go out a ways, 'cause of the red tide. You been fishing?"

"No."

"I'll get started on the bait," Mickey says, pulling a long bloody knife from a shelf in the cabin.

"Ain't too late to change your mind," Cappy says. "Last guy changed his mind halfway into the trip, eight miles off shore. That was not helpful. That was an inconvenience. You sure you don't want to change your mind?"

Danny looks back at the long dock, the row of boats, the rusty warehouses, and the little houses on the hill behind them—all warm and sleepy and just waking up to the red light, the tide of dawn.

"Sure. I mean yes. I mean no," Danny says. "I don't want to change my mind."

PART II

A RIPPING, PUFFING, RATTLING NOISE

THERE ARE BIRDS UP THERE

Danny wakes up someplace in Indiana under a huge tree. There are birds up there, fluttering nervously from branch to branch and chirping crazy—they may have woken him up, or they may have known he is awake. There is a wind, or a presence of wind, rustling around up there; but where he is, lying on his back, legs crossed at the ankles, arms crossed on his chest, it is quite still. "It is all very nice," Danny says to himself out loud. "I wish I could stay here a while." But then he hears a truck—that truck-grinding-its-gears-up-a-hill noise—from somewhere beyond his feet. He gets up and folds the cardboard sheet he slept on and stuffs it into the top of his pack. There are bugs all over him, but they are harmless little green bugs.

Danny stretches out and stares back toward I-70. There is a wall of corn stalks between him and the highway, and there is a dirt road—two muddy tire tracks through the corn—and at the field's horizon, way out in the distance, is the highway. Danny remembers how the night before he did not see the dirt road—he was pushing through the corn stalks in the dark, and he clotheslined himself on a low tree branch, which is how he found the tree he slept under. Danny feels for his ribcage—his T-shirt is ripped, and there is dried blood where there wasn't before, and he can't find the cut or scrape that caused the blood. Danny is feeling pretty good all over. Thirsty, but pretty good. The sun is rising over a row of trees in the opposite direction from the highway and sparkles up the water drops clinging to the cornstalks. Then, a couple of crickets. Then a million crickets. Danny steps onto the dirt road and shoulders his pack. His wet socks squish in his wet boots. He starts walking toward the highway, but it disappears in the corn. He comes to a T in the road, another dirt road. The corn is just over his head. It is getting hot and a little crowded. And he is getting more thirsty. The ground is damp, but there are no puddles or creeks. He follows the dirt road that feels a little more downhill. He stops for a moment to wipe the beads of sweat from his forehead. Then he hears something, a new sound. Something mechanical is tearing a hole somewhere through the corn—a ripping, puffing, rattling noise. It comes fast. Danny tries to guess which way it is coming from, and then he starts running.

THREE MOONS RISING

"So I've done that three moons rising thing," Driver Guy tells Danny. He stops what he is saying to take a long, long drag off his cigarette—a Newport, Danny thinks. He grips the top of the steering wheel with one hand, the cigarette hand, the ashes an inch long, the white filter squished between yellow fingers. Smoke curls around the cab of the truck like rotten teeth. "That time, you know, I was out past Reno someplace, out past everything, but the closer I got to Fernley, the farther away it got."

Driver Guy tells Danny this like he's told him this before, but Danny has only been in his truck since Kansas City, and they aren't even in Salina yet—just long enough for him to ask Danny his name, ask him if he's left-handed, tell him he can tell when people are left-handed, and then tell him that his people all call him Driver Guy. Now Driver Guy pulls a white pill out of his denim shirt pocket and washes it down with something that looks like a melted blue slushie in a Styrofoam cup, then he pops another pill.

"Hey, you hungry? You want some cheesecake? I got a whole goddamned truck full of cheesecake. So, where was I. Yes. Yes. About the time the wife leaves me, I come back from a long run back east, what's that shithole called? Oh, yeah—Philadelphia."

Driver Guy takes another long, cold drag of that sweet menthol smoke. The red lights of traffic streak up a long hill. It looks like a fistful of crayons. Rolls of hills lead to rolls of hills, orange cornfields, as the sun sinks in the rearview. The ash from the cigarette splits, mercifully, from the cigarette filter and sprinkles itself all over Driver Guy's pant legs. He brushes them off slowly and with great deliberation, taking his hand off the wheel for just a little bit too long.

"Oh, yeah," Driver Guy says. "What was I saying?"

Danny has forgotten what he was saying. Driver Guy looks up suddenly, righting the ship, and reaches for the pack of cigarettes. He pops a new one in his mouth and dislodges the world's biggest silver lighter from his other denim shirt pocket. He cups his hands around the cigarette to light it, even though not a wisp of air is circulating anywhere in the cab of this truck.

"You were saying about your wife, when she left you," Danny says, but his eyes are fixated on the swerving roadway ahead, the taillights in front of them, the headlights flashing inches from their right.

"Oh, yeah, the wife. Oh, yeah, her. Well, she took off with some shit down there in Texas." Driver Guy's face gets all waxy. He plugs another pill.

Then Danny remembers. "You said something about three moons rising," he says.

"Three moons, what? What are you saying, boy?" Driver Guy scratches the back of his neck, real slow, his fingers making a noise like sand scraping sea glass. New smoke floats everywhere. "Three moons whatever, man. What are you smoking? What do you got in that pack there? Yeah. Like I was saying, Philadelphia," he says. "That may not be the end of the world. But you can sure as hell see it from there."

YELLOW PAGES

"Boulder's booming, Danny," the lady at Manpower Temporary Agency says, pulling his application from the clipboard and handing him a blue slip of paper without making eye contact. "You need work, you come to the right place." She stuffs the application in a drawer without looking at it. The blue slip tells Danny where to go for his first assignment, a one-day job the next morning.

He arrives at the third loading dock on the mountain side of the plant—itself a huge, aluminum-sided, blue mountain. He is there at eight o'clock, as he was told. He is the only one there. The loading dock is closed, the big door pulled down shut. It faces a parking lot, empty, except for a huge dumpster pushed up against the fourth loading dock. And there is a car, parked alone, across the lot. There is a man in the car. The man sits with his head down, leafing through a pile of yellow forms in his lap. He doesn't look up at Danny. Danny stands there, staring up at the hazy mountains on the horizon, pretending he is enjoying looking at them.

What Danny really wants to be looking at right now is a cigarette. Danny ran out of cigarettes the night before, and he is itching for a smoke. He normally keeps a pack by the mattress and lights one first thing in the morning, before he unwraps himself from his surplus sleeping bag. Danny can't afford rent, food, or even beer, but he always comes up with eighty cents for a pack of smokes.

Until this morning. This morning he left his last sixteen dollars on the kitchen table in the tiny apartment where he'd rented a tiny room from a college kid who's roommate skipped out on him, with a note promising he'd have the other twenty-four bucks, plus next week's forty bucks, by Friday. Then Danny set off, down the hill and up Arapahoe, until he got here.

Now, standing on that loading dock, Danny is very cold. He sees that the man in the car is smoking. That bastard, Danny thinks. He is filling that car with smoke. Danny considers banging on his window and asking for one. But then, the man jumps out of the car, the cloud of smoke evaporating behind him into the snowy mountain air.

The man walks up to the platform and passes Danny. He pulls out a large ring of keys. He rattles one into the padlock. He pulls the steel door up. "Come on," he says, waving a fat arm at Danny. Danny follows him into a cavernous plant. Yellow Pages phone books tower in stacks eight feet high and at least a hundred yards deep.

"Where's the other guy?" the man asks.

"What other guy?"

"Goddamn it! The other guy I'm paying the agency for! Where is he?"

The pack of cigarettes in the man's shorts pocket makes Danny itchy. It looks like it might pop out, and he might not notice.

"I don't know," Danny answers.

"What did the agency tell you?"

"They told me to report here at eight o'clock."

"Well, I don't care how many of you people they send. I need an empty warehouse, not a warehouse filled with last year's phone books. I need you to get these phone books out of here and loaded into the trucks. I'm coming back here at five o'clock, and they better be gone. Trucks and phone books and you. You're on the clock. If not, I'm calling that goddamned agency and getting my money back, and you'll be out on your ass with the rest of those hippies living up in those caves in the mountains."

The man waves a fat arm up at the mountains, looks at them for a moment, and shudders. "I got to go now. You got your orders."

"Where are the trucks?"

"Oh, they're coming. Two big cowboys. And they don't like hippies, so you better watch your ass. Anything else?"

The man climbs off the platform and walks for the car, putting a new cigarette in his mouth.

"Can I have a cigarette?" Danny asks him.

"Sure you can," the man yells back. "Anybody can have a cigarette." He climbs into his car and drives away, leaving Danny alone with the phone books. Danny sits on the edge of the dock, staring up at the mountains. He is beginning to enjoy looking at them now. The snow looks like powdered sugar. The sun climbs up behind him and radiates the front range, and they take shape, each mountain with its own lines and patterns.

"I suppose I can make a run for it," Danny thinks, "before the truckers get here."

But then two big trucks pull into the lot, one behind the other. The driver of the first nods at Danny. He has a huge bushy beard and a vest. He turns and backs into the loading dock, the second driver close behind him. The first driver climbs onto the dock.

"Them there the phone books?" he asks.

"That's them," Danny says.

The driver pulls a pack of cigarettes out of his pocket, shakes one out, and points it at Danny. He takes one for himself and offers Danny a light. The smoke heats everything inside Danny.

"Well then, we better get started," the driver says. "Thanks so much for helping out."

"What do you want me to do?"

"Oh, don't sweat it, buddy," he says. "We got it covered." He pulls a palette jack out of his truck; the other driver has one as well. They load the full-stacked palettes onto the trucks, filling them quickly with phone books. Danny follows them around, occasionally picking up a couple of phone books that fall off the stacks. "Hey, thanks a lot there, bud," they say and offer Danny another cigarette. In an hour they are finished.

"You need a ride back to town?" one of the drivers asks Danny.

"No, thanks," Danny says. "I'm on the clock. I think I'll stick around for a while."

"Okay then, pal. Thanks for your help," the driver says. He throws Danny an almost full pack of smokes from the cab of his truck, and they drive off, back toward the mountains. When Danny opens the pack, there's a book of matches and a twenty-dollar bill.

JACKHAMMER

"This one's a week-long job," the Manpower lady tells Danny when he gets back to the office, "and we don't offer a lot of week-long jobs. So make sure you get out there early." Danny shows up with two other guys. One of them is a bent old man, and the other guy is drunk at eight in the morning.

The foreman comes in and looks them over. He doesn't say much.

"You know how to work a jackhammer?" he asks Danny. Danny says no. He says it doesn't matter. He takes a piece of chalk and marks out a three-foot-by-four-foot space on the concrete floor of the old strip mall they are demolishing.

"I need you to dig out the concrete here."

"How will I know I'm done?"

"When you run out of concrete, I guess." The foreman walks away.

Danny gets to work, wrestling with the throbbing jackhammer. Soon his stomach and shoulders are burning, and his lower jaw is vibrating. It takes a lot of time. The concrete is very hard. The other two guys are on wheelbarrow duty, wheeling blocks of broken concrete and bricks down to a truck. One takes the first wheelbarrow and doesn't come back. The other one takes the second wheelbarrow and doesn't come back. It grows hot. Sweat pours down the small of Danny's back. His hands start blistering. He is making progress. He keeps going. The regulars all stop for lunch, but nobody tells Danny to stop, so he keeps going.

The sun is slinking down, shooting rays through the dust Danny is creating. Around three o'clock, something happens—the blade hits something hard, and it creates a bolt of white light. Danny gets thrown back and lands on a soft pile of gravel. The jackhammer spirals into the air, the unplugged power cord twisting itself around the spinning projectile, and then crashes on the concrete floor next to Danny.

"What happened?" he asks the foreman, who is standing with a telephone, pushing the buttons.

"What happened was you cut through the phone line," he says.

One of the regulars comes over to check on the jackhammer. Nobody checks on Danny. "Hey, boss, check it out! He broke the jackhammer!"

Danny looks at the big thing he's spent the last six hours wrestling with. One of the handles is broken clean off. They all stare at it. Then they stare at Danny.

"How the hell did you do that? How the hell do you break a jackhammer?"

"Well, I guess you're done," the foreman says.

"Oh," Danny says. "You mean I'm fired?"

"Oh, no, not that. I mean you're done for the day. We got to rent us a new jackhammer."

"Yeah, it's a rental," one of the regulars says. "Kind of like you."

"We'll see you tomorrow, kid," the foreman says. As Danny walks down the board back to the street, one of the regulars shouts, "And stay away from them jackhammers!"

Danny goes to the Broken Arrow and stays there until closing time, stretching three Pearl Beers over how-many hours because he doesn't want to see the guy he is renting a bed from until he can pay him rent. The bartender is a funny guy and doesn't seem to mind. Danny tells him about the jackhammer incident.

"You're lucky it was a rental," he says. "If they owned it, they would have made you pay for it. Contractors out here are real sons-o'-bitches. I worked for a contractor when I got here, and I picked up his hammer by mistake, and he hit me in the face with it."

Danny is feeling all shaky from the jackhammer, like his stomach is all turned upside-down, and his ribs are sore. The room is vibrating, gentle but steady.

"This guy seems pretty okay," Danny says.

"They're okay today," the bartender says, putting a half-empty bowl of pretzels, left over from the people at the other side of the bar, in front of Danny. "But you watch your back. They're renting you for a reason, man, just like that jackhammer. They see you as a shuffler. They can always get a new shuffler."

BROKEN ARROW

All of a sudden Danny has a hundred-and-twelve dollars in cash in his pocket on a Friday night. The guy he's renting the room from is expecting Danny to show up with the sixty-four dollars he owes him. But Danny's hungry. He is so hungry he can't make a decision. He has been hungry all week, but now he is really hungry, and he has cash in his pocket.

Thirty minutes before, Danny was standing in a bank line, certain they weren't going to cash his check because he didn't have a state ID. He stood in line, covered in a film of sawdust and concrete dust that had soaked into his skin. The guy behind him in line, Mister Moustache, Mister Trim Real Estate Agent in an alligator shirt, was staring at Danny like he was on fire. The bank teller could have refused to cash Danny's check, he thinks now, because he looked like dirt. She could have asked for Danny's ID, but she didn't. She was kind, matronly, a lady who probably had a son out there on the Plains somewhere, packing boxes with gallon cans of paint or setting up Halloween displays at a Woolworth's. She didn't ask Danny for an ID. She smiled, counting out the twenties and ten and singles, as if she knew. "Here you are, dear," she said, pushing the bills through the teller window. "*You* have a nice weekend."

So now, thirty minutes later, Danny is at the corner of Pearl and Canyon watching college kids drive into town and office people drive out. I've worked hard for this meal, Danny thinks, watching the last glint of sunlight from the west backlight the front-range mountains above town. He thinks of the handful of restaurants on the strip: the diner, the Greek place, the Chinese restaurant. He settles on the Chinese place—he's walked past it every night after work, staring at the grilled birds hanging in the window, his stomach sucking into itself, holding out for this paycheck moment. Danny walks past the Broken Arrow. He runs his fingers through the thin wad of bills in his pants pocket. He hears, when he passes the door, two beer bottles clink together, a sad country song bleating from the juke box. He wipes his hands on his shirt—the smell of sawdust and cement, again, rise all around him—and he peers into the bar. Is his bartender in there? No. Is the guy he is renting from in there? No.

"*You* have a nice weekend," the bank teller said.

Danny hasn't eaten a real meal in some time, but just one frosty, cold bottle of beer never hurt anybody, he reasons. He stands in front a second, squinting at the street of lights, so clear now in the darkness—headlights and stoplights and neon signs. He does a quick calculation. I can eat anytime, Danny tells himself. And he walks into that bar.

CAVE HIPPIES

So this shipping platform is a big, blunt, methodical operation. The big job involves stuffing as much equipment and material as possible deep into the bowels of huge beat-up trucks that inch backwards and seal themselves against the tough rubber stumps cushioning the factory from the outside world. Danny and a couple of ghost-men load unit after unit after unit by hand and strap them together row after row after row. Stacks of panels and generators and mounting kits all have to be squeezed together perfectly to make weight-shift impossible; the trucks have to wind their huge overloads high up over mountain roads to make their deliveries.

The panels are pressurized glass and sharp steel frames wrapped around pipes and insulating foam; each weighs one hundred pounds, and they have to lift each one at the dock off a huge pallet, making sure they never touch the grimy floor. They heave them up onto their shoulders and wobble into the hulls of the trucks and set them in neat rows. They have to ratchet the rows together and seal them so they won't shatter on their way to Scottsdale or Platte or Salt Lake.

By the third row, Danny's hands are laced with cuts and his arms have gone numb and his palms are all shiny and smooth, and he walks out and there is another stack on a palette, forklifted fresh from production—sometimes the steel frames are so hot he can't touch them—but Danny and the ghost-men always get the trucks loaded, and they always get the orders right.

They roll down the big truck gate, and the trucks push off, and they stand there a minute watching the trucks snake out onto the industrial park road and onto the highway, rolling into the foothills that sweep away like waves and disappearing in a curtain of snow that brushes this place day after day for the whole eleven weeks Danny works there. They stand there watching until one of the boss men on a forklift yells at them to clean this crap up. And then another truck starts backing itself in, and they have to start all over.

A shipping-and-receiving job at the Novan Plant pays $4.25 to start, but if somebody makes it twelve weeks, it goes to $4.50 with medical. Nobody ever lasts twelve weeks. Danny gave it his best shot.

On the other side of the cavernous building lays production. They get paid by the unit. Guys run from station to station on an assembly line assembling magnificent machines with hydraulics and spray guns and power drills all hanging from power cables spiraling from sliding sockets attached to the rafters. Hissing and popping noises swirl through the building. The production guys flow like little mountain streams into a huge cataract coming Danny's way.

When he first got here, he met four production guys, mountain hippies living together in a cave somewhere nearby. They chant strange biblical scripture while they work. For the first two weeks, Danny eats lunch with them at a crowded little table in the lunchroom. When the bell rings, Danny runs out to the lunch truck; two ladies come around in one of those metal lunch trucks and sell watery coffee and stale bologna sandwiches with yellow mustard in Styrofoam packets that flutter across the parking lot like little plastic tumbleweeds. The two ladies look like mermaids, and the men line up politely. The hippies, in front of Danny, nod piously to the ladies and buy a bag of peanuts to share between them. They also bring some kind of strange rabbit stew they cooked the night before and share it, passing it between them, using one wooden spoon.

"Man, you," their leader starts at Danny back in the lunchroom, peanuts and beans falling out of his toothless mouth and sticking to his beard. "How much are you paying for rent? You shouldn't pay the man rent, man. You should live in a cave."

"Yeah," the second-in-command says. His eyes are fried from bad speed some years ago but are now relit with the light of Jesus. "Yeah, man, there's some pretty awesome caves up there, man. You should check out the cave situation. Seriously, you should check it out!"

Two others chime in something about John the Baptist or the Good Samaritan or something about somebody, but Danny has to stuff his face. The bell is already ringing, and he has to be back at his station before the bell stops ringing or the boss man will "dock his ass at the loading dock" or something he said day one, and before Danny knows it, he is back in the dark cavernous hollows of another truck.

He wants to check out that cave situation—he really, really does—but one day the county shows up and cinder-blocks the cave hippies' cave. They never show up at work again.

DAWN

After the first plant paycheck, Danny has enough money to ride the town bus out to the plant. The first morning he tries it, it's already colder and darker than it seemed the prior week. Danny doesn't have a winter coat, but he has an idea that he'll put away five dollars every week. But this Monday, Danny is already down to about twenty dollars, and he needs five dollars for the bus, back and forth, through Friday.

Before dawn he walks down the hill in the dark for the bus terminal. He pulls on the door, but it is still locked. The clock in the station says it is ten after six. The first bus doesn't come until six-thirty. He stands there stomping his feet for a minute, pulling his tattered denim jacket around him, but that isn't working. He stands there, waiting for somebody to open the door, but nobody comes. He bangs on the glass door. The wind is whipping down from the mountains, cutting through his coat and up his sweatshirt, which has holes in the sides and the armpits and a really stupid Oregon Ducks logo on the front. He doesn't even remember where he found the sweatshirt, but it is the only one he has. He hunches against the wind, and then he looks up and sees a light across Arapahoe and up a ways. It is the neon light of a diner. Acropolis Diner, it flickers, it beckons. Danny runs for it. Just a coffee to go, he thinks. As he runs across Arapahoe, the smell of the town rises up to meet him—burning firewood and desert trees and mountain snow. The diner door flies open in his hands. A lone waitress stands behind a counter looking at Danny. Something is cooking. Potatoes and onions. He sits at the counter by the register. All the stools are empty.

"What can I get you?" The waitress yawns. She looks like a drug-addled biker lady dressed like a diner-waitress for Halloween, but Halloween is still a week away.

"Just a coffee, please, to go," Danny says.

She brings it over, and Danny sits there with it. He doesn't want to go back out in the cold; he still has fifteen minutes until the bus. He turns and looks out the plate-glass window, back at Arapahoe. Pink light is filtering into the glass windows and lighting up the storefronts across the street. A single stoplight swings in the wind over an empty intersection. Everything—the scene outside, the stillness inside, the steam rising from the Styrofoam cup—all freezes for an instant, motionless. Then the waitress reappears. Danny thinks she is going to kick him out, but she doesn't. She points to his sweatshirt.

"Nice duck," she says.

"Thanks," Danny says.

SHIPPING

After a few weeks, Danny grows accustomed to waking up before dawn. But this morning is different from previous mornings. A new coldness presses him down into the mattress. Waking in darkness, his matted hair feels frozen to his pillow. His lips are cracked, and his ears sting. His hands, swollen and sore from the prior day's load-out, are stuffed between his thighs. He lays on his side, fetal, in his nylon sleeping bag. He bought the sleeping bag at a thrift shop, thinking he might need it someday. It is six inches too short for him, and it is thinly lined with faux-flannel duck hunters and dogs.

Danny disengages himself from the bag. He rushes to dress himself in every layer he can find in the predawn stillness. There is the Ducks sweatshirt, an old wool sweater, a raincoat, and army pants. He hurries into the little kitchenette and turns on the electric hot plate to warm his hands. The picture window is frosted over. He picks a hard heel of bread from a stale loaf and holds it over the warm plate, then stuffs it into his mouth. Still chewing the hard parts, he painfully turns the bolt and the doorknob and steps into the alley. A wind pushes down from invisible mountains, fluttering up his pants legs and stretching its fingers down his neck. The air smells richly of snow. He runs stiffly for three blocks, downhill, to the corner. The bus appears, its empty interior throwing beams of neon light out onto the street.

"Morning," Danny say to the driver, as he does every morning. He drops fifty cents into the steel machine. The driver says nothing. He gives Danny the same look every morning. The look says, "I'm here now driving a bus because I have to, because there are no real jobs in this town. But I'm a man who thinks a lot and will be doing something much more industrious as soon as I choose to do so." He pulls the bus door shut.

Danny sits down in a hard plastic seat. The super-heated, super-lit energy of the empty predawn bus soaks into his bones. The bus squeaks and grinds its way in wide, arcing turns through the downtown's blinking yellow lights, then its sleepy outlying settlements. Eventually the squat brown apartment strips give way to gas stations and fast-food satellites before stretching out into the complex, a maze of monolithic, windowless aluminum buildings out in the flatlands, marked by digital-looking names and numbers.

An alien pinkness begins to fill the back window. The mountains, now barely luminous from the rising sun ahead of the bus, are stained with the first real snowfall of the year. Danny stares at them like he always does. They are so close and so far away. The bus crosses 200th Street. At 210th Street, Danny pulls the cord, although, alone on the bus, he certainly can say something to the driver: "This is my stop," or "I get off here," or "210th Street," or "Same shit, different day." Instead Danny says, "Thanks," pushes through the twin exit doors in the back, and steps out into that weird pink light, growing weirder by the second. The bus hisses and pulls away, as it has for weeks, traveling empty for another few blocks before turning to haul its first batch of workers headed back into the city or up to the ski mountains behind it.

The complex starts where civilization stops. Beyond the complex, a long row of desert buttes jut up against each other in endless waves, rolling like the sea, but speckled with dead trees, or a barbed wire fence that stops and starts in the middle of nowhere, or abstract piles of human refuse-like tires piled atop shattered crates, all stuffed into a refrigerator.

To get to his job, Danny has to cut across the parking lot of a huge herbal tea packaging plant. Even at this early hour, its parking lot is filled with Volkswagens and old vans. Fat men with beards and bandanas and earth shoes sit at picnic tables provided by their employer on the edge of the rolling docks, sipping tea out of huge mugs while waiting to load trucks with little airtight boxes of tea. They wave to Danny every morning as he walks by. But Danny never waves back. He never waves back or salutes or shoots them the finger or anything. Even if somebody told him that something opened there, and they start at eight bucks an hour and knock off at three p.m., and they take all the breaks and drank all the free tea they want: No, thanks, Danny tells himself every morning. They can take their goddamned herbal tea and kiss Danny's ass.

"Late again!"

Darrell yells this at Dany as he approaches him, hurrying across the production floor to shipping. The huge white clock with black arms above the plywood shed reads 7:41. He points to it, swinging his feathered mane for effect, like he's pissed off or disappointed. He is twenty-six with full silver braces, half Danny's size, and a huge Steve Perry fan. The look is a tribute to his hero, Danny learns in the weeks he is here. There are white sneakers and tight, frayed jeans, a gold chain, and a rib-clinging Journey concert T-shirt, out of which spring two gangling white arms spotted with little black beads of hair.

"The bus was late again," Danny says, although he should probably be on a bus fifteen minutes before the one he rides each morning.

"Screw the bus!" Darrell yells, more for Spotley's benefit than for Danny. "Just get here on time." He turns to Spotley and shakes his head. Darrell is concerned about his job—there have been mistakes and blown orders he tries to pin on Danny and others, but invoices don't lie.

Spotley is the one Danny has to worry about, not Darrell. He is bigger, wiry and bone-necked, with a blond home-cut shag. Spotley warned Danny when he started that it was nothing personal, but Danny getting hired cut into his bonus pay—twenty-five or thirty bucks a week—and he is out to get Danny fired. This day might be the day. There is a rumor that someone is coming in from the main office to speak to some people; business drops with the cold weather. And today two big trucks are in the dock for the big load out to Tempe; they have to be loaded and out before a projected blizzard, now packing itself into huge black clouds behind the summits, comes clocking down the slopes.

"We need twelve more crates," Darrell yells over the forklift generator he's priming, "then start packing up generators. You think you can handle that, Dickhead?"

Danny goes to his corner of the shipping platform, pulling the pneumatic hose behind him to hook up to the air hammer.

Spotley crosses his path, an eighty-pound generator on his shoulder. "You better watch your ass today," he growls.

"Thanks," Danny says, plugging the hose into the hammer, which makes a series of clicking noises as it pressures up.

"YES!" Darrell yells, swinging down off the roll bar of the forklift cab. He runs to the shed and turns up the radio. "Doo, wah, doo-wah!" he yells, mimicking the opening chords. He grabs an imaginary bass guitar, then hops up onto a four-foot stack of crates Danny built the day before. Spotley picks up an imaginary lead guitar and jumps up next to Darrell. They stand on top of the teetering stack, legs spread, air guitaring, making wild poses for an imaginary arena full of screaming adolescent girls. Darrell's braces sparkle against the dark stacks of plates, crates, and machine parts all rowed up twenty feet high and a hundred yards deep, from the loading dock all the way back to the production floor, where twenty or thirty floor men in earphones and safety glasses work feverishly to finish the order before the trucks roll their gates.

Danny takes a stack of dry pine planks and pumps nails into them until he splits the square posts, one crate into five, five into twelve. After some time, he sees the beat-up back of a truck bumping up against the gate, making a huge scraping sound. Danny looks down at his hands. They look like sliced oven mitts. His palms are smooth and thick and shiny—one big, hand-sized callus on the face of each hand—and his fingers are laced with a hundred corrugated cardboard cuts, stung with glue and chemicals.

"Trucks are in now," Darrell yells, running to get on the forklift. "We need to get the two loads out before it hits." The clock reads eight-fifty. Spotley waves Danny over to start pulling cardboard cases out of the stacks. Sitting up in the saddle of the forklift, Darrell yells orders, but he is only half-interested in what he is saying; instead, he looks down the production floor, glancing at a man wearing a tie and talking to several people from the production crew. The man looks like a big Okie with a mop of blond hair and massive red cheeks. He holds a clipboard and explains something to the crew, who stand with hands on their hips, trying to comprehend something on the clipboard.

Darrell starts rolling back and forth with the forklift, picking up stacked crates from the back and running them up, almost on top of the men. "Come on!' he screams at no one and everyone, weaving from production to shipping, steering the plates and crates through the labyrinth. Spotley and Danny continue loading and stacking three-by-eights, then four-by-eights, into the truck, row after row, steel banding each row. They run from the truck to the plates but can't keep up. Danny's arms go dead. Spotley says nothing. Danny remembers when Spotley tried to start in on him yesterday in the lunchroom, something about not saying "hello" fast enough. There was a vague threat or promise about something bad happening to Danny's ass after work in the parking lot, but there was no room in the overheated lunchroom, between chairs and people punching in and out, to clarify what was said. By the time Danny got to the parking lot—his crate quota filled, but two hours after Darrell, Spotley, and the others had punched out—it was dark and empty.

Now Danny stops for a moment before picking up another plate. "Pick it up!" Spotley yells. "Pick it up!" But Danny can't stop looking up the long aisle because he knows something is about to happen. Darrell, looking nervously over his shoulder at the meeting, is roaring toward them. A stack of eight freshly made four-by-eight glass-and-steel plates—each representing three hours of the production crew cutting, bending, polishing, spot-welding, pressurizing, heating, cooling, insulating, wiring, sealing, and shrink-wrapping—are unbalanced, shifting precariously on the teeth of the lift. By the time he turns, it is too late. The forklift goes up on two wheels and swerves to the left, crashing straight through the plant wall and into the production floor of the adjacent plant, where a huge printing press is spitting out vacation brochures for the "Gateway to the West." The whole wall folds flat onto the press. Through the hole, Danny sees sparks and flames shoot from the big blue printing machine, and the forklift, smashed beyond repair, laying on its side with the glass-and-steel plates spread out like dead birds.

Darrell climbs back through the hole, looks first at Danny and Spotley, then up at the production crew, and, finally, at the man with the tie.

"Whoops," he says.

The next morning, when Danny walks into work at seven forty-three, the man with the tie is sitting in Darrell's plywood shack. "You're late," he says without looking up from a stack of invoices he is ruffling through. Darrell is nowhere to be seen; the hole in the factory wall is plastered, sealed, and painted shut.

"I won't let it happen again," Danny says.

"Don't," the man with the tie says. And for another nine weeks and four days, Danny doesn't let it happen again.

EMERGENCY

Danny is sitting in an emergency room. It is very late at night or very early in the morning. There was a nurse, somewhere at a desk behind a glass window, but she has disappeared. There is one wheelchair. There are twelve very hard plastic chairs facing each other in two rows. There are two swinging doors. There is a poster on one wall, behind the desk: a cat hanging from a horizontal bar. "Hang in there, baby," the poster announces, "Friday's coming!"

Duffy slumps next to Danny in his chair. He holds his right hand in his lap with his left hand. In the center of his right hand, right in the middle of the palm, is a three-inch nail. The nail protrudes out the back of his hand, but very neatly; Danny tried to pull it out some hours earlier with pliers, but it wouldn't budge. Not a lot of blood. But a lot of swelling— Duffy's hand is now an angry red football sitting in his lap with big red swollen fingers.

"Still hurt?" Danny asks.

Duffy doesn't answer. The pot he smoked during his lunch break wore off hours ago. His mouth is hanging open. He is staring at the cat poster.

"Do you want me to tell you another joke about Jesus?" Danny asks him.

"Look, man," Duffy says. "You really don't have to stay. I'm going to be fine."

"We've been waiting four hours. I'm not leaving now." Danny feels bad; he was the one who showed Duffy how to plug the pneumatic hammer in after Duffy came back from his lunch break with that glazed look. It was his second day on the job. Never use a pneumatic hammer when you're stoned, someone told somebody once.

Boom! The doors swing open. Danny turns, expecting a doctor or a nurse. It is an elderly couple being led in by an orderly. The woman slumps into a chair, looks at Duffy and Danny, and clutches her purse. Her husband sits next to her, holding a yellowed dish towel to the side of his head.

"Will it be much longer?" Danny asks the orderly.

"We're very busy tonight," he snaps.

"But nobody's here."

The orderly glares at Danny. He is a massive man who probably played college football with dreams of going pro but ended up being an orderly at a welfare hospital.

"Look, man," he says, "what do I care? I just work here."

"My friend here just needs to see somebody," Danny says, pointing to Duffy's hand, which now looks blue, like a blue catcher's mitt.

"If he doesn't like to wait, he should go someplace else," the orderly says, disappearing back through the swinging doors.

Danny turns and faces the woman, still clutching her purse, now staring at Duffy's hand.

"Hello," Duffy says. The woman's face melts.

"My son died for drugs," she says.

"Oh, boy," Danny says.

"Oh," Duffy says. "Sorry."

"My son died for drugs! There was a bitchery there in the paper, saying it was a suicide, but I knowed better." The old man takes the dishtowel from his face, slowly folds it, and stares down into it intently. Then he picks it up and holds it up to the other side of his face.

"I had to wear a sign at the county fair," the old woman continues. "I done told everybody it wasn't no suicide. My son died for drugs!"

"Wow," Duffy says, scratching the back of his head uncomfortably with his nail-free hand. The woman only seems to get more agitated, muttering to herself. As her voice rises, the old man winces.

"I done heard his voice from the graveyard, telling me, 'Momma, I died for drugs.' I done heard it!"

"Okay," Duffy says, rising slowly from his chair, clutching his nail-hand. "That's it. We're done here."

"But we have to see a doctor," Danny says. "We have to get that nail out of your hand."

"My son died for drugs!" the woman repeats, like she is about to start over.

"I'm sorry," Duffy says to her. "I'm sorry about your son." He turns to Danny. "And you," he says. "I'm sick of your funny business."

Duffy walks out of the emergency room, toward the parking lot, then the road back to town; Danny can't keep up with him, puts his arms up, and walks back toward town.

STRAY CATS

The six of them pour out of the Broken Arrow and squeeze into Spotley's Datsun. They are going to the Novan plant Christmas party at the Elks Lodge in the next town. Spotley, at the wheel, is fuming about something. He grips the steering wheel tightly, on and off, like he's choking it. He makes an accelerating U-turn under a string of Christmas tinsel hanging from a big red stop light. He turns up a side street, the headlights illuminating a row of trailers strung up with cheap little Christmas lights, then a lot full of junked cars, then the desert.

"Hey Spotley," someone yells from the three bodies pressed against each other in the back seat, "we have to stop someplace and get drunk first."

"There's a roadhouse on the way up there," someone else says. "We can stop and get more lit up there."

Danny is pressed up against the passenger seat door. Somewhere outside his blackened window there is desert and, beyond that, the mountains. Danny shares the front seat with Spotley and another large person who works in production; he hasn't said a word since they all met at the bar right after work. Tinny music strings itself out of a little cassette deck in

Spotley's dashboard, the same Stray Cats song, repeating itself over and over again. The car is carrying a heavy load, creaking and groaning on the hills. There is a rattling sound when the bald tires run into the sand laid down for the season's first big blizzard, due to sweep down the mountains in just a few hours. Outside of work, Danny realizes, he does not know these people. They all work in different stations. Except for Spotley, who used to work with Danny in shipping, before he went to receiving. Spotley can drive a forklift better than anybody.

"Hey, Spotley," someone yells from the back seat. "What is this crap you're playing for music?"

"It's the Stray Cats," Danny says.

"Do you got something else?" the voice asks. "Do you got the new Styx album?"

"It's the Stray Cats," Danny says. "Spotley likes the Stray Cats."

The car goes silent for a moment. "The bar is right up here on the right," another voice says. Danny looks out the window. A neon sign glows—a blue martini, then a prospector shoveling gold, then a blue martini. "Gold Mine Saloon" a sign blinks over a white door. There are no windows. One pickup truck sits alone in the parking lot.

"They better have a juke box," the music complainer says, unfolding himself from the back seat. "It better have Styx."

They walk into the bar. Six skinny kids, Danny thinks, who work in a factory, who think they're bad-asses, walk into a bar. The bar is empty. There is nobody there.

"Hello?" one says.

"Maybe it's self-serve," another says.

Christmas lights blink over shelves lined with bottles. A plastic Santa stands at the corner of the bar, smiling at them, holding a bottle of Schlitz where there should have been a Coke. Spotley climbs over the bar, grabs five bottles, hands one to each of them, takes one for himself, and climbs back over the bar.

"What are you doing?" Danny asks, staring down at a strange label, a pyramid circled by giant black birds.

"Ride's leaving," Spotley says, taking a swig from his bottle and walking straight for the door. He walks out. Danny hears the car start, the strained little whining of the Datsun's engine. He looks at the others, who look back at him. And then they all run like hell for that car.

PART III

THAT
BOX-LIKE
CONTRAPTION

EUSTICE SOMETHING McCULLICK

Crossing the state line into Pennsylvania is a lot like crossing an ocean—these rolling hills, this concrete roadway like waves disappearing into a vast, distant sea. Dried and broken cornstalks, parting like the stiff wake of the boat Danny is riding in, like he is going to some far-off destination. It is Christmas Day, and he is going to make it, unless he is thrown through the windshield of this station wagon first.

"Here you go, Babe! Have a shot of this." The huge man next to Danny, driving the wagon, just called Danny "babe." He has a red face and a mountainous red beard, little woodchips sticking out of it. He's wearing overalls and boots. Tools and pipes and things clang around in the back well of the wagon. At the crest of each hill, they are lifted into the air, the great car accelerating into open space.

Before it crashes down, Danny sees everything—a blue ridge of mountains in the distance, little clumps of trees, and rows and rows of dead corn—and then the car splashes into the trough. The car is moving way too fast for this road, Danny realizes. Something's got to give.

The bottle his new friend has handed him tastes like sour apples. It makes his throat sting. Danny hands it back to him. "Thanks," Danny says.

"Not at all, Babe! I'm celebrating."

They ride up another hill. The driver takes the bottle, squeezes it between his legs, and reaches into the back seat. "Say, babe. You all want a beer?" He pulls two bottles of beer out of the back and hands one to Danny. "Only you don't have an opener, do you? Shoot. I got an idea." He swings his door open into the seventy miles-per-hour headwind. "Hold the wheel here, will ya, babe?" Danny reaches over and takes the steering wheel. The driver pops the cap off his beer bottle, then Danny's, and hands him the foaming bottle, just as a huge truck barrels up over the lip of the hill toward them. He pulls the door shut as the truck's horn blares past.

"So what are we celebrating?" Danny asks him, while wiping the foam from his pants.

"Well, first of all, it's Christmas, and I'm four days off that crap job I've been working up here for the last six months. I'm building that hospital right back there where I picked you up. And second of all, I'm headed home to Virginia. And third of all, my wife just had a baby, a beautiful baby boy, so I'm told. And so how's that for something to celebrate?"

Danny looks over at him and he looks a little more crazed, his eyes going everywhere.

"Here you go, Babe," he says, handing Danny the bottle again. "What do you say? You'll drink to *that*?" Danny chokes another burning shot of sour apples down. "What you say your name was again, Babe?"

"Danny," Danny says.

The driver reaches out his free hand to shake Danny's vigorously. With the other, he takes the bottle. The steering wheel oscillates back and forth, seemingly following the edge of the pavement. "Well, my name's Eustice Something McCullick. But everybody calls me 'Babe.' Hold on now!"

The car rises up one more time at the crest and takes flight above the hills. A beam of light shoots from the clouds in front of Danny, illuminating a little herd of deer standing in a patch of dirt by the side of the road, looking for something to eat in the dead stalks surrounding them.

"Hold on now, Babe!" the driver yells again, and the car crashes down once more, leaving them floating between the earth and the air.

THE FIELD

On the far side of Gettysburg, way out on the far edge of the battlefield, Danny finds this place he calls The Field. It is behind a little clump of trees where the park service runs a summer theater. That is the summer, but now it is winter, and the tourists are not here, and Danny has the snow-brushed meadow to himself. It is just a little sprawl of a dug-up wheat field and a tangle of trees clinging to a frozen creek bed, and then an opposite hill climbing up into the orchards. Beyond the orchards are scrubby, piney little mountains. Every day he can, Danny walks out there, sits in that field, and watches the winter colors sweep across the earth. Sometimes a veil of snow brushes down from the sky. Sometimes a herd of starving deer wanders from the forest. Blackbirds screech and fight over dead clumps of last year's corn. More often The Field is totally, completely quiet. The first week of January isn't so cold, and Danny can sit there for hours, watching afternoons settle into evenings, shadows settle into the earth.

Danny has met a guy who has him cleaning carpets some nights. He should be working more, he knows, or at least looking for full-time work. But all of that is behind him in that little town; and all of this is up here in this little field. When Danny works, he daydreams about The Field. He tries to imagine what it looks like in the spring or in the fall. He imagines The Field as a rich green blanket. He knows it is park service land—part of the battlefield that circles the town—but he starts to think about how he might buy it, build a cabin there, raise chickens or something.

One afternoon Danny starts walking out there when he sees a guy he calls Raincoat Stevie. When Raincoat Stevie isn't washing dishes or goofing off in a bar, he loiters in the town square wearing a raincoat. Now Danny runs into him, and he is standing in front of a parking meter, staring into it with great intensity. There is no car in front of the meter. It occurs to Danny that Raincoat Stevie should come with him to visit The Field.

"Hey, man," Danny says. "You want to go for a little hike, man? I know this place. I call it The Field."

"Sure thing, that sounds great," Raincoat Stevie says, but he seems reluctant to leave the meter. Danny waves him along, and he breaks away. They walk together under bare trees. The air is still, but it has that feeling, like a big cold front is coming in fast. They walk to the end of the road, where the town stops, and the battlefield park starts, just as suddenly. They climb over a split-log fence, next to a pair of rusting cannons, and enter a squishing field of mud and water.

"Where did you say we're going, man?" Raincoat Stevie asks after slogging for a hundred yards across this first field. He looks cold. He huddles in his raincoat. Danny looks down at his sneakers, which have huge holes in the sides and are soaked through, just like Danny's.

"Over there," Danny says, pointing to the massed clump of trees surrounding the theater at the edge of the horizon.

"No way," Raincoat Stevie says. He looks at Danny directly for the first time ever; his eyes are like empty milk saucers. "I won't make it. And that place out there is hell, man. That's where they buried all those arms and legs."

"Nah," Danny says, picturing The Field in all its serene and wintry glory.

"Arms and legs, man," he continues. "That's where they set up the field hospitals. The farmers kept plowing them up.

They stopped planting in that field because of the arms and legs. Nobody goes out to that field, man. I'm serious."

"Come on," Danny says, trying to sound reassuring. "It's beautiful. You'll see."

"No, man, I got to go to work." Raincoat Stevie hunches up, like a cold wind is passing through him, although the air is warm and thick and smells like melting dirt. "This place creeps me out. This whole thing's a big graveyard." He turns and starts squishing back toward town, toward work. Danny watches him climb the fence and disappear into the safety of the town. Then he pushes on for The Field.

THAT BIG RUSSIAN COAT

January becomes February. Winds rip down from the foothills, screech through the bare apple trees, and circle the old house. They creep through the floorboards and rattle the windowpanes. The landlord never asks for the rent, so Danny never asks about heat. He finds clear plastic sheets and tapes them over the windows. He finds a space heater that smells like meat; a prior tenant may have used it to cook hot dogs. Danny leaves the oven running all night. It doesn't matter. It keeps getting colder and colder.

This is when Danny sees that Big Russian Coat. It is on a hanger in the back of the Moravian Thrift Shop. It is thick and knee-length and baggy and matted, old black herringbone on the outside, red felt on the inside. Danny is afraid to try it on. Then he pulls it off the hanger. It drapes itself over his shoulders and wraps itself around him. That Russian Coat! That Big Russian Coat! The old Moravian lady is alone behind the counter, pulling things out of paper bags and folding them.

She knows Danny only ducked in there to warm up for a minute. She knows he isn't going to buy anything. She never looks up at him. Danny doesn't want to ask her. He only has three dollars in his pocket. He puts the coat back on its hanger. He says, "Thank you," but very quietly, and he pulls the door open. The wind shrieks up Chambersburg Street. Danny wraps his old sweatshirt around his head like a turban, tucks the ends into his frayed denim jacket, stuffs his hands in his pockets, and starts walking.

There is no way Danny can afford that Big Russian Coat. He has been spot-working for a carpet cleaner, but nobody wants their carpets cleaned in the winter. Everybody Danny used to know in town has drifted on to another town, looking for work. The mills are all closed. This cold snap won't last forever, he tells himself. The cold has to break.

He walks all the way out to the Get-Mor Factory Outlet. Get-Mor sells surplus and irregulars from the closed textile plants. Inside, it is warm and smells like cleaning fluids. The two ladies who run Get-Mor are moving slowly and laboriously from bin to bin, folding things absentmindedly. They know their days are numbered. They hum along to tinny country music on an eight-track behind the register. Danny spends some time pretending to look for things, only to warm up. He pulls a huge, knockoff, irregular, padded flannel shirt out of a one-dollar bin. He walks to the register and stands there.

"Jest a minute," one of the ladies, rolling two mismatched monkey socks into a ball, yells across the showroom. She gives up on her sock-monkey ball. She walks slowly to the register, tilting ten degrees to starboard. She looks at the flannel shirt tag, then thoughtfully scribbles something in a notebook next to the register.

"Well then," she says. "That will be two dollars."

"But it only says one dollar," Danny says, holding the tag up.

"Well then," she says. "That will be one dollar."

Danny hands her one of his three dollars.

"Thank you," he says.

She folds the dollar bill and stuffs it under the register drawer, then walks back to her bin. Danny glances at the notebook to see where she has written down, with surprisingly neat penmanship, three words: "Sock Monkey Balls."

Danny pulls the flannel shirt on over the denim jacket and the other layers, rewraps his head, and walks back to town. This time he is walking straight into the wind. His cheeks stinging in the cold, his hands numb in his armpits; the wind cuts through everything. He turns onto Chambersburg Street, and splinters of ice particles cut into his face. He passes the Moravian Thrift Shop again. He looks in at the coat through the picture window. It is still there on its hanger. What the hell, he thinks. He walks in and tries it on again, pulling it on over all the other layers. It wraps itself around him, a little tighter this time, with the new layer underneath. The old lady looks at Danny. He expects a frown, but she smiles—a big silver-and-amber smile, like Danny is a boy she once knew.

"It looks very becoming on you, young man," she says.

"Can I ask how much it costs?"

"Two dollars," she says.

Danny wears that Big Russian Coat home, and wind can't cut through the layers. He is air-tight against the cold. He sleeps in that Big Russian Coat for a week.

During that big cold snap, a mother-son team opens a laundromat on Carlisle Street. They open it up with little checkered flags and "Battlefield Laundry-Grand Opening" signs and two rows of brand-new washing machines and two rows of dryers. During the first week, nobody goes in there. Another week goes by, and nobody goes in there. Every time Danny walks past, he sees the mother and son taking turns standing behind the counter, staring through the plate-glass window or folding a single towel, again and again, with great deliberation. Nobody ever, ever goes in there.

Danny becomes preoccupied with the new and empty laundromat because, while he loves the Big Russian Coat and spends every waking and sleeping moment in it, it does carry a strong smell—like cat litter or cat urine or something else. Danny needs to wash it, along with a bundle of filthy laundry piled at the foot of his bed. Either the mother or the son glances up from their towel folding when Danny walks by, and they stare at him like he's a shuffler. Danny only needs a pocketful of quarters, which he will have as soon as he gets a steady job. And then, he reasons, he won't be a shuffler, and he'll be able to wash all the laundry he wants.

And a week later, he gets lucky—he knows a guy who knows a guy who is washing dishes at the Dropkin House Tavern. One night the second guy just drops dead, face-down in the rinse sink. And the guy he knows put a word in to the boss, and Danny gets the job.

Danny convinces himself that things are looking up. A real job! A steady paycheck! And he works a few shifts, and he likes the job! The boss seems really nice, and the waiters and the cook seem really nice. Best of all, he has been good at very few things in his life, but one of those few things, as it turns out, is washing dishes. There is that box-like contraption, that metal-mouthed machine. There are hot hissing noises and a power hose. The dishes go in, lined up in racks, all dirty, and come out all steamy clean. Danny works in his own quiet corner of the universe. All the bustle of the restaurant rat-race is behind him.

On Friday afternoon, the boss's wife hands him his first paycheck. She has her son with her—a ten-year-old boy, bored out of his mind. She is very Christian and polite, and makes a special effort in front of her son to treat Danny like he's not a shuffler. But the boy knows. The boy stands next to her and rolls his eyes. The boy knows Danny is a shuffler.

Danny runs over to the bank, opens a bank account, cashes forty dollars, and leaves fifty-five dollars to write a rent check. His forearms are a little achy, still getting used to the work, and his hamstrings are a little tight. He rushes over to the Johnny Reb and drinks his first, then his second, then his third cold pitcher in weeks. The snow is melting in the square, right outside the bar's big picture windows. A truck drives around the circle, slashing an arc of snow-dirt against the abandoned cars. At closing time, Danny walks home, past Battlefield Laundry, closed with its gate pulled down. Tomorrow, he thinks. Tomorrow.

At home he climbs into bed, bundled in that Big Russian Coat, and stares up at the ceiling. He hasn't been drunk in a while—he tried to sober up when money got real short before Christmas. And Danny hasn't eaten hardly anything because of the money. Now the bed starts spinning—gentle at first, then wildly, like he is on a life raft at sea. He starts reciting Hail Marys. Mary calms the ship, and he spins off to sleep.

Late the next morning, Danny wakes up; it is his first day off in a week. It is warm enough, so he opens the windows. He gathers up his laundry in a huge ball and wraps it up in that Big Russian Coat. But then he puts it down because now he is hungry. He goes to the Lincoln Diner and sits at a booth and goes for the works: cream of broccoli soup and a turkey club with a side of apple fritters, then a cherry cheesecake with a Coke and a pot of coffee.

After paying the bill and tip, Danny's running low on cash, so he rushes to the bank to take out another forty dollars. On the way he crosses through the square. He can see a game on the TV above the bar at Johnny Reb. After taking out the money, Danny walks back. Three pitchers later, with the sun is setting over the orchards to the west, he walks out. He stops at the 7-Eleven for a six-pack, rushes home, gathers up the laundry, and drags the giant ball to Battlefield Laundry.

"How are you doing today?" he says to the son, who is folding the same towel he's been folding since opening day.

"We close in an hour, you know," he says without looking up from the towel.

All the beer Danny drank in the past eighteen hours, after drinking nothing at all for far too long, presses down against him. He takes the huge bag of laundry—that Big Russian Coat, two pairs of army surplus pants, fourteen socks (none matching), two flannel shirts, T-shirts and sweatshirts and the rest—and stuffs everything into a washer. He presses down hard on the lid to get the whole load in, but the lid won't shut.

"I can't close the lid."

"Supposing you can maybe do two loads of wash."

"Supposing I can't."

Son is folding that towel so tight it is like a paper airplane.

"Can I just turn on the water and see if it shrinks down so I can close the lid?"

"Don't care much what you do or how you do it," Son says. He licks his lips and stares at Danny. He has a thin moustache and wears a polo shirt from the local state college— Waynesburg or Shippensboro or something. "The Battlefield Laundry is a self-service laundry, so I suppose you can do whatever you like."

Son walks out the back door, leaving Danny to the machines. He opens and drains a tallboy. He rattles the quarters in his pocket. He buys detergent from a slot machine. He puts four quarters in the washer and pushes down on the pile. Nothing. He opens and drains another tallboy. He climbs up and sits on the washing machine lid. Still nothing. He gets up and stands on top of it, his head hitting the tile drop ceiling, and rocks back and forth. This does the trick—the door closes, and the machine starts.

Danny reaches down, grabs and drains another tallboy, and then another. Standing on the running washing machine is kind of fun, and no harm done, he thinks, rocking back and forth on top of it while it rattles and whirls beneath him. It's like surfing, he thinks. Washing machine surfing. He starts singing in rhythm. "Hooga chaka, hooga hooga chaka." He looks out the picture window. Wrapped up in a muffler and a ski jacket, a boy on a bike is staring at Danny.

"Hooga chaka," Danny sings through the picture window at the boy. "Hooga hooga chaka." The kid rolls his eyes and then pedals away. Only then does Danny recognize him—the boss's son. The job is as good as gone. He squats down, opens, and drains another beer.

"Git the hell offin that machine," Son says behind Danny.

Danny turns, and he is standing there with his mother, staring at Danny, holding a shotgun.

Now Danny doesn't feel so drunk. He climbs down off the machine. "Okay, okay," he says.

"What do you have to say for yerself?" the mother asks.

"I'm very sorry."

"You finish up that load," she says, "but after that you got to leave. We don't tolerate no such behavior in the Battlefield Laundry." She looks to her son for reassurance, and he nods enthusiastically—the muzzle of the gun pointing from Danny's knees to his stomach and back again—and then she turns back to Danny. "Self-service or not."

Danny climbs down. They all stand there in silence together, the shotgun still pointed at Danny's knees, while the washing machine moves from wash to rinse to spin and then shuts off. He doesn't ask to use the dryers.

"Well, thank you, I guess," he says. "Good luck with your new business."

Back home, Danny piles the clothes on top of the stove and turns it on. This will never work, he thinks, slowly sipping his last beer. He falls asleep on the kitchen floor. Those spins, those spins. Hail Mary, full of grace.

When Danny wakes up early the next afternoon, his clothes lay wrinkled on top of the stove, all clean and dry, and that Big Russian Coat smells only like detergent; a good thing, because the wind is howling out there again, and it looks like a new snow is blowing in from the hills.

AUGUSTA AND GRETA

Every so often Danny is visited by one of two witches who drift into Gettysburg from the east and wander off to the west and then, sometime later, drift back into town from the west on their way to the east. The first is named Greta, and she is tall and fair, and she wears big cowboy boots and long hand-sewn dresses and a cape, and she always walks with a big wooden stick, and she is always followed by a pack of stray dogs. The second is named Augusta, and she is small and lives under a mountain of thick black hair, and she wears work boots and baggy pants and a snorkel jacket, but she also has a big wooden stick, and she is always followed by a pack of stray cats.

Danny thinks they know each other, but he never sees them together, which may be on account of the dogs and the cats. But regardless, somehow, he gets to know Greta, who sleeps on his floor, wrapped up in her cape, with her cowboy boots on and sleeping dogs all around her, when she passes through town. And Augusta too, with the work boots and snorkel and cats. They insist on sleeping on the floor, even though there is a perfectly soft and comfortable couch Danny dragged up from the street some weeks before. Danny only has to move the piles of newspapers, but they won't hear of it. Neither one of them. He often asks each if they know the other, but they just stare at him quizzically until he changes the subject.

And they cook things! Like, Danny comes in from some bar, and there they are at one in the morning, one or the other, cooking something, grains and sauces, things they find in their bags. They make a bowl for Danny and another for the dogs or cats. This all goes on in this crazy, collapsing building Danny is living in. The front door doesn't have a lock or a doorknob. The place is freezing. Danny sits at the table and gets drowsy eating that great hot food. Augusta or Greta watches him and the animals eat, stirring a pot or sizzling some seeds they pull out of a pocket, but they never eat any themselves. And they are both very quiet. To fill the void, Danny does all the talking. Which he is not, at that time in his life, very good at.

"Um," Danny says, "can you tell me your dogs' names again?

"There's Ampithoe and Dionne and Egavore."

"Oh. Where are you from again?"

"I came from Taneytown. I'm on my way to Biggersville."

"Oh, cool! So, um, I'm off tomorrow. I'm thinking of going out to McPherson Ridge to hang out in that bar. Um, it's pretty cool; they converted a chicken coop into a bar." Danny prattles on and on, Greta or Augusta, dogs or cats, the hot, grainy porridge sinking into him, until he wakes up—laying fully clothed on top of his bed—and his visitor is long gone. This goes on through the winter. But in the spring, a crazy thing happens. Danny comes in one night and finds Greta and Augusta and the dogs and cats all having this crazy fight in the kitchen, seeds sprayed over the plastic table, a pot of something knocked over on the stove. They are really fighting, red hands clutching each other's shoulders, shoving each other into the walls, dogs barking, cats screeching at the dogs.

"Um, hey! What's going on?" Danny asks. They turn and glare at Danny. They are red-faced, wild-eyed, and their hair is everywhere.

"You need to leave this place now," Greta says.

"Oh, um, cool! I'll come back later."

"No!" Augusta says. "You will *never* come back to this place."

And Danny doesn't ask. The looks on their faces fill him with terror. He runs down the stairs and starts walking. When he comes back the next morning, all signs of them are gone.

DEAD WOMAN HOLLOW

For a few more weeks, Danny holds onto his job washing dishes at the Dropkin House Tavern. The Dropkin House is an old stone house in the middle of town that was converted into a hospital during the Civil War. Later, it was restored as a tourist restaurant for out-of-towners who came to see the battlefields. Out-of-towners aren't coming this year on account of the economy, and they certainly aren't coming in February. There aren't a lot of dishes for Danny to wash, and four weeks after he started, they fire him and close the Dropkin House.

During Danny's last week at the Dropkin House, he gets friendly with a waitress everybody calls Cashtown Annie. Cashtown Annie is from Biggersville, another orchard town in a string of orchard towns running along this side of the river and that side of the mountains, but they are all the same. Cashtown Annie, however, is one of a kind. She is louder than the other staff; she drops things, and she laughs a lot. They make her wear a frilly wench dress and apron that she makes fun of. She complains about how cold it is and insists on wearing a red hunting cap with a bill and earflaps, even in the dining room. And she has a huge red pocketbook that she refuses to put down; she has cheap plastic sunglasses and a dozen Bic lighters stuffed in it. The Dropkin House manager is a skinny little moustache guy who is very particular about the comportment of his employees; but this particular winter, employees are as hard to come by as customers, so they let the hat and the pocketbook go.

Cashtown Annie comes in and eats her shift meal with Danny, leaning against the dishwashing machine, trying to soak its heat into her bones. She talks a lot. She calls Danny "Frederico," even though that isn't his name. She has a remarkable nose—a real Karl Malden number—and she has huge brown eyes that don't register any emotions ever. With her hunting hat on, she looks pretty crazy, leaning against the stainless steel machine, eating a pork chop with her fingers, and going on and on about her ex-boyfriend from DC, who has some connection or other to the music world; she'd once been backstage for the Bad Brains or Minor Threat or Black Flag or something.

Cashtown Annie gives Danny advice about all the people in this town—"You should get to know them," "You should stay away from him." She tells stories about witches in the woods, ghosts right here in the Dropkin House, and an old lady whose body keeps washing up in a creek by her house. They buried her up in a hollow, and for years after, she keeps washing up in the creek. They call the hollow "Dead Woman Hollow," and they call the creek "Marsh Creek;" it is the same creek that rambles through the center of Gettysburg. "If you see a dead old lady floating around in that creek, don't you ever go try to pull her out of the water! And don't never set foot in that creek! Don't you never! Because if you do…" The manager yells her name. Cashtown Annie slams down her plate and returns to the dining room.

Danny never finds out why they call her Cashtown Annie. In all, he probably only talks with her three or four times at that job. She punches out an hour before Danny does; some strung-out guy picks her up in a beat-up old car and drives her back up to Biggersville. When Danny punches out an hour later, he walks alone in the dark, up an alley, the late winter winds slicing through him. He stops at the Billy Yank and drinks three or four dollar pitchers by himself, and then he goes home. He wrestles himself into his sleeping bag, pulls the old coat and other things over his head, and waits for the spins to start. For a while there, he sees Cashtown Annie—big eyes, big nose, funny hat—spinning in front of him, laughing; then it's an old woman, face-down, floating in a creek.

Cashtown Annie gets fired at the same time Danny does; when the job at the Dropkin House ends, Cashtown Annie disappears from his spins. But the old lady's still there, every night, spinning.

Winter turns to spring. The snow melts away. The orchards surrounding the little town lay still; the budding apple and cherry trees are out of work. Flower petals blossom and blow through the town's empty streets. Everything smells like steamed dirt.

This is the time that Danny meets Sir Henry.

Danny has seen Sir Henry around town, and he certainly knows about him. Danny is scared of him. He is a head taller than Danny with long dreadlocks and teeth lined with gold that shimmers when he laughs. He laughs all the time—a heavy, booming laugh that echoes up and down the streets, between the little frame houses. His laugh rattles the window frames behind the rusting steel gates in the long-closed jewelry store and the long-closed clock store. All the stores on Chambersburg Street stay closed after the farmers got bought out and the plants and mills closed and everybody had to get up and go live someplace else. Danny hears that laugh, and wherever he is, he freezes.

One time, from his apartment window, Danny hears Sir Henry going back and forth with somebody on the street.

"You there! What is your name?" Sir Henry booms.

"Uh, hey there," another voice quietly responds. "Um, they call me Bill."

"Bill man! Ha! Ha! I must ask you—what is it that brings you to this forsaken place?"

"Um, nothing. Well, I'll see you around, I guess. I got to go pick up my old lady."

"Very good! Very good! Bill's old lady! Ha! Ha!"

"Well, yeah, I guess I'll see you around."

That laugh! Ricocheting up and down the narrow passages between the buildings. Is it getting closer, or is it getting farther away?

It is Cashtown Annie, Danny remembers, who told him to keep away from Sir Henry. "That Sir Henry guy? You keep away from him, Frederico!" she told Danny once in the dishwashing room at the Dropkin House. "He's caught up in some drug-runner business. He's selling jack. He's driving jack up from Baltimore. He's works for some crazy-ass jack dealer," she says, looking at Danny with those big brown eyes, unregistered. "He acts all friendly to everybody, but believe me, you keep away from him."

By early April, Danny is living on a box of canned vegetables. Carrots and peas. Creamed corn. He is running out of cans. Landlord George is sending his boys out for Danny, to shake him down for two months' back rent, and Danny has to climb in and out his back window to avoid them. George's boys scare Danny as much as Sir Henry does. He sees them standing in front of the 7-Eleven, sucking Slurpees with a straw, staring up at his front windows.

Once out that back window, Danny scampers down the alley between the ice factory ruins and the main street, then crosses at the apple crate factory, now all boarded up. He cuts over to the railroad tracks and follows them into the twilight. Danny walks until he can walk no farther. He stops for a moment in the darkness, panting, saying, "What the hell, what the hell," to himself over and over again. Then he turns around and heads back for town.

One night Danny gets back to town, and he passes a dumpster behind Charlie's Texas Lunch. Something smells pretty good in there. Danny stops and stares into that dumpster. That is where Sir Henry finally corners him— staring into that dumpster.

"You there! What is your name?"

Danny tells him.

"And what brings you to this forsaken place?"

"I, you know, live here."

That laugh fills the dumpster and echoes around. It makes Danny's head hurt.

"There is no food to eat in there, Herbie."

"My name's not Herbie," Danny says. "It's—"

"You need good, hot food, Herbie, is what you need. Come with me. I am cooking hot food. You are welcome. You are welcome. Ha!"

Danny is hungry, so what the hell. He follows Sir Henry up a staircase in the back of an old gas station. They then cross above the alley on a fire escape bridge that leads to a rooftop. The bridge creaks and bends under their weight. "Ha! Ha!" The alley below them is piled high with rusting chrome fenders. On the other side of the rooftop is a window with thick red curtains. Sir Henry climbs through, and Danny follows. The curtains close behind him. He is in a room that looks like somebody pillaged the previous decade. There is plush, thick red carpeting, a tired leather couch, black light posters of foggy, neon green dragon-mountains. There is a kitchenette along one wall with a stove. On top of the stove, four pots are hissing.

A woman is sitting on the couch, staring at the TV. "Lady!" Sir Henry yells. "This is Herbie! My old friend Herbie! I have brought him for the dinner."

"Oh, what? You brought home another stray dog?" she says without looking up from the TV. She is watching a rerun of *Hogan's Heroes*.

"No, Lady! Ha! Ha! Not a stray dog. Herbie. My old friend Herbie."

"I don't remember you talking about any old friend named Herbie," she says. She unfolds herself from the couch and walks through a door to another room, pulling the door shut behind her. Danny never sees her again.

But the food! The food smells so good. There is a pot with some kind of stew. There is a pot with some kind of cabbage. Sir Henry stirs one, and then he stirs another. He is laughing as he stirs.

"Just a little more curry, Herbie!" he yells, dumping half a container of McCormick's into the pot, stirring it, and then dumping in the other half. "Just a little more pepper! Ha! Ha! Lady, oh Lady. Ha! Man," he says. "I have got to figure out that lady. Okay. Dinner is served. *Dinner is served!*" he yells at the door, which remains closed. Sir Henry shrugs, puts a huge plate of steaming everything on a plate for Danny, puts another one in front of himself, and they sit down at a little table by a window, looking out at the silver rooftops and telephone poles spread out haphazardly everywhere.

And then they get to talking. Sir Henry tells Danny about a man he knows, who knows a man, who is looking for somebody who is good at building things. "Is Herbie good at building things?" "Sure," Danny lies. Then Sir Henry tells him about a lady with a farm out in the hills who he does some work for, and who gave him a baby billy goat, and how much he loves this baby billy goat, and how, one day, he is going to drive Danny up to that farm to visit his baby billy goat. The job, the goat, and the laughing—"Ha! Ha! Ha!" But that's all Danny remembers because all that rich food makes him sleepy, and he can't keep his eyes open.

MISTER PATIO

Mister Patio is not the only Schmuckleman in the county, but he is the only one who ever got hit in the face with a patio brick.

The Schmuckleman name is all over the orchard barns and silos to the west. Mister Patio is the last of a long line of Schmucklemans who had a cow farm on the outskirts of town before the Civil War and bought up a bunch of the orchards after the war. Three years before Danny shows up in town, the dad fell under his tractor, and the mom sold the whole operation to National Agriculture, which, once they got a foothold, swept through the county like a plague. The banks came in and pulled the carpet out on all the family farms that tried to resist Nat Ag. The Schmuckleman clan came out of the deal cash-rich but landless and scorned; the mother and first two sons turned to religion, but the third son chose to immerse himself in the rich array of illicit pharmaceutical products traversing the county. Religion or drugs, neither helped. There was a curse on that family for selling out their land, and the whole bunch was dead in five years.

The Schmuckleman family story, Danny cannot verify. It came to him third-hand through the muddled mythology of the fall of the town, interwoven in whispers at bar booths or in awkward reunions waiting in line at the 7-Eleven. But the Mister Patio part—the hit-in-the-face-with-a-patio-brick part of the story—is the gospel truth. Danny just has to look at this guy—cleft lip, nose bent to the side, one hollow cheek, messed-up teeth. This guy clearly got hit with a brick. A patio brick. Square in the face. Danny can still see that face hours after he sees that face. Sometimes Danny thinks of that face, and he just can't get it out of his mind.

Danny first notices Mister Patio's face through his back kitchen window; he often sits in the kitchen and watches the morning opera unfold in the ice houses. The ice houses are a low, crumbling line of ten tiny brick houses set up and away from Washington Street with the big ice plant, long closed, leaning up behind them. The ice plant is in the process of collapsing in on itself. Somebody buttressed its north side so it wouldn't fall onto the railroad tracks, but the rest of the building caved in during the big snow in January the winter before. Huge steel rafters stick up from the wreckage at right angles, like crazy teeth. Danny stares at them often through his kitchen window that faces out into the accidental courtyard, ice houses to the right, ice plant in front, and a jumble of irregular apartment houses to the left. The rafters frame the trees on the long ridge in the distance. It all looks like a jumble of picture frames without the paintings.

From the ice houses, you can't see the ice plant or the trees. The ice houses have no backyards or back windows or kitchen porches. They each have a front door leading out into a gravel parking lot, across Washington Street from the Agway and the 7-Eleven. Twenty or thirty people live in the ice houses, but they rotate frequently. They all come down from the hollers and hills to the west of town. As the farms and orchards close, the people who worked them for years either migrate away or come to town looking for work. There isn't any work in town, and there is constantly a pile of people's belongings in the parking lot after the landlord sends his boys to evict another family.

From Danny's back window, he notices Mister Patio, mostly because of his face, but also because he seems like a permanent figure. One Friday night somebody comes over and starts a fight in the parking lot. Mister Patio comes out his front door carrying a lug wrench, staring at them. The fight breaks up immediately, and the visitors get in their car and never come back. After that, Danny sometimes sees Mister Patio lumbering down the street. He has a way of walking like there is an invisible steel pole embedded in his ankle and running straight up to his neck. Danny always crosses the street when he sees him coming. Everybody does. People walk off the sidewalk and cross into traffic whenever old Mister Patio comes down the street. It is just something people do.

Mister Patio has two older brothers who drive into town on Saturday mornings in a big red pickup truck and trailer and park at the Agway across the street. One morning they climb out, hitch up their pants, and walk across the street to check in on little brother. One brother pulls the screen door open, and the other one knocks on the door. They wait a long time, knocking and knocking.

A little toddler in a full diaper sits on the little step in front of the next door, chewing on a corner of a rolled-up newspaper. "Say there, little fellow," one of the brothers, who Danny thinks is named Abel, says. The toddler keeps chewing thoughtfully on the newspaper. Then he throws it with two hands into the wet gravel. He pushes himself up from the step, toddles over, and picks up the paper—the full diaper perilously close to but not quite releasing its contents—and then circles back to squat on the step, chewing away where he left off a moment ago. The other brother at the door, who Danny thinks is named Isaiah or Isaac or something, knocks even harder.

"All right now, I'm coming," a voice belts out from beyond the curtains.

"Come on, little brother," Abel yells. "It's time for your wellness check."

They call him "little brother," but come on, Danny thinks, watching all this unfold through the broken corner of his kitchen window.

The door jerks open with two heavy pulls, and Mister Patio sticks his head out. The big brothers ask him a series of short, pointed questions. "You all right?" "You been drugging?" "You need something to eat?" "You gonna call Ma?" Mister Patio shakes his head. "You tell Ma I'm out soon," he says. "You tell her I'll be coming out soon." The two brothers hesitate—they are older, but softer; since selling out to Nat Ag, teams of day laborers are bused in to do the hard work for them. Their shirts are untucked over their growing bellies; gold crosses on chains sparkle from their necks. Next to them, Mister Patio, shirtless, looks like a coiled spring. He runs his fingers through his hair. They all put their hands in their pockets and stand there, rocking. Then they all look at the toddler, who has been watching them from next door the whole time. The toddler throws the damp, chewed newspaper toward them, gets up, and slips through his own screen door.

"Okay then," Abel says. "I guess we'll be going."

The door closes. The two brothers cross the parking lot. At the street, they stop and look both ways, holding a hand out toward each other to prevent the other from darting into the street. They cross themselves. Then they climb into their truck and drive off.

One morning Danny wakes up to a thumping coming up the stairs; thinking it's George's boys, he grabs his pants and boots and reaches for the window. He hears someone stop at the top of the stairs, a small landing that opens to the little kitchen. It is always dark at that landing with doors and hallways leading in multiple directions; whoever designed this old farmhouse must have done so with unwelcome visitors in mind.

"Herbie!" Sir Henry yells from the kitchen. "Oh, Herbie. What is it that you are doing? Where is it that you are hiding? Come out, come out, Herbie!"

Danny comes out and finds Sir Henry sitting at the kitchen table, staring out the window at the ice houses.

"Herbie!" Sir Henry announces. "I have talked to my friend! He is a good man. And he has talked to his friend! And he, too, is a good man. And you will have this job. You will have this job tomorrow, Herbie. I told them you are good. I told them you are a good man. I told them you are a master carpenter. So you only need to tell the man that. He will meet you in front of the chapel at nine o'clock tomorrow."

"What?" Danny asks, pulling his pants on, first one leg, then the other. "But I'm not a master carpenter. I'm not even a master dishwasher. I can't…"

"That is why, what I tell you. You will master the others. You will be the boss man. Ha! The others will be your helplings. This is what I told them. There will be others there as well. You are the master carpenter, Herbie. Master Carpenter Herbie. The chapel on Littlestown Road. Ha! Ha! Ha!"

Danny tries to protest, but Sir Henry squints out the window with great intent.

"Say, what is this? What am I looking at? Are these the ice houses I am looking at? It is! It certainly is the ice houses I am looking at. Ha! Ha! Ha! But it is curtains, it is curtains you need. I will bring you these curtains. Hello, Master Carpenter Herbie, you must put your pants on. Please finish. There is something I must show you."

Ten minutes later Danny is hurtling through space in the passenger seat of a rust-coated Pinto with the hatchback window blown out and a garbage bag fluttering behind them. The windows are all gone; only the half-shattered windshield remains. An old Bob Marley song gargles in an eight-track. Sir Henry mumbles along, leaning over the steering wheel, a giant packed into a tiny cockpit. The pinto chassis is a little bent; as a result, only three wheels are on the road surface at any given time, and the car really wants to drift into oncoming traffic. Sir Henry announces "Here it is, I think! Oh, Herbie, yes, yes. Ha! Ha! Ha!" and swerves off the main road, just missing a row of mailboxes, and onto a dirt road climbing a hill.

They pass an old, boarded-up barn and then another. It is a warm spring day. Leaning out the Pinto passenger window to smoke his last cigarette, Danny is overwhelmed with the smells—buttered corn, apple butter, salty sweat, burning gas and oil, rotten apples, sticky asphalt, stale beer, microwave hot dogs—circling in and out of the car, even though the farms are clearly shut down. The car rocks from one wheel to another. Dust sprays out everywhere. They roll up and down one hill, then up and down another. They come to a T in the road, dirt roads leading left and right. A boarded-up farmhouse stares down at them, its shutters waving in the breeze.

"Herbie!" Sir Henry yells with great enthusiasm. "We are someplace near Biggersville, I think, and somewhere near Aintsville, I think, but we are nowhere. Herbie!"

"Can you please stop yelling?"

"Herbie, I believe I am lost! I know not to go left. I know not to go right."

Danny flicks the cigarette butt way out toward the boarded-up house; sadly, it does not start a conflagration. "Where exactly are we going?"

Sir Henry grimaces at him—a row of perfect gold teeth. "We are going to the Lady's farm," he says. "We have to find that farm! If I do not feed the Lady's chickens, I will be relieved of this world. I must feed the chickens. I must see my little billy goat. Herbie, I love that little billy goat. I have to see him. I have to feed him."

"We'll find it," Danny says. "Let's go up the hill. There's got to be a farm up here. A real working farm."

"Oh yes, a working farm, a living farm," Sir Henry says. They drive to the left, up and over a hill, and there it is. Sir Henry walks to a small pen where a dozen little goats bleat at him. He picks one up and cradles it in his arms. He takes Danny to the chicken coop and tells him how to feed the chickens. Danny feeds the chickens.

The next morning, walking over to the little chapel, Danny tries talking himself up, running through the types of things he'll need to say to convince somebody that he's knowledgeable about carpentry and supervising people and all that. But when he gets to the chapel, nobody's there. There is a hand-written sign taped to the door where somebody has written in old English letters: "Coming Soon! The Olde Chapel Summer Theater Festival." On either side, somebody has drawn a smiley mask and a frowny mask. Danny bangs on the door.

"S'open," somebody mutters behind the door. Danny walks into an open church space, all the pews and chairs pushed to one side and light streaming through a stained glass window. In the center of the chapel, in a lone chair, is a kid slumped over like somebody shot him and left him there yesterday.

"What's up?" Danny says to the kid.

"What's up?" he says back, opening his eyes wide for a minute, then closing them. It smells like bird poop, and it is so hot inside the little chapel that drops of water forming on the stained glass drop to the stone floor and make a sizzling noise.

It's not too late. Danny turns for the door, but then a man walks in from a side door. He's wearing a red ascot with mirror sunglasses perched on his forehead. In the room behind him, there is a pile of lumber—all warped and water-damaged, two-by-fours and firing strip and five-eighths-inch particleboard and sheets of Styrofoam and other stuff. Ascot Man looks at Danny, and then he looks at the kid in the chair, who's holding his chin in both hands, resting his elbows on his knees. The kid is wearing a black Molly Hatchett T-shirt. A fly flutters in front of his gaping mouth for a second, then flies straight in. Ascot Man turns to Danny.

"You must be Herbie," he says. "I have been informed of your prolific talents."

Before Danny can say anything, he starts waving a hand around, telling of his dream of opening a world-class regional theater starting right here in this little chapel, and this and that and something about somebody named Ernest. Danny points to the kid.

"Is this Ernest?" Danny asks.

"Don't be silly. This is Billy," he says. "I'm speaking of our opening play, *The Importance of Being Ernest*. I feel it's critical to open with a popular piece that brings the community together through laughter. After which, I suppose we'll explore the Bard. But first, we'll open with *The Importance of Being Ernest*. Which I fully intend to open in three weeks. Which is why you two, at this moment, are so important."

"The importance of being Billy," the kid mumbles.

"I'm picturing a thrust stage," Ascot Man goes on, "twenty feet from the altar. It must be squeak proof."

"Squeak proof?" Danny asks.

"Yes. Squeak proof. You know how to make a stage squeak proof, don't you? I was told that you are very experienced at making things." Ascot Man pulls a rolled-up blueprint from under his arm and rolls it out on the floor; he and Danny squat above it. Billy stays in his chair.

"I took the liberty," Ascot Man says. "These are the plans. The tools and the materials are in the back. You will have two weeks to build the stage. My first casting call is tomorrow."

"So that's it? Just build the stage?"

"Well, the stage, the lighting grid, the set. But first I need the stage built. We will be rehearsing elsewhere until two weeks from today, and then the company—my little theater company—will take up residence in this hallowed space. I need this space to be ready. I need it to be *Ernest*-ready."

Ascot Man stands up and waves his arms dramatically at the stained glass, the empty little choir loft, the pigeons. He puts on a wide-brimmed straw hat, rerolls his blueprint, and hands it to Danny.

"I'm putting my trust in you, Herbie, Master Carpenter Herbie. And you, Assistant Master Carpenter Billy. Our fate is in your hands. I have faith in you. I have faith in both of you." He turns to leave.

"But what if I don't have everything I need?" Danny asks.

Ascot Man stops, then turns around.

"Everything you need is in the back room there, but here, just in case." He counts out five twenty-dollar bills and hands them to Danny. "These are for expenses, only to be used for expenses. Get what you need, but keep the receipts. You'll be paid one hundred dollars for the job in two weeks, when the job is complete. I have faith in you both. I really do. Adieu," Ascot Man says, bowing slightly and then exiting.

Billy lights a cigarette. "Thank god," he says. "I thought he'd never leave. You got any idea what he wants us to build?"

"Not a clue," Danny says, fingering the bills in his pocket. "Tell you what," he says, handing him two of the bills. "What do you say we split this up?"

"Okay, I guess," Billy says, taking the forty dollars. "But I think we should split it fifty-fifty."

"But I'm the master carpenter," Danny says. "You're only helping."

CHARLIE'S TEXAS LUNCH

Charlies Texas Lunch is nowhere near Texas, and there is nobody there named Charlie, but they do serve lunch. Danny went there for lunch sometimes when he was working, but then he ran out of money. There is a counter with about eight stools and two booths, but nobody ever sits in the booths. The same skinny guy works behind the counter every day. He is a funny guy, but not ha-ha funny. He is a fry cook and a grill cook and a counter guy all at once. He never breaks into a sweat, no matter how hot it is in there.

Cashtown Annie told Danny all about him earlier, back at the Dropkin House. "Who, Chicken Man? He's an AA guy, he's a big time John Bircher. You definitely need to stay away from him." But Danny can't stay away from him because the food there is so good and cheap, and when he can afford it, he can afford it. And Charlie's Texas Lunch has cans of beer in a little refrigerator for fifty cents a can. Schaefer, Rheingold, Yuengling.

Today, with sixty dollars in his pocket, Danny walks straight into Charlie's Texas Lunch. "Hello, sir," he says to Chicken Man. "What's for lunch?"

Without making eye contact, Chicken Man points up at a chalkboard with the specials of the day: Texas wieners and beans, fried chicken and beans, or pancakes with scrambled eggs and beans. The beans have bacon in them, Danny remembers. "I'll have the wieners, please," Danny says.

Chicken Man says nothing. He wipes his hands on a towel and turns to the grill. He acts like he's never seen Danny before or like he was just there yesterday. Danny can't figure it out. Why aren't we friendly, he thinks? What makes him and Chicken Man so different? Danny wolfs down the wieners and beans and washes them down with three cans of Rheingold. A bead of sweat hangs from Danny's nose, but he leaves it there; he can tell it drives Chicken Man nuts. He angrily pushes a pile of onions around on the grill.

Danny puts down a twenty. Chicken-man picks it up and gives him fifteen back. "Well, see you tomorrow, I guess," Danny says. Chicken Man pretends he is doing something else. When Danny gets up, Chicken Man clears the plate, then wipes the counter down angrily with a dish towel.

Back on Chambersburg Street, it is turning out to be a nice day—big, bulbous clouds drifting to the south of town—and Danny starts walking, up toward the battlefields this time. Outside of town the air is hot and buzzing with midges and dragonflies; the trees lean over him, whispering to one another. Danny finds a dirt road that leads through the woods along a ridge; at the end there is a crazy statue of a barefoot muscular man standing over the fallen body of another, swinging the broken barrel of his rifle at the sky. Danny stands there for a while, looking at the statue, until the mosquitoes come out. Then he walks all the way back to town. He walks straight to the Johnny Reb, swinging through the saloon doors, and orders a pitcher of beer. Sometime later, Danny leaves the Johnny Reb Lounge. It rained really, really hard while he was sitting in the bar, but he didn't know how hard until he came outside. Water is flooding straight down Baltimore Street, circling the town square, and draining down past the burned ruins of the old hotel. The water is all sparkly from the streetlights and the traffic lights. Danny wades ankle deep to cross the square. Seeing the water is draining deeper on the other side, he takes a right turn instead of a left, figuring he'll circle back for home.

At the corner of Mummasburg Road, there is a bridge over an aqueduct where three people are leaning over the rail and staring at the waters raging beneath them. It is too late to turn around or cross the street. They are really deep into whatever they are looking at. Danny tries to slip past them, but a woman turns around. In the dim light cast from the town's lights, he recognizes the hunting cap. It's Cashtown Annie.

"Hey, it's Frederico!" she yells, pointing at Danny, even though he is only two steps away from her. She is standing next to Mister Patio and some other guy, a stringy looking guy with long, matted hair in a trench coat. "Frederico! Come check it out! The phosphorous! You got to see the phosphorous!"

Danny still has no idea why everybody calls her Cashtown Annie. He also still has no idea why she calls him Frederico.

"Check it out! Check it out!" she says. "Look into the water! The phosphorous!"

Danny looks over the bridge rail. There is nothing but blackness filled with bubbles, dark forms racing past. The water is very high, almost touching the bridge.

"I don't see any phosphorous."

"You got to look close!"

"I see the phosphorous," Mister Patio says.

"I definitely see the phosphorous," the other guy says.

"Ain't it something?" Cashtown Annie asks.

"Oh, yeah, now I see it," Danny lies. "There it is."

"You must never touch the phosphorous," Cashtown Annie says, staring down, transfixed. "You can look at it. You can admire it. You can even reach for it. But don't never, never touch it."

The three of them stare deeply down into the water.

"I sure won't never touch it," the other guy says.

"We're watching for the dead woman," Cashtown Annie explains to Danny matter-of-factly. "This here's Marsh Creek.

Sometimes she floats all the way down here. Sometimes she just keeps on going. They found her once in Chesapeake Bay."

Danny leaves them there and makes his way home. As he climbs the stairs, he smells something cooking. He turns the corner into the kitchen, and Sir Henry is standing over four pots on his stove, stirring something into something. On the kitchen windows, he has hammered a row of red velvet drapes. "Sir Herbie!" he yells. "A beautiful stew! A stew to celebrate! Master Herbie! Master Carpenter Herbie! Ha! Ha! Ha!"

They sit down to eat. The stew is so rich. Everything smells so good.

"I am very sad today, Herbie," Sir Henry tells Danny. "The bank came to take the nice lady's farm. The chickens are gone. The farm is gone. The nice lady is gone."

"I'm sorry to hear it, Sir Henry," Danny says. He doesn't want to ask him about his goat, so he changes the subject. "Hey, what kind of stew is this?"

"It's curry stew, Herbie."

"Oh! Yeah, the curry. But what kind of meat?"

"It's billy, Herbie."

"Billy?" Danny puts his spoon down.

"It's billy goat, Herbie."

It is so good Danny can't stand it. And Sir Henry keeps right on eating. So Danny picks up his spoon, and he keeps eating it too.

A couple days later, a funny thing happens. Danny is walking down Chambersburg Street, and he hears somebody yell, "Hey, Frederico! Hold up a minute!"

Mister Patio hobbles up to him with that half-walking technique he uses to get around. Then he bums a smoke off Danny. He wears a torn-up Hawaiian shirt, unbuttoned, and long heavy work pants smeared in oil.

"Working hard, or hardly working?" Mister Patio asks. The moment he has the cigarette lit he is looking up the street, down an alley, into a bar window, over Danny's shoulder. Like a rooster. Never any eye contact. Danny tells him he is working.

"That's what old Cashtown Annie said. That Frederico—always working."

Danny is nervous this might lead him into working on something he doesn't want to work on, so he changes the subject. He asks Mister Patio what he is up to.

"You know, this and that. Got my eye out. You know. Stuff like that. Hey, you seen Cashtown Annie 'round?"

"Nope."

"How 'bout Vlad, you know?"

"I don't think I know anybody named Vlad."

"Vlad. From the bridge the other night. Vlad the Impala. We call him that because he drives an Impala."

"No, sorry." Danny shrugs.

"Old Vlad's been all messed up. He ain't been right since his dad bought it. You hear about his old man? They found him lying half out the front door. He went right through the screen door, man. Ain't no dignity in that. Well, thanks for the smoke there, Frederico. You take her easy," Mister Patio says, and then he hobbles up the street.

VLAD THE IMPALA

So for a while there, it gets hot—really, really hot. The corn stalks are burning up all around the east side of town, turning brown and black and crumpling on their stalks, and the corn hangs limp and burnt out of its brown husks like dead things with no teeth. The air in town smells like popcorn, Danny thinks, walking across the 7-Eleven parking lot. He buys a six-pack of tallboys. When he walks out, with the ice-cold beer cans gathering condensation in the bag in his hands, a car pulls off of Chambersburg Street. Danny knows the car; it's a rust gray Impala without a front fender. The windshield wipers are going even though it hasn't rained all week, and one headlight is permanently on. Turning into a parking lot, the Impala makes a squeaking noise, belches out a blast of yellow smoke from its undercarriage, and rolls to a stop.

"Hey, man," the driver yells after rolling the window halfway down, as far as it goes. "I been looking for you."

"Yeah, sure," Danny says, cradling the beer under one arm and stuffing his hands into his pockets. "What's up?"

Danny remembers the guy. He looks all strung out. He is the friend of Cashtown Annie. The bartender at the Johnny Reb once warned Danny about this guy. "You see that guy?" he said to Danny once, pointing out at the town square at a guy sitting in a beat-up old car, staring out the windshield at the traffic light, even though the car was parked. "You stay away from that guy. That's Vladimir somebody. He's one of those drug people out of Biggersville. Never have anything to do with that guy."

The bridge that rainy night, the car in the Dropkin House parking lot. Vlad the Impala. Here Danny is now, standing in this hot parking lot talking to Vlad the Impala.

"Hey, man," Vlad repeats. "You want a ride someplace? You need a lift?"

"No, I'm good thanks," Danny says. "I live right across the street."

"Well, listen. You think you can help me out with something?"

"Oh, listen, man. I don't know. I mean, I got to go to work."

"With a six-pack of beer?"

"What, this? This is for later."

"Come on, man. Let's go for a spin."

"Okay."

Danny climbs into the passenger side. The car looks like Vlad has been living in it for a while. It smells like a damp ashtray. He has the air conditioner pumped up to full blast, only hot air is coming out of the vents. Vlad the Impala is wearing a trench coat and sneakers. He appears soaking wet. Long, stringy hair sticks to his beard. He pulls out a cigarette and hands Danny one. Danny pulls two beers off the ring, hands him one, and opens his own.

Unexpectedly the sky turns black, and it starts to rain. This happens a lot in August: A curtain of darkness appears, it pours, then it stops, and the water drains out of the town, and it is even stickier than it was before. Vlad pulls the old Impala out onto Washington Street, and the windows all go wash-out and the windshield wipers aren't working and the traffic light at Lincoln Street goes all green, yellow, red all at once and headlights of other cars streak away to one side or the other. Danny sits in the passenger seat holding onto the broken seatbelt, certain that he is about to go straight through the windshield. Vlad, fumbling to pull a cigarette out of a soft pack, while lighting a match, while cracking the tallboy between his legs, while brushing ashes from his denim leg, manages to do all this without driving into anything or anybody. And then, like magic, the rain stops, and the sun bursts through the clouds. And the windshield wipers squeak on. They leave muddy brown streaks on the windshield. Vlad turns them off.

They drive up and over the ridge and leave town. Big black clouds lumber up and over the ridges in front of them, leaving white puffy tentacles of fog dragging their fingers through the distant orchards. The fields are lit with that weird green light, that tornado light.

"So, ah, where are we going," Danny asks Vlad.

"Out by Biggersville," he says.

"Oh. So what's going on out by Biggersville?"

"Well, it's like this," Vlad says. "Last month I sold my old man's meat freezer to this guy he knew down in Aintsville. But my old man's house is up the hill in Biggersville. The thing is huge, you know? But I got to get it down to Aintsville."

"So what are we gonna do? Tie it to the roof?"

"No, man, you joke! It's way too big to put up there. It'll scratch the roof! But I got this other idea. It's only about ten miles or so. I think we can just sort of, you know. Row it down there."

"Row it? What do you mean, row it?"

"Well, thanks to this here rain, that there creek's gonna be all swelled up in about fifteen minutes. So we'll just push it out into the water, and...you know. Row it, I guess."

"But it's a meat freezer. It's not a rowboat."

"Oh, it's seaworthy, you'll see. It's air-tight. I'm sure of it." Vlad lights a new cigarette with the butt of the old one, hands it to Danny, and lights one for himself. "Yes. My old man left four deer carcasses in there, unplugged, for a month after he died, and I couldn't smell a thing until I opened it."

They come to a V in the road; ahead, a blue car sits parked on a bridge. "Let's take the farm road," Vlad says and swerves the big car off of Three-Town Road and onto a mud track climbing a hill.

As they get on toward Biggersville, they pass farmyards where the banks have dumped the houses' contents into the front yard. Somebody has come back and arranged the dumpings like they are living rooms: couch here, lounge chair there, coffee table smack in the middle. Moss and mold creep up the upholstery. Screen doors swing open into black, hollow interiors; nobody's home.

As they get closer, Vlad explains how he's living in his car these days, sleeping in the driveway of his dad's house, because he is still scared to go in there at night, even though they found the old man lying right through the screen door, more outside than inside.

"But you don't never sleep in a dead man's bed," Vlad says, shaking his head. "That's what Cashtown Annie always told me. You don't never sleep in a dead man's bed. You don't never wear a dead man's shoes. Let's see. What else she tell me."

"Man," Danny says, cracking his second-to-last beer and draining half of it before handing Vlad the last. "She sure filled your head with some interesting material."

"That she did," Vlad says. He turns off the car, but it turns itself on again. Smoke fills the interior. Danny gets out. Vlad bangs the steering wheel with his palms. The engine dies. He gets out. "She filled my head with many things. Many wondrous things. Let me see. Where was I. Dead man's bed. Dead man's shoes. Yes. Don't never drink a dead man's beer. Yes, she did. Yes. She told me that. So the meat locker's in the garage," he says, loping toward a corrugated door attached to the side of the house.

Danny can't stop staring at the screen door, half-broken, swinging open into a yard filled with fluttering newspaper bits and beer cans. What a way to go. He follows Vlad into the garage.

"Hey, man, you want another beer?" Vlad asks. There are cases and cases of Schaefer beer stacked in one corner of the garage. In the other is a big meat locker. A back door leads down a small hill. Danny can hear the water bubbling up. Vlad walks down the hill and comes back up. "Water's up," he says. "No time like the present." He starts pushing, and Danny starts pulling. The meat locker slides easy across the grass down the hill. They pull it up on some rocks next to the creek, Marsh Creek, the same one that starts in Dead Woman Hollow and gurgles straight through town. It is disgorging all of the sifting waters from a steep cleft in the mountains, just up behind the orchards. The water is chugging, brown and cold and fast, rushing under a distant bridge, southward toward Aintsville.

Vlad runs back up to the house and comes back with two inner tubes half-filled with air, a long rope, two poles, and a case of Schaefer. Danny watches Vlad walk back to the Impala, pull the trunk open, and pull out a brown backpack. He comes down and hands Danny a rusty can. Danny wipes the top off with his sleeve. "Thanks," Danny says. "So what exactly are we doing here?"

"Well, now," Vlad says, handing Danny one of the wood poles. "I guess you should climb in first, and I'll push off, then I'll climb in second is all."

"So maybe we should just push it out there—I mean, without us in it—and we can, you know, just guide it down the creek to Aintsville?"

"But how we going to steer it?"

"It's a creek. Where's it gonna go?"

"Now look, man, look. I need you to help me out. Old Mister Patio woulda helped me out, but he can't leave town because he's on house arrest. He told me you were the man for the job. He told me you were Mister Reliable. He told me you know how stuff works. So you got to help me make this work. You're the man for the job is all. You're Mister Reliable. Old Mister Patio told me so."

"Okay, I guess," Danny says.

They push the meat locker to the edge of the water. Danny climbs in. It rocks from left to right. The door falls on his head. He holds it open with one hand and pushes off on the wooden pole with the other. Vlad climbs in behind Danny. They are sucked down under the bridge, spinning wildly, plunging into the raging torrent. This goes on for about three minutes, surprisingly loud water churning through low-hanging branches, surging over rocks. An old man sits at the end of a little dock with a fishing pole in his hand, but he isn't fishing. Danny waves. He waves back. The meat locker dips down a cascade. The old man disappears. The water rocks them back and forth. Brown water starts filling the locker. The locker keeps spinning. The poles keep getting stuck.

"Push harder! Pull harder! No, not that-away! This-away!" Vlad yells.

Danny is in the back, watching the brown water swirl around them. Then Vlad's pole sticks, and Danny swings around to the front. Then he sees the branch, a low-hanging branch from a fallen tree. His head is smacked with rotten apples. The branch lifts him out of the meat locker. The last thing he sees on the surface is Vlad, poling madly, brown water surging into the locker. For a second, Vlad comes out clear and in slow motion, like a final photograph, standing in the well of the sinking meat locker, trench coat shining in the splashing water, hair everywhere, a frantic look in his eyes.

Danny bobs from the branch until the branch breaks, dropping him in the brown water once again. Then the water pulls Danny down. He imagines for a second that he hears the Dead Woman cackling, cackling, pulling him down with her icy fingers. And then Danny supposes for a time that he has drowned.

THREE-TOWN ROAD

By the time Danny gets back to town, it is dawn, and he is almost dry. Sir Henry is in his kitchen, staring through the curtains at the ice houses. He does not appear to notice Danny. Danny goes straight to bed and sleeps for at least a day. When he wakes up, he starts bouncing from bar to bar. There are six working bars in town; Danny visits each one twice. Just before sunset, he is coming up the back alley when he sees two legs sticking out from under a parked wreck of a car, a Dodge Roadrunner, that had been sitting in the alley for some time with four bald, skinny flat tires. Danny recognizes the legs, and he tries to slip by, but then he hears that voice: "Say, come over here a minute." Danny goes right over. When he does, he sees Mister Patio through the open hood. He is lying underneath two-thirds of a rusted engine, that face all tensed up, trying to unbolt something from something else.

"So whatever happened out there with Vlad the Impala? He's sort of pissed off is all. Said you screwed up his meat locker deal."

Mister Patio pulls a socket wrench off a socket whatever and taps the heel of his hand against something with old brown wires sticking out of it. There is a sizzle sound, and a tiny little lightning bolt shoots out and hits his pinky, which turns red and then black in just a few seconds. Mister Patio doesn't seem to notice; he just keeps plugging away with the socket wrench.

"I screwed up? I didn't screw anything up. Meat freezers aren't boats, man. They are not designed to be paddled down creeks. What did he tell you?"

"Well, now, that's what I told him! He said he may have lost something. He was wondering if maybe you found it and wasn't telling anyone."

"Did he tell you the creek was up ten feet? Did he tell you I almost drowned, and he left me there, and I had to walk all the way back here?"

"Well, now, don't get all sore at me! I told him it might not work. But now he's all sore as hell at you."

"Yeah, well, I didn't do anything."

Mister Patio's pinkie is swelling up like a little football; he keeps working the socket wrench with that hand, holding his pinkie out like he is drinking tea.

"That's what he said! He said you didn't paddle fast enough. Anyhow, just thought I should tell you. In case of, you know. Somebody comes looking for something, or there's trouble, or something."

"What are they going to be looking for? What are you talking about, trouble?"

Mister Patio climbs out from under the car, stands up, wipes his hands on his grease-coated pants, and signals for Danny to give him a smoke, which he does, and he lights it for him. Danny looks out above the ice houses; a line of brown clouds is building up just to the west of town, tumbling up and over themselves, flashing in the fading daylight.

"Well, as it turns out, he was delivering the meat locker to Cashtown Annie's old man, and, you know, it was a pretty important thing, you know, this meat locker, and Cashtown Annie's old man got the whole story, and he may send some boys down here looking for you is all."

"But I didn't do anything," Danny repeats.

"That's what I told 'em! Anyway, you should be on the lookout is all. Say. Was Cashtown Annie up by your place?"

"Who, Cashtown Annie? Why would she be up by my place?"

Mister Patio takes a long drag of smoke. He surrounds himself with smoke. A rumble of thunder comes from the piles of bricks and burnt timber surrounding them, closing in all around them.

"Somebody says they saw her is all. Could have been anybody."

"I haven't seen Cashtown Annie since that night on the bridge."

"That's what I told them!"

"That's what you told who?"

"Anyhow, you keep an eye out. There's some people. They's looking for something is all."

A couple of big raindrops hit the bricks—hiss, hiss. Mister Patio looks at his finger curiously, then swivels back under the car and disappears.

"Maybe it was Sir Henry that they saw," Danny says. "Sir Henry hangs out in my kitchen sometimes."

"Yep. We know."

"Who's we? Who are you talking about?"

"People is all. There's some people around. You keep an eye out."

Mister Patio stays under the car as huge raindrops pelt the vinyl roof. Danny makes a run for it, but by the time he reaches the front door, he's drenched. He tiptoes up his stairs and peeks around the corners; nobody's there. Then Danny goes into his kitchen. He finds Sir Henry sitting at the little plastic table, one finger on the curtain, watching Mister Patio through a small crack. Nothing is cooking on the stove.

"Sir Herbie, yes! I am waiting for you. I must speak to you," he says without looking up. "There are some people who are looking for you, Herbie. This is no joke. Ha! Ha! Ha!"

"Yeah, I've been meaning to talk to you about that," Danny says, sitting down at the table, dripping water. He is so exhausted that he can hardly keep his eyes open. "That job you sent me to do. I sort of screwed up. I mean, the guy was an asshole, and he sent some asshole to work with me."

"Screw them, Herbie!"

"Yeah, well, I sort of did, but I mean, it wasn't my fault. But I sort of never showed up."

"Herbie, screw them. *Screw...them...Herbie*. Ha! Ha! Ha!"

"But, you know, I sort of took some money, and I didn't do the work. So I suppose Ascot Man is looking for me."

"Who is this of what you speak? The Ascot Man, who is this?"

"The guy you're talking about? The guy who's looking for me?"

"Herbie, you speak sometimes in a sideways manner. I do not always understand that to which you speak. I do not know this Ascot Man." Still looking through the curtain, Sir Henry's eyes open wider, wild, headlights through the rain. "There are people who are looking for you. And they are looking for this Cashtown Annie. Have you seen this Cashtown Annie?"

"Why does everybody keep asking me if I've seen this Cashtown Annie?"

"She has a gift that she is supposed to bring to me. The gift is from the farm lady. Maybe she has this gift. Maybe her friends have this gift. But you must help me find this gift, Herbie. You must—"

Sir Henry jumps from his chair and runs down the stairs; he is on the street, in his car, in seconds. Danny watches through the curtain as he races up the alley, and then he disappears into the sheets and sheets and sheets of rain. Then

Danny puts his head down on his arms and falls fast asleep, right there at the kitchen table.

Danny wakes up sometime the next day, still at the kitchen table. It is really, really hot. He peeks out through the curtains; the Roadrunner is still sitting in the lot next to the ice plant, but he doesn't see Mister Patio's legs sticking out. He gets up slowly. He really needs a beer. He still has eight dollars.

He walks down to the 7-Eleven and pulls out a six-pack of Rheingold. At the counter, he looks at the town newspaper. His eyes adjust to the headline. "Two-Car Crash on Three-Town Road," the headline says. "Two Dead, One Injured, One Missing," the subhead says. "Good Samaritans Rescue Area Man." Danny picks up a paper, goes back upstairs, drinks a beer, and opens the paper. There is a picture of Chicken Man, but he is wearing a blazer and a tie.

As he explained it to the newspaper, Chicken Man, who is really Hubert something from Aintsville, was driving back from a church meeting in the rain when he saw an old car turned sideways on a bridge. As he slowed down, a Gremlin T-boned the sideways car at a high speed. He reported thinking he saw a woman jettisoned from the old car into the creek, but when he climbed down the embankment, he could not see her in the surging waters. The men in the sedan, an old-model Impala, had no pulse.

Hubert pulled a local man from the smoking Gremlin, who then tried to crawl away. Hubert ran to a farmhouse to call for help, but it was abandoned. When he returned, two men in a blue sedan with out-of-state plates were lifting the crawling man into the back seat. They told Hubert they were taking the man to the hospital. The hospital, however, reported no intakes the prior evening, and nobody found a lady in the creek.

Danny pulls one of the curtains off the window, wraps himself in it, and stares out at the Roadrunner. He sits there for the day, then the night, then the next day. There is an ashtray that never stops smoking in front of him. Danny starts coming around when a beam of afternoon light bursts through the clouds and drinks up the crumpled ruins of the ice plant, windowless, roofless, the sunbeams settling softly on the wet charred beams and rusting machine parts.

Danny lights his last cigarette with the stub of the prior. He ponders going out for a new pack, an act that will take some motivation. It will require pulling his pants on and bending down and finding a boot under the table and pulling it on and lacing it up and finding the other boot and pulling it on and lacing it up. Then it will require walking down the stairs, crossing the street, walking over to Charlie's Texas Lunch, because they have an eighty-five cent cigarette machine, and pulling eighty-five cents out of his pocket without having to ask Chicken Man for change. Then he'll have to click the change into the coin slot, pull the knob, pull the pack of smokes from the slider, look up and smile at Chicken Man, who never smiles back, and walk all the way back up the stairs.

"Just gotta do it," Danny says to himself out loud, and then he dozes off again with the cigarette getting hot and then hotter, burning his fingers and then dropping to the floor.

And then he falls asleep, sitting straight up for about an hour. And then he wakes up real sudden. It is dark out, and the room is dark, except for little orange embers still glowing on the spot where they burned into the cheap kitchen flooring.

Danny wakes up because two sets of heavy boot steps are coming up the stairs from the street. Crap. George's boys. He must have left the front door open down there. Danny jumps up, ready to go for the window, but he is too late; they are at the top of the stairs, squinting at him in the dim light. There are two of them. They are not George's boys.

"Mister Patio!" one of the two men in front of Danny says. "We're looking for Mister Patio. You Mister Patio?"

Danny flicks on the light on the table. With only one dim bulb, it casts a soft yellow ray of light on two short men in big black leather jackets and big black leather boots. They are both gaunt and unshaven, their eyes red and bulgy. One has neat blow-dried hair, and Two has a big, funny moustache. They both spend an awful lot of time on their hair, Danny thinks. Wow. He really should have locked that goddamn door.

"My name's not Mister Patio," Danny says.

One starts looking around. Two watches Danny in the dim light.

"Looks like you got a little fire going there, Mister Patio," he says.

Danny stomps out the embers. His socks smoke for a second, then stop.

"My name's not Mister Patio."

"Oh, yeah? Where's Mister Patio then?"

"I never heard of anybody named Mister Patio," Danny says. "Why would I know anybody named Mister Patio?"

"We know all about it, Mister Patio. We've been looking for you. We're looking for a girl named Cashtown Annie. You know where at's Cashtown Annie?"

"Aints who?"

"Cashtown Annie."

"Why do they call her Cashtown Annie?"

"I dunno. They call everybody something, I guess." The guy looking around stops looking around. "Anyways, you know her?"

"I guess I might of heard of a girl named something Annie, but I haven't seen her in months. She moved down to DC, I think."

Danny doesn't like the way the two guys are looking at him. They don't look like trouble—they look like two guys who are trying to look like trouble. Danny reaches around behind him, just in case, but can't find a beer bottle or a broom handle. His hand locks on the ashtray.

"So you ain't Mister Patio, and you ain't seen Cashtown Annie?"

"I don't know anybody named Mister Patio, and I never did, and I told you: I haven't seen Cashtown Annie in months."

Danny thinks they might try to jump him; instead, they both lean on the wall, dejected.

"Well, dang it. You got any weed?"

"No. I don't smoke weed."

"You got anything stronger than weed?"

"No, man. I don't do nothing like that."

"You know where we can find something like that? We done driven all the way down from Harrisburg. Friend sent us. Told us to find Mister Patio or Cashtown Annie. Here," the one says. He hands Danny a folded-up grainy photograph of a young woman in a varsity high school jacket, smiling, next to a car. It is not Cashtown Annie.

"Oh, yeah. That's the Annie I used to know," Danny says. "Haven't seen her in months."

"Well," One says, "I guess we're just gonna have to hang out here until she gets back."

"I don't think she's coming back," Danny says. "She left months ago. I don't hardly know her."

"You know, you look hungry, pal. What did you say your name was?"

"Herbie," Danny says. "Herbie Frederico."

One looks at Two. "What do you say I go across the street to that 7-Eleven, find us something to eat."

"You're in for a treat," Two says to Danny, handing One a ten dollar bill. "This guy's an ace cook."

"I don't think the stove works," Danny says, still gripping the ashtray behind him. He can smell the ashes. "The landlord turned the gas off."

"We'll come up with something," Two says to One. "Come to think of it, I'll come down with you."

They both putter down the stairs. When the screen door slams, Danny gets up and pushes his way up the dark corridor. He hears the bedroom doorknob unlatch. Annie is sitting on the edge of the bed. She is slowly, methodically pulling on her cowboy boots. She's been sleeping, on and off, since she got here. Danny looks through the curtains at One and Two down on the street. They are standing next to a blue sedan in the 7-Eleven parking lot, talking through the window to two other guys.

"All clear now?" Cashtown Annie attempts a smile.

"All clear now," Danny says. Those eyes, those eyes. Even in the darkness, nothing registers in those eyes—not sadness or fear or hope or hopelessness. Danny pulls everything off the bed and stuffs it into her red pocketbook; then he stuffs the red pocketbook back into her brown backpack. He helps her up by the hand, just to guide her, because she can't get up by herself. Danny helps her climb out the back window, and they slide together down off the back roof. They walk together, side by side, up the back alley behind the ice factory, then up to the railroad tracks. Then they walk single file, step by step, up the railroad tracks forever.

And this time Danny really, really never goes back. He helps Annie get on to where she needs to go, and then he heads out toward where he thinks he's got to go.

PART IV

DEEP
HYDRAULIC
WHISPERS

STICK OF GUM

Downtown Saint Louis is all boarded up. Fresh Reagan-Bush re-election posters are glued up on the frayed plywood walls everywhere, promising four more years of prosperity. After spending the night stretched out in the Greyhound station, Danny climbs onto the bus for Denver. It's an empty bus; he drops his backpack in the seat next to him and stares out the window. The city fades away and becomes rolling fields. The air from the vent smells like burnt corn and pumpkins.

Danny forgets the recent past and starts remembering, instead, another time on a bus, a long time ago. He was eighteen. He remembers standing outside a bus station in Boston, waiting for the bus to Wolfeboro, New Hampshire. He was on his way back up to the summer camp where he was working as a dishwasher for twelve hours a day and practiced catching short passes for one hour a day. On his one day a week off, he was busing down to Boston, sleeping on Big Brother's college couch, and wandering Boston alone, piddling through used bookstores.

Danny remembers that he was standing in line with a string backpack over his right shoulder. His shoulders were still aching from practicing with his friend's dad, who was his high school football coach, Coach Beano, who was also the camp director. "You're going to work for my dad this summer?" Beano asked Danny the prior spring. "What would you want to go and do that for?"

At the beginning of the job, the first week of July, Coach Beano told Danny he could have the starting tight end job in the fall, but only if he worked all summer on his cuts and his hands and, afterward, if he could do a hundred push-ups. All summer long, six days a week, for his one free hour, when the other dishwashers were swimming in the lake before the dinner shift, Danny and Coach Beano were on the camp's superheated sports field, running and catching and dropping and push-upping. The six-week payoff for this version of hell: by late August, Danny had grown his first set of shoulders.

But back to that bus stop. A line was forming, and Danny had the string backpack over his right shoulder, and in his left hand he was reading Kerouac's *Desolation Angels*, the part about being alone on a fire tower in the Cascade Mountains, and that's when he noticed the girl.

The girl was standing in the back of the line. She was a little older than Danny, maybe nineteen, maybe twenty. She was dressed like somebody who works up in the mountains. Hiking boots, rag socks, cut-off shorts, and a big backpack with all sorts of stuff dangling out of it. The girl had beautiful strawberry hair pulled up under a crisp blue bandanna. Danny's shoulders slunk when he saw her. He shrunk back to his pre-push-up form. He was nothing, a dishwasher-ball catcher at a crummy camp. The girl was the mountains, and Danny was the foothills. He put the book away, tucking it back into his string backpack, and stared down at his boyish sneakers.

The bus came. Danny sat in the middle and stared out the window. Boston became Lawrence, and Nashua became Manchester. Buildings became houses, and houses became trees. He was eighteen and alone in a narrow aluminum tube, hurtling through the woods. He had one week to go, and then he was done at the camp. The dishes and the ball-catching lessons would be behind him. School would start, and maybe he'd be the starting tight end, and maybe he wouldn't. But he already knew he wouldn't. It would be back to the bench for Danny, shoulders or no shoulders.

"Stick of gum?"

"Stick of what?" Danny said reflexively. The girl was standing in the aisle, trying to hand Danny a stick of gum. The girl had freckles. So many freckles. Her freckles had freckles. And she was smiling.

Danny looked around. The rest of the bus was empty. What to say? What to say?

"Um, sure," he said. He accidently took three pieces of gum; then he stuck them all in his mouth. "Thanks."

"It's just such a long and boring bus ride," the girl said, and then he looked ahead, up through the windshield as the bus lurched off the highway and up a ramp. "Do you go to school up here?"

"Me? No, I'm working up here." It was real hard to talk with all that gum in Danny's mouth. "At a camp. I'm a dish catcher. I mean, a tight washer."

"Oh, that's great," the girl said. "That must be pretty hard work."

"Yeah. Pretty hard."

What to say? What to say? The bus pulled into a diner parking lot. It hissed and bent down, and the door popped open.

"Well, this is where I meet my ride," the girl said. "See you on the bus next time, I guess."

The girl walked off the bus. She stood there for a moment in the parking lot, that backpack with all the things dangling from it over her shoulder. Then she dropped her backpack and sat down on it, staring out across the street at the distant rim of mountains, a blue haze wrapped in a blue haze.

The bus continued on its way north toward Wolfeboro. The diner was in Tilton, Danny remembers. He's pretty sure it's Tilton. As the bus drifted north, Danny told himself that when he came back the next week for the last time, the girl would be waiting at that bus stop. He told himself the girl would smile when she saw him, all those freckles, all those freckles. This was meant to be, Danny convinced himself. This was meant to be. He imagined he'd tell her about all the cool things he was reading about, all the places he wanted to go.

But a week later, when Danny's last bus pulled into that parking lot in Tilton, the diner was closed, and the parking lot was empty. The mountains shimmered blue in the distance, but the girl was nowhere to be seen.

MILL MALL

In a strip mall on the outskirts of Denver, this Manpower lady taps her pencil on a paper form sitting in the middle of her desk. Danny sits in the chair, fidgeting. The office stinks of perfume and something close to alcohol. It is 9:25 in the morning, and Danny doesn't know if the alcohol is coming from him or from her. If it's coming from him, he is sure she can smell it.

"Buddy, let's be honest," Manpower Lady says.

Danny thinks to himself, Does she think my name's Buddy? Does she think I'm somebody else? She is wearing a yellow pants suit with a white frilly blouse and a broach, like she probably used to wear at her job at the bank, before they closed the bank.

"You checked here on your application 'construction experience,' but the roofing company said you didn't know nothing about construction."

"The roof was coated in ice," Danny says, "and they gave me a pitchfork to take off all the shingles. No harness, no rope. I was three stories up. I wasn't going to—"

"The roofing company is one of our most important contracts right now," Manpower Lady says. "Three Brothers Roofing has been with us for three years. They are a very reliable contract. So, again. You said here on your application that you have construction experience. Do you have construction experience?"

Danny looks through the window slats behind her, where a pickup truck is speeding up the main street toward downtown Denver and a logging truck is speeding out of town, out to the highway, to the mountains, shimmering in the distance like mushrooms. He thinks for a second the two trucks are going to collide. They do not collide.

"I got about three-quarters of those shingles off, in the ice, without a harness, with a pitchfork. That roof was a forty-five-degree angle, three floors up. If I fell—"

"Construction experience?"

"Not a lot, no, I guess. I ran a jackhammer once. I sort of broke it."

She takes her pencil and marks a long black line through the place where Danny checked "construction experience."

"Given the conditions, I'm surprised I got as far as I did."

Manpower Lady puts his file away in a cabinet to her left, then pulls out a drawer in a cabinet to her right. Turning around, she leaves a line of orange makeup powder on the crease of her blouse. She opens the file. Then she turns to Danny and smiles.

"You like kids, don't you, Buddy?"

"Um, I guess so. Why?"

"No reason. But about this special job. There's a special job that's come up, which I can't really tell you about until you get there, because of our confidentiality protocols. But it pays six-fifty an hour, which is our highest rate this season, and it's full time. And it's not a construction job. Only, I can't tell you what it is because of confidentiality and all."

"Oh. Okay." Danny does that quick calculation thing he does in his head—$6.50 times forty hours. Soon he'll be out of here, out of this flop-house living, lonely, lonely place, and on to someplace else. Danny rubs his chin, like he's thinking about it. "Okay, I'm in."

Manpower Lady runs forms out of a big nine-point printing machine. She has Danny sign a few things, a blue sheet and another sheet that she rips the tabs off the sides of. She hands him the blue sheet. "You need to take these out to the Old Mesa Mill Mall and go to the main office. Now, don't get all mixed up—the Old Mesa Mill Mall is the old mall on the south side of town, not the New Mesa Mill Mall they are building where the Old Mesa Mill used to be on the north side of town. And when you get there, you'll report to a man named Phil. Oh, wait until you meet Phil. He's something else."

Manpower Lady stares at the paper on her desk, chuckling to herself. Danny starts chuckling too, although he doesn't know why, slapping his sore hands on his knees. He takes the papers, and he folds them neatly and puts them in his shirt pocket. "I'll call Phil and let him know you're coming," Manpower Lady says. She looks over the file, stamps some things, and puts it in another drawer. She chuckles one more time, shaking her head. The whole time Danny is there, she doesn't look at him.

"You remember where you're going?"

"Old, Mesa, Mill Mall."

"Thank you, Buddy!"

Outside the sun is gleaming off of everything—Indian summer. Danny's ten-speed is where he left it, leaning against the wall of the abandoned department store next to the Manpower Office. He bought the ten-speed, used, the chain a little rusty, for fifteen dollars at the Salvation Army, thinking he could get some exercise while he was here. Within a week, it became his lifeline to the strand of temporary job opportunities on the outskirts of town, wherever Manpower sent him.

He pushes and rides off toward the south side. The little mill houses and double-wides drift away. Soon he is peddling through cleared prairie fields, tumbleweeds rolling themselves slowly into barbed-wire fencing. The beer is wearing off, sweating itself through his shirt and out into the clean desert air. The fields are barren, but there are sticks everywhere, painted different colors with numbers on them, like they sprang up from the weeds. Old, Mesa, Mill, Mall. Old mill. New mill. Mill Mall. Mesa Mill.

For some inexplicable reason, a traffic light hangs in the middle of the empty prairie, where a country road crosses a state road. Danny stops at the light. An old man on a bike appears, rides up next to him, and asks:

"Working hard, or hardly working?"

The old man is caked in desert dust and has spilled something like motor oil all down his left pants leg. His lips are parched and cracked. He has a desert beard and a baseball cap with a beaver on it, swinging a baseball bat.

"Me? No. I'm on my way to work," Danny says, patting the blue paper in his shirt pocket for no particular reason. "You know, out at the Mesa Mill Mall."

"The Mill ain't thisaway, it's thataway," the old man says, taking his hands from the handlebars and folding his arms. "And if you think there's work to be got there, you're mistaken. They closed all the mills, couple years ago."

The old man stares off toward the mountains, squinting at something in the distance.

"It's a shopping mall. They just called it the Lava Butte Mill Mall, I guess."

The old man wipes his mouth with the back of his hand, like he's just drunk something, even though he hasn't.

"Say, you got anything to drink?" the old man asks.

"No, nothing like that."

"Well, I gotta find me something to drink," he says. "You take 'er easy."

The old man looks at Danny for a minute, waiting for him to say what he is supposed to say. Then he pushes off, straight into the middle of the state road. Two trucks coming from opposite directions converge on him, but when they pass, he is still there, a stick figure on a bicycle, peddling up the middle of an asphalt strip in the desert.

Across the state road, the county road passes a golf resort that's under construction and a condominium complex that's coming soon, a stack of cinderblocks and rusty pipes sticking out of the dirt. Then it rolls down a hill to a place where the natural world still has a hold on the earth. Climbing up over stilted pine trees, the sun spreads out over dried wild grasses, all bending back onto themselves, preparing for the coming snows. The mountains are getting whiter every morning, the snowpack advancing down the eastern slopes, inching toward town. A marquee sign appears: The Old Mesa Mill Mall at Mountain's Edge.

Danny rides up a steep driveway and into a parking lot about one-quarter filled with station wagons and pickup trucks. He leans his bike against a lamppost in front of a big mall entrance. White plastic flowers and green plastic vines hang from a flowerpot hooked to the lamppost. He pulls on a big glass door, but it seems locked. He can see people in there, walking real slow, back and forth, along what looks like an indoor sidewalk, but he can't pull the door open. He bangs on the door, but nobody notices. He walks around the huge yellow building to the back of Sears, where there is a loading dock with an open steel door. A tall, thin man stands next to the steel door, smoking. He is wearing sunglasses, a black turtleneck, and a black beret. Behind him, through the door, Danny sees two big, beefy men in flannel shirts pulling boxes out of shrink-wrapped crates, one by one, and loading them onto a palette.

"Hello there," Danny says to Beret Man. "Are you Phil?"

"I most certainly am not Phil," Beret Man says.

"Can you point me to the front office? I'm looking for—"

"Yes. You're looking for Phil. You made that quite clear."

Beret-Man blows a plume of blue smoke around himself creatively. He pulls up a walkie-talkie. "Here," he says.

"Um, yes. Can you—"

"You're not the first, you know."

"I'm not the first what?"

Beret Man waves his thin white fingers through the door behind him. "You can pass through my workspace. I give you permission. Only don't interrupt my people. And for God's sake, don't touch anything."

Danny enters the workspace, where the two big men stop and stare at him.

"Well, lookie here," the first one says. "Looks like Phil got himself a new one."

"I ain't been naughty!" the other one says.

"What are you talking about?" Danny says.

"You'll find out, you sure will," one says. The other one holds his belly, chuckling.

Danny walks past them, through the store, and into the mall's big gallery. The same people walk slowly along a circular indoor sidewalk. Huge fake plants hang from balconies. Half the store spaces are empty. A little man in overalls is climbing up and down a ladder, taking down banners that read "Autumn Attitudes" in fancy script with leafy montages, and putting up banners that read "'Tis the Season" with snowflakes and waving Santas. In the middle of the gallery is a half-assembled Santa's village with lights strung up and fake Christmas presents stacked up under a fake Christmas tree next to a big red chair.

Danny walks around the mall until he finds the office. He walks through one steel door and then another steel door. Another little man in a white shirt and a bristle moustache is going through a stack of boxes. His head is polished bald, and a huge gold crucifix jangles from a gold chain on his neck. Christmas ornaments lay around him everywhere.

"I'm looking for Phil," Danny says.

"Well, you found him!" Phil says. He looks Danny over, top to bottom. "What the blazes do you want?"

"Um, Manpower sent me?" Danny pulls the paper out of his pocket and tries to hand it to him. "They told me to report to—"

"You're late! What the blazes! I sent for you an hour ago. The guy they sent yesterday never showed! Now you show up late! And look at you! What the blazes? Is this all they got?"

"Well, sir, I'm here now. Can you tell me what you need me to do?"

"Don't be a smart guy. You know what to do!" Phil starts stacking boxes on top of other boxes. He hands Danny a box. "They told you the particulars! Didn't they tell you the particulars?"

"They didn't tell me any particulars. They only told me—"

"We don't have time for the particulars! We've only got two minutes! Put this on!"

Danny opens the box. It smells like urine. "You want me to put this on?"

"What the blazes? What did they send me? I'm calling Manpower right away. Any bum. Any bum would be grateful. What the blazes! You got two minutes. I'm back in two minutes. You better be ready. You better—"

Phil doesn't finish because he slams the door shut. Danny stands there looking into the box. What he really wants is a beer. It's eleven in the morning, and he only wants another beer. He is so thirsty. He thinks of the old man out there on the state road. He wonders if he found something to drink. He wonders what he is drinking. He wonders where he found something to drink.

But then the numbers come back to Danny: $6.50 times forty times how many weeks. He takes a deep breath. When the door bangs, he is dressed and ready. His face itches. Now he smells like urine. He follows Phil out into the gallery. Phil is whispering the particulars to Danny, but none of it is registering. The Christmas lights, now strung from the balconies, swirl around Danny.

Thirty or forty children are standing by the Christmas display, their parents standing behind them with Polaroid cameras. When they see Danny, the children start jumping in unison.

"Santa!" the children shout joyfully. "It's Santa!"

GINA THE HAIRDRESSER

Danny is back in Boulder, walking up Arapahoe with his head down, looking for money and things people drop in the gutter next to the sidewalk. He just needs to find enough change to call Big Brother up in the mountains and see if he can set Danny up with work or a couple of bucks or a place to crash a few nights, when he walks straight into his old roommate, Gina the Hairdresser. Gina moved out here a few years back to be with some guy, and the guy is with her. The guy looks like a rock star—leather jacket, square-toe black boots with the metal ring and straps, a faded Eagles T-shirt, and a black strap with a silver cross around his neck. He has a mountain of hair on his head. Gina is dressed all the same, with a Dead T-shirt under a foothill of flippy curly hair. Danny sees her before she sees him, but it's too late.

"I can't believe it, it's you. What are you doing here?" she says.

"You know, I'm just passing through, I'm in transit, I'm just visiting some people."

"Cool. So this is Stevie, he works at the record store on Pearl Street, he's a guitarist." Stevie flashes a set of perfect white teeth and half waves. "I heard you went back East or something," she says.

Danny looks up for a second at the mountains behind Gina and Stevie, and they look all dreamy, like he is looking at them through tinted glass.

"Yeah, well, the back-East thing, it didn't really work out."

"Oh. Cool. But where are you staying?"

"Here and there, you know," Danny says. But Gina can tell—she's a hairdresser and she knows everything about everybody; she listens to what people say, and she knows instantly what they are really saying. And she is a worried mother. Everybody she knows, everybody whose hair she cuts, they are like her babies. Danny remembers this about Gina. It's like a power she has.

"You know, you got to be careful in that bus station," she says. "The cops are all over that bus station. You want to come to dinner? Stevie and me were just going to dinner."

"Oh, no, thank you," Danny says. "I got to go catch up with somebody."

"But it's my treat, and I insist," Gina says. "It's my birthday. I'm taking everybody out."

"Okay then, I can't say no to that."

Danny walks with them to the restaurant, and they get a booth. Stevie orders a pitcher of beer and then another, like he's buying, but Gina's buying. He tells some story he tells everybody, about a rock star who came into the store and how they jammed together. When the food comes, Stevie pulls a denture plate out of his mouth, hides it in his pocket, and eats with his hand over his face. Stevie transforms from the cockiest person in the world to the most bashful. Gina tells Danny about her new life. Stevie doesn't say anything.

HELLO, FRASER

Danny hitches up into the mountains to find Big Brother, who is working as a cook up in a restaurant in Fraser, next to the Winter Park ski resort. Danny hasn't seen Big Brother in years. Big Brother told Danny he can get him a job on the mountain as a ski lift operator and in the restaurant as a dishwasher. It's all shift work, he says, but he knows a guy who rents trailers cheap, and Danny can make a bunch of money in two months, and he'll be on his way.

Danny hitches over the pass, riding in the back of a van sitting on steel bars and engine parts. The driver yells to him from the cab that he's going to weld his goddamn airplane back together as soon as he pulls it out of the goddamn tree he crashed into last summer. The van swerves back and forth; through the crack of the back doors, Danny sees that he is climbing higher and higher, and a straight, weightless terror sweeps through him: no guardrails, up against nothing but air. The driver is pretty drunk and singing along with country music on the radio. And then they plummet down, down into the valley on the far side through a canyon of plowed snow, eight, ten feet high, with little tree tips poking out up top. The driver stops and swings the van doors open to let Danny out—they only open from the outside—and the cold and the snow is blinding.

"Here's your stop," he says, "unless you want to come up to Granby and help me pull my goddamn plane out of a goddamn tree."

He drives off. Danny is standing in the middle of a two-lane road with packed-down mud cutting its way through the walls of snow. In one direction is a mountain. In the other is a bigger mountain. I'm screwed, Danny thinks, shivering in the cold. There's nothing here. I'm going to freeze to death.

Danny starts walking. He finds a shoveled-out parking lot filled with jeeps and trucks. Smoke rises from a building. Fraser House of Fondue, the sign says, with old wooden skis hammered on either side. It looks very Bavarian. Danny walks into the bar and asks for his brother. A man in a black suit is at the bar. He looks Danny up and down, his face all screwed up; is he going to send Danny back out into the snow to die? But then he grins.

"Are you Danny, the little brother? You ain't so little. You here to work?"

He tells Danny the boss is out, but he'd be back that night. Then he tells Danny where to find Big Brother. "Oh! He's off today. He's probably at home." Danny asks where he lives. The guy points out the window, up a side road he hadn't seen before.

"Up the ski road, I guess," he says. "Hey, you look frozen. You want something?" The guy in the suit disappears into the kitchen. Danny stares at the rows of bottles of alcohol behind the bar. So many kinds, so many colors. The guy comes back. "Here you go," he says. He looks left and right, like someone is looking for him. Then he whispers, "This one's on the house." He hands Danny a hot chocolate in a Styrofoam cup.

"I'll bet he lives up there. All them workers do," he says.

"Thank you," Danny says. He drinks the hot chocolate in the parking lot—it is the best thing he's ever tasted. Then he jogs up the ski road to try to find Big Brother.

BULL WHEEL

Danny walks straight up to the hill, his sneakers slipping in the packed snow. He walks all the way up to the plywood shack with the big sign that says "LIFT SHACK," and he bangs on the door. "S'open!" two voices yell at once. He jerks the door open and walks into darkness. As his eyes adjust, Danny can make out silhouettes of two men. The first, a little man with a beard, is hunched over a pile of forms with smoke streaming out of his mouth and nostrils. The other, a tall, thin man with a weathered leather cowboy hat, stands looking at Danny.

"Hello," Danny says to the standing man, who nods. "Is this the lift shack?"

"You seen the sign out front?"

"Yes."

"Then I guess this here's the lift shack."

"Sorry I'm late."

"Don't matter to me. Nobody put me in charge."

"You're very late," the sitting man says without looking up.

"I know," Danny says. "Sorry. I couldn't get—"

"Fill these out," the man says, handing him a pair of forms. "They're release papers. Don't get hurt. This here's Droop," he says, nodding to the man with the hat, rubbing his hands next to a space heater. "Droop's gonna show you around. He's been waiting for you."

Danny fills out the forms. Droop fidgets with a chain attaching his knife to his belt with one hand; with the other he runs his fingers through his moustache.

"S'at all you brung?" Droop says, pointing at Danny's feet. "Gym shoes?"

"You best get started," the sitting man says.

Crossing the base of the mountain, Danny slips along, following Droop. Droop's big insulated boots crunch effortlessly across the snow. Slush soaks through Danny's canvas sneakers. Danny trails him across a blinding field of ice, clutching the battered big Russian Coat, with the buttons gone, around his chest. Droop lifts a yellow rope. Danny ducks under it. He follows Droop to a large bush-faced man standing at the lift base, watching skiers climb onto the lift.

"Tiny." Droop nods.

"Nuther new guy?" Tiny says.

"Yup." Droop gestures. Danny steps into place.

"You have a nice ride," Tiny says.

"Yup. Take 'er easy."

The cold steel seat clips Danny's legs just behind the knees. Droop pulls the safety bar down. The chair takes them up into the sky. Droop tugs a worn ski glove off with his teeth, reaches into his parka, and pulls out a crumpled pack of Marlboros. He offers Danny a cigarette, then a light. He spits down at the skiers. Danny looks down at them. They are everywhere, descending the glowing white trails. They wear white and pink and yellow suits. They have hats, padded gloves, and goggles. They stop, throw their heads back, and laugh. They spread their arms out and gesture, the sharp poles swinging in every direction.

Droop nods down to Danny's left.

"That there's the bunny slope," Droop says. A pile of skiers are sprawled on their seats, wobbling down the slushy hill. "You always start on that bunny slope. You don't wanna get stuck working the bunny slope for long though if you can help it."

Danny turns to see the base lodge, now far below, then the brown valley beyond, then the hills—miles and miles of endless hills rippling north and east until they disappear. Danny lets his legs swing freely.

"Droop, come in," a muffled voice chatters on a walkie-talkie.

"Droop here."

"Droop? You there?"

"Droop here."

Droop looks at the walkie-talkie, shakes it, and clips it back to his belt. "Thing ain't worth crap," he says. He points down to the long, bandy slopes winding in and out of the woods below. "That there's the intermediates. That there's advanced. That there's the mid-station," Droop says, pointing to a small red booth. "That ain't so bad to work in there, the mid-station. Some skiers get off at the mid-station. Some skiers get off at the summit."

They glide up to the summit. Droop lifts the safety bar. Danny leans forward and slides off the chair and down the ramp. Droop strides across the clearing, where more skiers disembark from the chairlift and fan out in all directions. Danny follows Droop to the summit booth.

"Another new guy?" the teenage operator, scratching a neck caked in pimples, asks.

"Yup," Droop says. He lights a new cigarette with the butt of the old one and leans on the door frame. "Lookit," he says to Danny, surveying the top of the mountain. "You work up here, you get some situations. Skiers like to fall down. Skiers don't get off the lift, you gotta stop the lift and get them down. Sometimes they get stuck by their coat; that there's what we call a coat hanger. You sorta got to unhook them. Sometimes they get stuck by their leg; that's what we call a leg hanger. You sorta got to hold them when you unhook their leg so they don't fall on their head and sue our ass. Sometimes they get stuck by their neck; that's what we call a neck hanger. I don't know what you do when you got yourself a neck hanger. Sometimes they get stuck up by their arm."

"Is that what they call an arm hanger?" Danny says.

"Look, numbnuts. You don't need no college diploma to work up here," Droop says, looking Danny up and down. "You just need some good common sense. And you need to git to work on time or the Captain's gonna stick your ass down on the bunny slope every time."

"I couldn't get my car to start," Danny lies; he's never had a car.

"We all got problems."

"You don't wanna git stuck working that bunny slope," the operator says with a grin. His front teeth are missing.

"I got one more thing to tell you, numbnuts," Droop says, "and then I'm done telling you things. Whatever you do up here, them skiers get stuck or they don't get off, you stop the lift, and you get them down. Don't ever let them ride the bull wheel."

"The bull wheel?"

Droop gestures to a large grinding circular machine that turns the cables and chairs around and back down the mountain. Its base is surrounded by red bamboo poles and police tape. "That there's the bull wheel. They git that far and somebody's gonna get hurt. That'll whip 'em around and grind 'em up, and we'll all get our asses sued. Don't ever let 'em get to the bull wheel."

Danny stares at the turning, humming wheel.

"And one more last little piece of wisdom," Droop continues, looking down at Danny's soaked-through high tops. "Don't come up here in gym shoes. Go get yourself some boots. It gets pretty damn ass cold up here."

The walkie-talkie cackles again. "Droop? You there?"

"Droop here."

Droop walks out, slamming the door behind him.

The operator stares at Danny.

"They call me Hawk," he says. "What's your name?"

"Danny."

"You know, Danny, one day I'm gonna ride me that bull wheel."

"What?"

"I'm just gonna ride it. That bull wheel. While nobody's lookin'. Hey, let me ask you something. Do you like girls?"

"Um, sure," Danny says.

"Cuz there sure is a lot of girls up here," Hawk says. "You just wait and see."

Droop returns Danny to the base of the mountain. He walks Danny to the bunny slope, points to the on-off button on the J-bar lift, and walks away. For eleven hours Danny disentangles housewives and children from J-bars dragging them up the hill. There is no time to roll a cigarette or have lunch or a cup of coffee. Finally, at dusk, the skiers just seem to disappear into the lodge. Danny presses the button, and the J-bar stops. He walks over to the lift shack. He asks the man, "Is it time to punch out?"

"It's time," the man says, not looking up. "See you tomorrow at eight."

Danny walks out to the parking lot, which is empty. He walks the four miles back to town, squishing along the snow-plowed side of the road. In his little mini-trailer, there are no messages on the answering machine. He puts the plastic telephone next to his futon on the floor and pulls his sleeping bag up over his head.

For the first week, Danny works twelve-hour shifts on the bunny slope. He finds a pair of abandoned insulated boots in one of the electrician's shacks by the J-bar; although they are too big, he masters running up and down the hill in them, chasing the flailing skiers and rehooking them onto the J-bar.

One morning they send Danny to the mid-station. He rides the lift up through a dense fog alone, before the skiers have lined up. In his boots, Danny slips like a puck down the mid-station ramp and up to the little shack. Inside there's a chair, a small red telephone bolted to the wall, and a shelf. On the shelf is a frozen cup of coffee. He sniffs it; it's chewing tobacco. He opens the door and heaves the cup into the woods. It lands on the untouched snow, straight up. There is a loud electric heater; once on, the shack fills up with moist heat. It's still early; while the chairs squeak by with their safety bars raised, there are no skiers. Danny pulls off his nylon hat and gloves and puts them on top of the heater.

A stack of tear-off accident reports are stapled to the wall. A scribbled note in magic marker on the plywood wall states:

An axident riport MUST be filed out inTIREly

eech time you shot down the left.

DO NOT SHOT DOWN THE LEFT.

Next to the forms is a red button on a metal box, with wires running up to a hole and out to the large lift pole just above the ramp. The windows start to mist. Outside the fog lowers, just below Danny's eye level. He can make out the tips of trees, the rippled tops of clouds spreading in a straight line out toward the next wooded ridge. The chairlift sends rows of empty chairs past him, all toward the summit.

A human form rises out of the mist in a bright red baseball cap and a black Ski Liberty crew jacket. It's Hawk, swinging his feet beneath him. "Hey, man!" he yells to Danny as he glides by. He points to the logo on his jacket. "Check it out!" Then he flips up his safety bar and sits up on the edge of the seat, flailing his arms and legs. Danny waves, then looks down, pretending he's filling out a form.

"Hey, Danny!" Hawk yells again. "Check it out! I got a promotion! I'm a ski lift senior operator now!"

As Hawk passes, Danny pulls his torn, zipperless army jacket more tightly around him. He can hear the icy wind pulling around the little shack, reaching up under the sodden floorboards, trying to blow the space heater out. He looks down the valley. The clouds untangle and rip themselves open. He can see the ski lodge, the bustling parking lot filling up with cars, a line of brightly clad skiers at the base of the mountain waiting for the lift to open. He cranes his neck to look up the hill; he sees Hawk, ascending, disappearing into the sky.

"I'll call you!' Hawk yells.

"What?" Danny yells back, swinging the door open.

"I'll call you!"

"You can't call me," Danny yells. "It's an emergency phone! It's only for emergencies!"

Hawk disappears above the trees. Danny pulls the shed door shut. All the heat is gone. He rips an accident report form from the wall, pulls out a pencil, and begins sketching the trees on the back. He focuses on how the branches lean in like bony fingers toward the chairlift pole, how the bare hills behind it are framed by the cables and chairs. The first skiers come up on the lift. He keeps drawing. The emergency phone rings five times. Danny ignores it at first, then decides he'd better pick it up.

*

"Are you gonna let me know when the girl with the pink snowsuit is coming up or not?"

Two hours have passed. It's Hawk's tenth call. "Oh, sure," Danny says.

He is running out of accident report forms for his drawings. A pile of them lies crumpled on the floor.

"Cuz she got off again, and I'm not going to get a chance to talk to her if I'm sitting here at the controls and not out there on the ramp when she gets off."

"Why do you want to talk to her?" Danny pictures Hawk up at the top of the mountain, abandoning the control console, trying to stop a skier who's getting off the lift so he can talk to her. This can't be safe, Danny thinks. He should really call somebody from ski patrol.

Just as he decides this is a good idea, someone knocks on the door. He quickly hangs up the phone.

"How you doing?" It's ski patrol. "You got a light?"

"No, sorry," Danny says; he ran out of matches an hour before.

A cigarette hangs from the patrolman's red face. He's wearing an all-red body ski suit with a white cross on the back, Ray-Bans, and the beginnings of a blond handlebar moustache. He looks angry. He leans on his poles, the unlit cigarette hanging from his lip, watching skiers pass above on the chairlift.

"Seen any good accidents lately?" Danny asks.

"Nothing today," the patrolman says. "But last night we had a beauty. Two broken legs. Dumbasses ran right into each other. Up on the black diamond."

"Wow."

"Took us an hour to get them untangled and down. They ended up in the woods. All wrapped up around a tree. They were howling. One of them said he was going to sue my ass. Texans."

"Huh."

The patrolman starts to push off, then turns around. "You know you're not supposed to be on the emergency phone, right?"

"Oh, yeah. I know."

"Okay then," the patrolman says. He uncrosses his poles and digs in. Over his shoulder he says, "Because if I catch you on that emergency phone again, I'm going to have to report you."

The fog has burned off. The sun has climbed above the trees, dripping the frozen fake snow from their branches. The phone rings, on and off, for a long time. It must be around lunchtime, Danny thinks. He's drawn the view of the treetops on the back of eighteen accident reports that he's decided to keep and tape to the wall of his trailer. Each drawing is a little different, Danny thinks, and yet they are all the same. I wonder if anybody would get this, Danny thinks, leafing through page after page. I wonder if anybody would see the difference. Danny looks out at the chairs drifting by; if he stares at them long enough, he realizes, he can invert their silhouettes so they appear to be going backwards. If he really focuses—if he screws his eyes down to little slits—he can make the empty chairs on the far side go up, not down. It's an illusion. He can make all the chairs turn around on the lift. And the skiers too. If he squints, he tells himself, maybe he can make their fronts become their asses.

Danny starts to nod off. His head falls against the cold plexiglass. The phone rings, and he picks it up.

"Why is girls so stuck up?" Hawk asks.

"You have to stop calling me."

"It's like I keep trying to talk to her, and she's all like, you know, shruggy about it."

"I'm sorry to hear that," Danny says. He hangs up. He focuses on a teenager in rental boots, blue jeans, and a hooded Texas Longhorns sweatshirt, approaching on the lift. She is staring at the mid-station ramp, her eyes open in terror. She hasn't pulled the safety bar up. Her ski tips are pointed straight down toward the ground. "Pull the tips up," Danny says quietly to himself. "What are you doing?"

She inches up in her chair, looks at Danny, and yells, "How do you git offin this thing?" Her ski tips latch into the ice, a foot below the lip of the ramp, and catch. Instead of falling out, the chair holds her. It lurches downward, straining the cable, then springs into the air. She hurtles up and out of it, like a high diver, but her skis catch again on the safety bar. Fifteen feet in the air, the chair snaps back into its place on the cable. She drops through the space between the bar and her seat and falls until her chin cracks against the foot bar, jerking her head back. She then falls limply down, ten feet, to the soft snow in the trees.

Oh, my god, Danny thinks. He hits the red switch with the palm of his hand, again and again. The chairlift lurches to a halt. Oh, my god. He picks up the phone.

"I've got a code red, mid-station!" he yells into the phone. "Code red. A neck hanger."

"So I tried talking to her again." Hawk's voice comes through the receiver, a little high-pitched, like he's been whining. Hawk never realized that Danny had hung up on him. "And do you know what she done said to me?"

"Hawk, hang up the emergency phone! This is the emergency phone! I've got an emergency! I need ski patrol!"

"She done said to me that I don't talk to no boys that I don't know. And you know what I done said?"

Danny bangs the receiver on the wall. He looks out at the girl's body, lying face down in the snow. She hasn't moved. He has to go out there. "Hawk," Danny says into the phone. "I need ski patrol. Now. Please."

"I said, 'Well, how you going to get to know me if you don't never talk to me?' Oh, wait, there she is. I see her. I'll call you back." The phone goes dead. Danny presses button nine.

"Ski patrol," someone says.

"I got a code red at the mid-station," Danny says. "A neck hanger. She isn't moving."

"We'll be right there," someone says. "Don't touch her."

The phone goes dead, and the mountain goes silent. Danny wraps his scarf around his head, pushes the plywood door open, and steps out into the frigid air. He walks over to the girl's limp body. Her arms and legs and skis and poles are all tangled beneath her, like a roped deer.

"Are you okay?" Danny whispers.

The girl's head jerks up out of the snow; she looks at Danny, then up at the chairlift. Somehow she untangles herself, springs up onto her skis, and pushes off, snowplowing down the hill.

"I ain't never getting on a stupid chairlift again," she says over her shoulder.

Danny watches her descend the hill, mixing in with others snowplowing down the icy slope, then disappearing into the zigzagging crowd. A moment later four ski patrolmen arrive, pulling an emergency sled with medical equipment. At the same time a snowmobile hurtles up the slope, beneath the chairs. All converge on Danny, where he stands next to the girl's fallen-angel imprint in the snow.

"Where's the code red?" somebody asks.

Danny shrugs and points down the hill.

"She just floated away," he says, trying to pick her out among the white and orange dots on skis, slushing down the hill far below them. "She just floated away."

*

"It is time for me to extract vengeance on his dumb ass."

Hawk squeezes his fists around the steering wheel. This is two weeks later, nighttime, after closing. Danny reaches for his seatbelt. Hawk's truck headlights paint the parking lot an uneven, milky amber. Danny looks back and sees the mountain's bright spotlights recede into blackness.

"Which dumb ass?" he asks.

"Droop," Hawk says. "Chewing me out. Putting me on report."

"Really? What did you do?"

"Tried to ride the bull wheel," he says. "I was just staring at it, and it was turning round and round, and I thought, 'Why not. I'll just jump an empty seat and jump off the other side.'"

"Isn't that dangerous?"

"It's for fun is all. What are you gonna do up here if you don't have some fun."

"How did you get caught?"

"Ski patrol saw me and shut the lift down. They told Droop. He chewed me out good. Which I don't mind so much, except for some girls getting off the lift, and them all started laughing at me."

Hawk grinds the gearshift of his truck in a circular winding motion. The truck's bald tires spin and choke on the black ice. The plowed banks of snow glimmer icily under the headlights. Little mailboxes stick out like little pointed elf heads.

"Why do you want to ride the bull wheel?"

"Because it's got all that torque and stuff."

Hawk is sucking on a bottle now—maybe it's Mad Dog or Wild Irish Rose—and hands it to Danny.

"It's pulling all that weight and cable up that mountain, and you can see it when them chairs spin around. I want to be in one of them chairs and see what it feels like. I know it ain't allowed. I just get so bored up there."

"Yeah, but you'll get killed."

Danny takes a slug from the bottle. It's really bad. Is it maple brandy? Cheap port?

"That thing will throw you right off the mountain if you don't get your legs caught in it," Danny says.

Just as he hands the bottle back, a V in the road appears. Hawk lurches the truck into a ninety-degree turn off the shoveled two-lane highway and onto a smaller, half-plowed road. The truck fishtails, and for a second, Danny finds his face pressed up against Hawk's bristly neck. Thankfully, he swerves the truck back, fishtailing back into the other direction. "Sorry 'bout that," Hawk manages to say, but before he hurtles in Danny's direction, which will probably send Danny hurtling out the truck door and into the snow, a tree trunk appears in the headlights.

Well, Danny thinks, thank god for this. Thank god for both of us. The tree trunk appears to rise up and explode into the front of the truck. A new, bright white bolt of light flashes through Danny's forehead, and for all he knows, he's fallen sound asleep.

Another week passes. Danny is now a senior lift operator. He has a black Ski Liberty jacket and a badge with his name on it. Tonight he is positioned as the base operator of quad four, a four-person lift on the back side of the mountain. He rarely sees any skiers. When he does, they pop out of the woods quietly and slip onto the ascending lifts by themselves. Danny watches them climb up in the lights toward the summit. He is responsible for three buttons regulating the speed of the lift; he watches three gauges determining its tension, temperature, and oil. The giant lift makes a gentle humming, clicking noise. Its huge gears and bull wheel are housed in the same heated building Danny occupies. He reads a science-fiction paperback, totally against the rules, but there is no one on this side of the mountain to monitor Danny, and nothing ever happens.

A lone skier, clearly a beginner who's lost, hobbles out of the woods, one ski in her hand. Danny leaves the shed, walks to her, and takes her ski.

"Can you tell me where I am?" she asks.

"You're on the wrong side of the mountain," Danny says, helping her reattach the ski to her boot. "What you need to do is take this lift straight up to the top. When you get off, walk straight ahead until you see the other bull wheel. There's an intermediate trail from there, marked really clearly. It will take you down the other side of the mountain to the lodge."

"Oh," she says. She shuffles to the chairlift in her buckled skis, climbs onto a seat, and disappears. Danny is alone for the evening. It is March, and a damp fog has settled around the mountain from the melting snow. Black mud patches have been appearing in streaks on the trails, and it's too warm to make more snow. The mountain will be closed in a few more days, Droop told Danny.

Now the safety phone rings. Weeks after the accident—weeks after Danny's had any contact with Hawk—he still wonders if he should answer it. He picks it up. It's Droop. "Ten o'clock," he says. "Time to put 'er to bed." Danny sets the generator for full speed and the shut-down timer for ten minutes, pulls and locks the door behind him, and walks out to the lift. He flips the seat up on every chair that goes by, until the last, which he climbs onto. It jerks him quickly up into the darkness. As he whistles up above the trees, he looks out to see the dim lights of a ring of ski condos, like a string of pearls stretching out toward town.

At the top Danny climbs off and pulls the rope over the trailhead. He walks across the summit to the bull wheel. Here he is supposed to climb on a chair heading down with the person who's been manning the shed where Hawk used to sit.

Someone waves frantically to him. "Hey, man!" It's Hawk. He's no longer in a Ski Liberty jacket; he's wearing a ragged denim coat over a sweatshirt. Danny hasn't seen him since the accident. Danny knew he broke his nose. Danny heard he was back on the mountain, but demoted, on permanent assignment on the bunny slope. Danny has ducked him until now.

Hawk is standing at the summit shack by the chairs coming up the mountain, across from Danny. The chairs are zipping by between the two of them. Hawk's watching the chairs, looking like he's about to jump one, to ride the bull wheel.

"I told you I was gonna ride it!" he yells.

"Don't," Danny says.

"Jest watch me!"

Hawk lunges and grabs the bar of a passing chair, swings into the seat, and careens toward the bull wheel. His legs dangle beneath him. He pumps his fists in the air just as the safety bar crashes down onto his head. The chair rocks wildly, then spins into the turn. The bull wheel, waiting, pulls him into its wild, grinding turn.

Danny knows he shouldn't watch. But somehow he can't turn away.

GOODBYE, FRASER

Spring has come, and the huge banks of snow have melted into torrents of green water. Big Brother and Danny are the last workers at the Fraser House of Fondue, and they get to close up shop. Big Brother follows a typed list of instructions left by the owner, who took off for Denver a few days before.

Danny removes the metal grates from the prep cook station and hangs the long rubber floor mats up on a cable; he takes everything out of the pantry, cans and all, and stocks it in the unplugged freezer so the bears won't come looking for stuff when they wake up. The owner doesn't take chances with bears. He only keeps the Swiss House open from October through April, the heart of ski season, and closes as soon as ski patrol shuts down the last mud-streaked, water-gushed trail on the mountain. He shoots down to Denver to run another restaurant, leaving shlubs like Danny and Big Brother to wrap things up, promising them they'll have a job when they come back next fall, but the owner knows nobody's coming back.

Danny climbs under the dishwashing machine and turns off the valves. Check!

Big Brother shuts the gas off on the range stoves. Check!

Danny screws in the window plates. Check!

And then they are done. Big Brother reaches behind the freezer where he stashed six T-bones and a dozen frozen lobster tails. Danny climbs over the bar and grabs four bottles of twelve-year-old whiskey and a case of beer. He hits the circuit breakers, throws the keys in the mailbox, turns on the alarm, and steps out of the darkened, cavernous, unspeakably lonely restaurant where Big Brother sweated and worked and argued with waiters for twenty-four weeks, him being the head chef, and Danny fought with the dishwashing machine when he wasn't operating a ski lift up the mountain. They step outside, and the late-afternoon sunlight glares off the last dirty little mountains of snow, stuffed up between the pine trees and shoveled into corners of the mud-streaked parking lot. Water cascades from ledges high above them; there are black pools of water where there used to be mountains of snow. A truck blasts by them in the parking lot, sending an arc of water into the sky. Danny stands there, his eyes adjusting to the outdoors—mountain after mountain, still all white up top, and nothing but green trees and clouds. Danny pulls a beer out of the case for Big Brother and one for himself.

"Come on, man," Big Brother says.

"Where are we going?"

"Granby," he says. "Lets go up to Granby."

"Why go to Granby?"

"Why not go to Granby? Plus, we can cash our checks there. Plus, there's a place up there where they play jazz. I'm gonna hook up with a jazz band up there. Come on now, give me a push."

Big Brother's car needs to be push-started. It is an ancient, rusted hulk of a thing with an old choke knob under the steering wheel and the road visible under Danny's feet. Big Brother climbs in, and Danny starts pushing from the back. Big Brother throttles it a few times, and the engine turns over, a black plug of smoke coating Danny, then disappearing into the crystal spring air. Danny runs for it and jumps into the passenger seat. And they are off for Granby.

THE PASS

"Jazz?" the bartender says to Danny while Big Brother stands in a phone booth outside, trying to call someone in Denver. "Jazz leaves Granby each spring with the jobs and the skiers. Now, if I was looking for work right now," he whispers, leaning over the bar to speak, although the place is empty, "I'd head out for Oregon. Oregon's booming. Once the snow melts out here, nobody's booming nothing."

Big Brother drives Danny up to I-80, drops him at the ramp, and drives east toward Denver. Danny works the westbound ramp. A few rides and a cold night under an overpass later, Danny wakes up in Idaho. After a few hours of nothing, a truck stops at the top of the ramp. Danny watches it carefully. The driver's probably just taking a break, he thinks. Or checking a map. Or waiting for a partner to catch up.

"Excuse me, sir. Are you waiting for a lift?" a voice calls out.

Danny runs along the side of the truck. It hisses in a deep, hydraulic whisper. A door swings open. A hand reaches down and pulls Danny's pack in. He climbs up and follows it into the cool, dark cabin.

"Looks like you're going over the pass. You going over the pass?"

"Yeah," Danny says, trying to catch his breath.

"How are you doing today?" The driver starts doing that thing they do with their arms and legs—the jacks and balls and roasting of gears. The truck lurches forward. All at once Danny feels the huge, cold weight of whatever is packed into the trailer behind him pushing them up the hill.

"Name's Ezekial, but you can call me Z," the driver says, draping his huge, hairy forearms across the steering wheel. "Most folks call me Z," he says.

The truck rolls up the ramp. They swerve away from the huge vein of trucks still on the highway, pumping raw materials and eggs and hydrogen chloride up and over the next mountain ridge. They are in the only truck going onto the side road, up over the pass. Danny scans his surroundings. First there is Z, who is definitely bigger than him. Danny can jump out if he has to, but he'll lose his pack. There is a crucifix air freshener hanging from the rearview mirror. The cab is clean, like it has just been vacuumed.

"Is this a new truck?" Danny asks.

"Hardly that," Z says. "Had it eleven years."

"What have you got in the trailer?"

"Doors and windows. Lots of them." Z takes his hat off and scratches the top of his head. He's surprisingly bald for a man with a boyish face. "I build log cabins, me and my buddy up here." He pulls his cap back on. He smiles. "Say, would you like to listen to some country music?"

"Sure."

Z turns on the radio, and it's the same Danny's heard everywhere. He heard it when he was sitting at a counter in a Stuckey's with a cold cup of coffee, waiting for the old man next to him to push his plate away and leave so Danny could eat the last of his mashed potatoes. Danny heard it when he was trying to sleep standing up in a phone booth outside a gas station in a rainstorm. The song is about drinking things away, which really eats at Danny. But he pretends to enjoy it, and Z really likes it a lot, rocking his head back and forth, humming along, and tapping his fingers on the steering wheel.

The mountain pass gets steeper. Z effortlessly glides the truck around the first switchback.

"Would you enjoy a cigarette?" Z asks.

"Sure," Danny answers. "Thanks."

Z unwraps a new box with one hand, crumples the cellophane, and packs one out for Danny. Danny takes it, and Z holds out a lighter. Danny takes the lighter. He takes a deep pull. The smoke fills his sinuses and the depths of his lungs. It's been a while. Danny exhales slowly, blowing the smoke out his window. The silver guardrail spins past, framing browned stalks of dead field grass and, beyond them, a plunge down a ravine.

Can't jump now. It's too late. Danny takes another drag.

"Thanks," he says, handing Z the lighter.

"That's okay," Z says. "You can keep it if you like."

"The lighter?" It's silver plated, heavy, with a bronco leaping over a fence engraved on its front.

"Sure. Here," he says, holding out the cigarettes. "Take these as well."

"I don't want to take your whole pack."

"It's okay," Z says. "I don't smoke."

Danny pretends to listen deeply to the next four songs while Z wrestles the steering wheel. There are three more switchbacks on the way up, each tighter then the last, before the truck settles into the saddle. Snow-caked summits drift by in little waves. As the truck lurches forward into a steep valley, Danny feels the weight of the load it carries start pushing him down the first steep hill. At the end there's a guardrail, where the road U-turns back into the mountainside. Beyond the guardrail there's nothing.

"Do you mind if I ask you a question?" Z says, staring straight ahead.

"Nope," Danny says, lighting another cigarette with his new lighter. "Shoot."

"Do you believe in Jesus?"

"Yes."

"Really? And you accept him as your savior?"

Z downshifts twice; the smell of brake fluid and smoke fills the cab. He turns the truck in a wide arc. The force swings Danny from the bucket seat toward the center of the truck. He looks down at the rocks. The truck straightens out. Another switchback appears, two hundred yards farther down; the truck picks up speed.

"Yes," Danny says. "Yes. I really do."

"Boy, am I glad to hear that," Z says. "I'm really happy for you. Because I was lost for a really, really long time before I found Jesus."

"Where?"

"Where what?"

"Where did you find him?"

"Well, here, actually," Z says. "That's the reason I was thinking of him. I found him right here."

"That's great," Danny says.

The mountains on this side of the pass are beautiful and seem to go on forever.

"Yeah, well, what happened was—" Z takes a deep breath and downshifts. "You're not going to believe it, but, boy. What happened was this: Just ten years ago, when I was just starting out, me and my partner rented a flatbed, and we were hauling a load of logs over this pass. Only we got real drunk in town before we loaded up. Because we were lost, you know. We were lost souls. And the truck was a rental, and we overloaded it real bad. And we just made it over the pass back there.

"And we were coming down the hill, and my partner went to downshift, but something happened, and he couldn't get the gearshift back into four. He couldn't get the gearshift into anything. The clutch just stuck. And the truck just started rolling. Wow. Boy.

"So I tried, and he tried, and we tried together, but we could not move that gearshift into a gear. Fourth, fifth. It didn't matter. 'Hold on,' my friend said. I guess we were both saying things. Name in vain. Stuff like that. You know. Because we so were lost.

"We took that first hairpin back there doing sixty. I don't know how we did it. He took as wide a turn as he could. We lost some logs over the edge. If you look at the next turn, you can see them, stuck up in the air. But we made it. But then we came out of that curve, and gosh. We were still picking up speed."

Hiss. HISS! The truck pumps air around the axles. There's a soft jerking sensation. Danny looks at the wall of cracked stone in front of him, like a cleft lip, where the mountain to the right leans down onto the valley on the left. Z starts the turn.

"And so then we got real quiet. We stopped cussing, stopped the name in vain stuff, stopped everything. The truck was up to seventy, then seventy-five. We were leaning on the gearshift, both of us, with all our strength, feeling it bend. Looking at this big rock face growing right in front of us. And then my friend said, out of the bottom of his breath, 'Thank you, Jesus, for everything that you've given me in this life.' And the truck snapped into fourth gear effortlessly, just like that."

Danny can almost touch the stone rock face as it spins past him, as the truck's weight presses him against the door. "So you made it?"

"We made it," Z says. "We just barely made it."

In the gully before the next turn, Danny sees them; four logs, dried, petrified, sticking up from the earth like trees stripped of everything. Z is quiet now, lost in the next country song, tapping his hands on the wheel. Danny lights another cigarette and blows the smoke out into the valley. In two more turns, they are surrounded by trees on a flat stretch of road. Z pulls off at the first exit.

"Well, here's my exit," he says. "I live up here. Do you need anything? A hot meal? Anything?"

"No," Danny says. "I'm all set. But thank you."

"Thank you," he says, shaking Danny's hand. "And I'm really happy for you. I'm really happy you've found him too."

Danny climbs down, and Z hands him his pack. The truck growls and rolls away down the exit. Danny is left alone with a perfect view. He can see the two great snowy mountain peaks, the sheer ledges, the little trees popping up out of the ice. And he can barely make out the road he's just travelled. It's a thin scribble, a little black line winding back and forth, back and forth, back up and over the pass.

PROPANE

"Bend's booming, Danny," this Manpower Temporary Agency lady says, pulling the same application from the same clipboard and handing him the same blue slip of paper without making eye contact, just like all the other Manpower ladies before her. "All of eastern Oregon's booming. You need work, you came to the right place." She sends Danny out to a construction site somewhere on the outskirts of town for a long-term assignment.

Each morning Danny needs to be the first one on-site at seven-thirty. He doesn't have a car, so he needs to buy a bike and bike four miles up a slow incline, along the base of a huge mountain, through dazzling pine forests that sparkle when the spring snows begin to fall. Danny's first responsibility when he gets there is simple but extremely dangerous: He has to enter eight half-constructed units and make sure the propane heaters stayed lit overnight and are blowing heated air into the drying interiors of each unit. If the flame is out, but the gas has continued to blow and Danny tries unknowingly to relight it, he will explode in a huge ball of flame, possibly witnessed by the second man on-site, who might by then be driving up to the site in his heated truck. But if the flame is out because the gas has run out, he has to disconnect the empty propane tank, roll it down the stairs, and drag a new one—at least one hundred pounds—up the stairs from the lot. All this takes a lot of time and has to be decided alone. And Danny has to remember to bring his shiny new lighter.

Although it's spring, it gets cold, and then it gets colder. And then, one morning in April, it snows for real. Peddling up the hill, great puffs of air in front of him, his fingers freeze to the handlebars. Wow, Danny thinks. What is this now? What have I done? How did I get this desperate? He rides into the lot and down a rutted dirt road that will one day be a rich person's driveway decorated with wild plants and cactus and floodlights, but now still dark in the wintry morning light. He pushes open the temporary plywood door of the first unit, and he smells it instantly. Gas. The sweet smell of gas. There is nothing he can do. At least he smelled it. He climbs the stairs into what will one day be some rich person's great room. Plastic sheeting covers what will soon become a massive cathedral window. Danny turns the knob on the tank, still hissing. His head swoons. He peels the plastic sheeting away and steps outside.

The snow has altered the treetops beneath him, all plunging into a canyon, rushing, half-frozen water beneath him. Once this was a beautiful place. The boughs around Danny lean toward him, suppressed with the heavy snow, surrendering to this odd, asymmetrical stack of ski condominiums now dug into a once proud set of ledges at the base of the mighty Cascades. Danny looks out and is startled by a huge bird, an owl, that rises from a branch just a few feet from him and spreads its wings. The owl swoops away down into the canyon, appearing to turn its head back at him for a moment, as if to say, "I don't care what you build here. I'm not going anywhere."

ROSIE

From the back of the truck, Danny watches the first shafts of sunlight paint the side of the mountain in brilliant orange. The beam spreads above him, picking up floating ice crystals that swarm around the trees. The snow lights up, then turns to black water and dribbles down the slopes in big black stains. This is so beautiful, Danny thinks. This place is so beautiful. If only—

Bang! The truck hits a rut on the hard dirt road. Danny bounces up, then down on the toolbox. Kenny pulls the little cab window open and grins at him. A plume of cigarette smoke puffs out the window. "You still holding them propane tanks?" he asks.

"Yes," Danny says. He is holding in his frozen hands a steel cable that loops through the eyeholes of a dozen propane tanks, leashed to the truck's side rail. They are tight and cut into his palms, but he can't let go. He's been told what happens if he lets them go. "Fireworks," the boss once told him. "Happened to the last rental," he said, holding his hands up and giggling under his bushy moustache. "Look ma, no hands!"

Kenny drives straight into town and pulls the truck up in front of the McDonald's. He climbs out of the cab and slams the door shut. "Come on." He waves an unnaturally long arm at Danny. Danny follows him through the glass door to the counter. "Boss says I should buy you breakfast."

Danny sits down across from Kenny. Two stacks of pancakes in Styrofoam containers sit on plastic trays between them. "Boss wants me to talk to you about not being a rental no more," he says. A knot of homesickness clutches Danny's throat. He can't swallow his pancakes. He pushes the tray away. "He just wants me to ask is all. It's a good job once you go permanent." Kenny finishes his pancakes and sticks a plastic fork into Danny's. "Once I went permanent, they started paying me for all the overtime and all that. And nobody treats you like a rental no more."

"Thanks," Danny says.

"All Boss wants you to do is think about it is all," Kenny says. Somehow he stuffs the pancakes into his mouth while still smoking. "Let him know by tomorrow. Today he told me to bring you and the propane and them tools over to site four. They screwed up so bad they need a rental to come clean it all up."

The big truck turns out onto the flat paved road that runs through downtown Bend, then spills out on the road toward the river. Through the trees, Danny can see the neat little cluster of houses and stores around the old mill. He can barely make out smoke rising from chimneys, steam rising from a plant, and the roof of a diner. All he can think of now is that tray of pancakes they left there. He misses them. He is sad he didn't eat them.

Kenny pulls the truck in front of a two-story shell of a building in the woods. Through the woods next door, cars inch slowly through a drive-through window. Danny can't make out if it's a Wendy's or a Burger King.

Kenny sticks his head back out the window. "Well, we're here, I guess. Get your ass off the truck. Check in with a guy they call Rosie. Jest pull off four of them tanks. And don't lose them tools."

Danny enters a cinderblock fortress. A half-dozen workers with burnt faces and shaggy blond beards drop long steel bars onto a cement surface. They glare at Danny, then go back for another bar.

"You know where I can find Rosie?" Danny asks one.

"Nope," this one says, putting his large hands on his hips.

"Can you point me in his general direction?"

"I can," he says. "But let me ask you something first. Where you from?"

"Site seven," Danny says, nodding back toward the big truck. "From the site seven worksite. They told me to find Rosie."

"No, I mean, where you *from*."

"Back East."

The man turns and spits on the bar he just dropped.

"Oh, yeah," he says. "We heard all about you."

"Up here!" A voice comes from somewhere high up in the building's half-constructed skeleton, but Danny can't see anyone up there. "You come on up here! Don't pay them no mind."

A new bar clangs down. "Who's that?" another one asks.

"Shuffler," the spitter says. "They sent him over here from seven to do some poop work."

He spits again.

"Course, now we don't need us no poop worker. We got us here a shuffler."

"Up here now," the voice from above comes again. "Get on up here."

Danny looks up again at the roofless turret of the castle. Scaffolding made of planks and rope weaves through the top ledges. The sun has just started to bleed through the trees, blinding him. He sees the silhouette of a small man above him, waving a large forearm. "I guess you're looking for me," the voice says. "You must be that shuffler they sent. Get on up. There's a ladder out back. Grab that toolbox. Get on up here."

Danny climbs over a pile of half-shattered crates and broken cement blocks, through the frame of what might someday become a back door. Danny ascends the ladder with one arm, moving the heavy toolbox up against his stomach. He climbs over the ledge and lands softly on the wet wood of the scaffolding, which creaks under his weight.

"Y'ever see anything so screwed up in your whole life?" the voice asks.

Danny turns around, and Rosie is standing in front of him. His face is very difficult to look at. One eye is clear blue and stares right at him, and one has no pigment at all and stares down and away. There's a nose that's been broken so many times that Danny can't really tell where nose starts and forehead ends. The whole right side of Rosie's face drifts away from him. He's short but wide; two twisted arms dangle loosely out of a sleeveless Rebel Yell sweatshirt.

"Yeah, like I was saying," Rosie continues. "Some screw-butt contractor said we do it his way or whatever and git it done before the first snowfall, and guess the hell what else is new. So what's it do? It snows. And it all just fell out, the first frost, it just frigging cracked out, man. Set us back three weeks easy. We're screwed, man. We screwed this job up good."

Danny pulls his gloves on; they have grown stiff and cold in his pocket. "What do you need me to do?"

"I don't care what the hell you do," Rosie says, still staring at his ruins. "I ain't the boss man." Rosie turns to walk back to a corner where he dug a hole between two steel beams. Then he marches straight back to Danny, almost bumping up next to him. "But I guess if I was the boss man, I'd want you to take that sledgehammer over there and start breaking up the rest of that crap wall so we can reset it all over again. I'd probably want this whole job dug out and redone and set before it freezes out again."

"Okay."

Danny's arms and legs ache with hunger. He picks up the sledgehammer. It's heavy, and it hurts his hands still cracked and sore from yesterday, when he dug a foundation trench out at site seven. Rosie starts digging through the toolbox. Danny starts swinging. The cracking concrete feels good. It drops in little triangles onto the scaffold boards. He peeks down at the floor below; he can still hear the clang of the rebar men working, but he can't see them. He follows the lines where they interlaced the bars together.

"You ain't gonna get nowhere, just tapping at it like that," Rosie says.

"Sorry."

"Don't have to apologize to me none," he says, still pulling out tools. "Like I said, I ain't the boss."

Rosie screams out something like a whoop. It is so loud that Danny loses his grip on the sledgehammer. He traps it with his leg before it plummets off the scaffolding. He turns back to Rosie. He guesses Rosie must have hurt himself, but he is staring out over the precipice.

"Oh, baby," Rosie says. "Oh, baby. Will you look at that. Oh, baby, baby. Will you look."

"Look at what?" Danny asks. He peers over the edge. He can see the fast-food restaurant. There's a woman pulling the door open. She's wearing a green pants suit, like a flight attendant or a rental car agent. Her hair is tied up in an off-green scarf that matches her suit.

"Will you look at that," Rosie says. "Hmmm, hmmm. Oh, baby."

Danny picks up the sledgehammer and swings it fiercely. A square foot of the wall becomes sand; it slides down the wall of the building.

"Let me ask you something," Rosie says behind him. He waits for Danny to turn around. Danny takes off his work gloves, pretending to adjust them, so he doesn't have to look at Rosie. Then Rosie comes right up into Danny's face again.

"You got yourself a woman?"

"A what?"

"A woman! You got yourself a woman?"

"Yeah," Danny says, "I guess."

Danny starts to pick up the hammer again when Rosie makes a gesture for him to stop.

"I got me the best woman in the world," he says. "But she's in the big house right now." Rosie pulls a wad of something wet out of his sweatshirt pocket and stuffs it in the sagging side of his mouth. "It's all account of me she's in there too.

"Thing is, we were climbing out the back window of this here liquor store, and we set the alarm off, and the cops came in the front door. And you know what she said? She said, 'You run, Rosie.' And I said, 'No, sir,' right to her face I said it. 'No woman of mine's gonna take one for me.' And she said, 'You run, mister! You got a prior!' And she turned and shot one over their heads. That was enough for me, and I ran like hell. I just ran and ran, and when I turned around, she weren't there. She got eight years, and she's still up there, and she never once told nobody I was with her. Not once. I ended up in there later for something else, but I only got two years. Now I go up there and visit her sometimes 'cause she was so loyal and all that."

Rosie is still staring out at the fast-food restaurant. He spits a string of brown tobacco juice out onto the snow.

"Even though I pretty much got women anytime I want now."

Danny picks up the sledgehammer and swings it with such force that the whole wall collapses in a cloud of powder; when the dust clears, Rosie's still there.

"Now let me ask you something," he asks Danny. "You got a woman that would do something like that for you?"

Danny doesn't get to answer. The workers on the floor are screaming up at him; he has to go down and clean the rubble and plaster he's just poured down into their new foundation.

By the time Danny is done, Kenny's come back to get him. When Danny climbs down the ladder, Kenny stands there staring at him, his arms hanging at his sides, surrounded by the other workers.

"Looks like he pretty much screwed this job up worse," one says to Kenny.

"Stay away from them sledgehammers," one of them yells to Danny when he climbs into the back of the truck.

Kenny drives Danny back to the center of town.

"So you got to meet Rosie," he yells above the wind howling all around Danny.

"Yeah."

"Ain't he something?"

"He is."

Kenny pauses to light a cigarette.

"He tell you he used to be the boss man?"

"No," Danny yells back. "He didn't tell me that."

"Yeah, he used to be the boss," Kenny says. "Then he got all messed up, did some time. When he got out, the company still hired him back. Only he can't be a boss no more. For all the obvious reasons, I guess. But it goes to show you. This company takes care of its own," Kenny says. "When I heard that story, I signed right up."

The big truck pulls over on the town's main street, just across from the McDonald's.

"See you in the morning," Kenny yells. "You go right in and talk to Boss."

Kenny pulls the little cab window shut. Danny climbs off the back of the truck, which roars off out of town, its tire chains ringing on the pavement. The sky goes dark, and it starts to snow again; big white gobs float down like feathers. Danny stands for a second, not sure where to turn; then he can't help himself. He stares in through the plate-glass window of the McDonald's, now closed. He looks at the table he sat at, where the pancakes once steamed in their Styrofoam tray. He has some hope that they are still there. But the table was wiped clean many hours ago.

FIREWOOD

The phone wakes Danny up the morning after the construction company releases him. A guy named Marshall is calling. He got Danny's number from a guy named Ricky. Danny rubs his eyes and yawns. He can't remember a guy named Ricky.

Marshall needs some firewood split for his woodstove. He hurt his goddamn back or something. He's willing to pay somebody fifty bucks to split a load of goddamn firewood. It just got delivered the night before. He needs it split before it gets wet. He asks Danny if he knows how to split firewood. He sounds out of breath. Danny pictures this huge bear of a man, all beard and suspenders. Yes, he says. He has no idea how to split firewood, but he has a pretty good idea of what he can do with an extra fifty bucks. So he says yes.

He pulls on his sweatshirt and pants and starts walking. He walks all the way to the house. On his way, he walks through the boarded-up town. He walks past the little mill houses on the outskirts with wood smoke hugging the yards like little blankets. He starts winding up the hill. It was once the side of a mighty volcano. The volcano popped out of the desert floor a million years ago, carving black ruts of lava in the sandstone. The houses are built into the sunny side of the hill, multileveled, made of exotic woods. Or they are those terra cotta jobs, with those red pipe tiles they use for roofing out here. The houses have neat, arty little mailboxes. The yards are terraced with pink desert plants and blue cactus, tucked into little white rock gardens.

Up here Danny rises above the smoky, out-of-work little mill town. It is warmer up here than down there, but it is still cold. He finds Marshall's house number on his mailbox. He walks up and rings the doorbell. A lady comes to the door. She doesn't unlatch it. She speaks to Danny through the storm window. She holds a huge coffee mug in her left hand. "Oh, my," she says. "Marshall left the maul and the sledge in the back." She raps a fingernail of her right hand on the windowpane in front of Danny. "So you'll just want to go around back. Just follow that path around the garage to go around back. There's a pile of logs right there in the back. You'll want to stack the wood by the back door. Marshall's just gone to the store for a minute." She looks Danny over for a moment. Steam forms on the glass in front of her. Danny wonders if she might offer him a mug of coffee. "So," she says, "you'll probably want to get started."

From the backyard, the sky opens up to the mountains, spinning away in a row of snowy, crumbling teeth laced together by the morning fog. Huge old pine trees tangle against each other, clawing the slopes. The town is now far away, behind the house, below Danny. This is all right, he thinks. He picks up a solid round log in his arms and wrestles it onto a flat stump scarred from earlier. Picks up a thing that looks like an axe and swings it into a crack in the top of the log. So far, so good, he thinks. He picks up a thing that looks like a sledgehammer. He spits in his palms because he thinks he is supposed to. He can feel the lady's eyes bearing down on him through the curtains somewhere in the huge house behind him. Danny picks the sledge up over his shoulder. He swings it, putting all his weight into it, every pound of energy he can muster, his legs, his back, the bulgy things in his neck, all coming down in this wild swinging arc. And it comes down. And he misses the axe head. The sledge bangs on the semi-frozen tree stump. A bolt of pain shoots up his arms into his forehead.

"Oh, my," he hears through the curtains behind him. "Oh, dear. Does he even know what he's doing? Does he even—" and then silence.

She's right, he thinks. I can't even do this. I can't even split a piece of goddamn firewood. What am I doing here? Danny wipes his cracked lips on his sleeve. Who am I trying to kid?

He stares off at the mountains for a second, that sweet, clean line of snowy peaks. That tangled path that clears when the snow melts, winding its way back to all that once was. And then he think of the fifty bucks, and he combines it in his head with the last one hundred–dollar check coming from Manpower on Friday, and he starts thinking where that might get him—up toward Portland, Seattle maybe, maybe farther. There was the guy who knew a guy who ran a cannery up in Alaska; he has the guy's phone number. Big money. Danny spits in his hands again and picks up the sledge. He takes another swing, softer this time. It rings off the axe blade like a bell. A second shot and the log splits even. Then quarters. Then eighths. Then another log. Big money, Danny says to himself, setting the axe blade. Big money. Alaska. The sun rises high behind him. Logs to sticks. Logs to sticks. Water drips from the roof, from his face. The wood grows softer, lighter.

Danny is just about to swing again when a voice speaks behind him.

"Well, I'll be goddamned," it says.

Danny turns to face a tiny old man with a beard and suspenders, leaning on a cane and patting the huge stack of firewood by his door.

"You must be Marshall," Danny says.

PART V

HISSING STEAM AND A GLACIAL GREEN SEA

WINONA

Sitting this morning at the picnic table at campsite fifty-one in a no-name state park just outside of Anchorage, Danny tries to figure how long sixty-eight dollars will last. A lukewarm beer sits between his legs; cold tomato soup sits half-eaten in its can on the picnic table. Four to five days, he calculates. The cannery man told him to call back this week about a job, to check if there was an opening. If there isn't an opening, Danny has to make a decision: give up drinking, stop eating, or surrender the ten-dollar-a-night tent site and move into the woods.

Danny stares into the woods in front of him. They are dark and wet and mossy. I'll just stop eating, he reasons. He slugs down a last flat slosh of beer.

Behind him, the campground wakes up. Dense breakfast smells—bacon and biscuits and eggs—fill the woods around him. Camper generators hiss and grumble. Television jingles whisper through tangled branches.

He cracks open his last beer can, then puts it down. He turns. He's not alone. A sickly, pale woman approaches.

"Whoa," Danny says.

"Now I'm so sorry if I scared you," the woman says in a hollow voice. "I'm just looking for my dog. Have you seen her? Have you seen Pearl? She's white. She looks like a poodle, but she ain't."

The woman sits at the far corner of Danny's table. She stretches her opaque, bonelike arms, brushing a red strand of waist-length hair from her face. Then she points to Danny's soup can.

"Is that all you got to eat?"

"It's okay."

"It's hardly that. I bet you're starving."

"I don't mind."

"Everybody up here is starving. My husband's starving himself to death too."

"Your husband?" Danny looks around.

"Oh, he ain't here. He's out in the islands. I'm just coming back from visiting him. I came up with my parents-in-law, Darlene and Red. They're over in that camper parked just over there. We drove all the way up here, then the Navy flew us all the way out there to some island to visit him. To visit my husband? We flew all day and didn't see nothing but clouds and rain. There's nothing out there. He's just so awful lonely out there. I think maybe he's sick or something. My husband, I think he's sick or something? He lost sixty pounds. And the weather's just awful out there."

"Sorry."

"Yeah, well. We're supposed to head home this afternoon. After my mother-in-law gets to see those Natives do that dancing thing they do downtown. It's all just so boring. Red can't hear nothing, and Darlene won't let me drive." She takes a deep breath. "So I hope you don't mind me sitting here just for a little spell."

"When does your husband come home from the island?"

"Six months. And now I lost Pearl. She's all I got. My dog. Her and the kook-a-doos, and my sister's caring for them. You ever have a kook-a-doo? They are the best pets in the world. They just love you and love you. They're pretty, and they sing, and they make you so happy. I miss them so, so much. All eight of them. My kook-a-doos. Now there's Scarlet," she says and sighs. "And then there's Juniper."

An egg-shaped woman appears.

"Well, hello, Darlene," Danny's visitor says.

"You come on back to the camper now, Winona," Darlene says.

Winona untangles herself from her seat and walks toward Darlene, her arms flapping helplessly down to her sides in protest.

"But I'm just out looking for Pearl."

"Pearl will come home soon enough."

"Just don't want her tangling with no bear."

"She knows where to find us."

"Well, we'll see you around, I guess," Winona says to Danny. "If you see Pearl, give a holler."

Danny stares out the window of the municipal bus as it passes an Arby's, a Pizza Hut, a strip club, an Arthur Treacher's, four bars, and a hunting supply store. The bus emerges in a faceless concrete urban center. Danny spots a row of pay phones. There is no time like now, he tells himself. I just have to go call the cannery man. Danny jumps from the bus and marches across a parking lot toward the phones.

An old man in rags blocks his path.

"Give me some fucking money!" the old man yells.

Danny hurries past the old man and scampers up a broad street in search of another bank of phones. More men in rags accost him. One with long, matted hair and a black eye lunges at Danny and tries to punch him. He misses by four feet, falls down on the pavement in front of Danny, and curls up, fast asleep.

Danny breaks into a jog. He doesn't stop until he finds a safe, quiet phone booth in a Denny's foyer. He calls the cannery man. When he gives his name, there's a pause.

"Call me in a week," the man says. "Maybe we'll have something in a week."

Danny walks back into the campground, a new six-pack in a bag under his arm. The wet branches seem to reach out for him, grabbing at him. The rain has started again, darkening the pine branches and soaking through his clothes. It won't be too bad, he thinks. I'll find a place in the woods where I can see the town lights. I can make it another week.

Hunched, Danny almost walks right into Winona, who is standing by a camper at the park ranger office. "Well, there you are!" she says. "I came looking but couldn't find you. We found Pearl. We're headed out, but I wanted to give you something first."

"Let's hurry it up then, Winona," Darlene says, sitting in the driver's seat, one hand on the wheel, watching Danny.

Winona opens the screen door. Her bony white arms grapple with a large brown box packed with cans—corned beef, creamed corn, chili. "It's a bunch of food and all. We got it for my husband, but they wouldn't let me take it on the plane, and we aren't never going to eat it all, so."

"Anchors away, Winona," Darlene says.

"Got to go now," Winona says. "So long." She disappears into the camper, and Darlene steers it slowly out toward the southbound highway.

"Thank you," Danny says. But she's already gone.

EVERYTHING COMES TOGETHER

It's Monday night, and the rain has started again. Danny slips in his flat-soled boots up the muddy dirt road toward the trailer. He sees an old man ahead of him, standing in the road in the glowing light from an open front door. The old man's searching for something, first deep in his pockets, then in the mud around him. Rain drips from his hat and shoulders. He notices Danny, mutters, and shuffles painfully back to his door. He disappears into the ramshackle cottage, one of a dozen that line the path like little hats. A bare bulb illuminates the interior. The door shuts. As Danny walks past the cottage, he thinks about the big raincoat the old man was wearing—how warm it looked, how it was such a waste, how old people are insensitive to the wet cold and stay indoors most of the time here anyway.

Danny looks down and in the dim light sees a wad of crumpled dollars at his feet. He picks them up quickly and continues up the road, not looking back until he turns the bend. From there, through a cut in the woods, he can see the old man again, returned to the spot under the streetlamp. He peers down at the mud, clutching his unbuttoned coat, still muttering.

In Danny's trailer, it's colder and darker inside than outside. He pulls out the wad of bills and smooths them out in his cold red palms. There's a twenty, a ten, and eight singles. For one flashing moment, he thinks of last week's rent, now a week late, and this week's. Then he gets up and walks back to town.

The Foghorn bar has electric heaters. A longneck costs a buck fifty, and Monday night is dollar hot dog night. Sitting at the bar, Danny meets two small, scruffy men counting their change. They look cold, fearful of the cold rain outside. "We're shufflers," one says. "We just got up here." Danny buys them beers and hot dogs. There are four other people in the bar, three men and a woman, sitting closely together, folding blue papers and talking seriously. The woman has black hair that sparkles in the bar's neon lights.

Danny buys another round. He focuses on tearing the label off of each longneck. It takes a few hours to blow through the thirty-eight dollars. When he runs out of money, the two strangers go in search of another bar. He stumbles home, past the old man's cottage. If I see him, Danny thinks, I'll just walk by like nothing happened. But the lights in the old man's cottage are off.

It's Tuesday morning. Danny wakes up in his sleeping bag in the trailer. He gropes for his pants and stumbles out the door. The day before the owner left a single word scribbled on yellow paper taped to the door: "When?" Outside the air smells like more rain is coming. Danny runs stiffly down the hill. He stuffs his sore, cold hands in his pockets.

Twenty minutes later Danny arrives at the edge of the piers. Flat, squat, colorless buildings cluster together before him, canneries and processing plants and refineries and warehouses, all tangled together, already hissing steam, and behind them, the green glacial sea. At the loading zone, he is surprised to see somebody new. It's a little man with crazy red hair and a freckled little boy's face. He wears a RUSH SOLD OUT T-shirt. He's standing where Danny's supposed to be standing, stacking loose cans onto a pallet and wrapping them in plastic. Danny stops and glares at him. He does the same.

Danny walks into the supervisor's shack. Another stranger sits where his boss is supposed to be sitting, punching a red stamp onto a stack of clipped invoice forms. "You must be the one who forgets to punch the clock." the man says. "You remember to punch the clock?"

"Where's Mr. Johnson?" Danny asks.

"Johnson, well." The man laughs, showing strange yellow teeth with wide openings between them. "Johnson has been reassigned. I am Rumson. Did you meet Nickel on the way in? I would like to meet you both. That way we have extra nuts to bust. Three boats we have to load today. The next twenty-six in a week or so."

"I thought production was down," Danny says.

"Hardly. Who told you of this?"

"Johnson."

"Okay then," Rumson says, scratching a thinning scalp. "Let us go." He rises heavily from the chair. "First, there are more pallets to be needed."

Danny walks past Nickel to the bin of split pine strips and loads the pneumatic gun with two-inch nails. He starts pumping the stack, five pallets, ten pallets. Stray nails ricochet off the concrete floor; a few ding off the steel rafters. Occasionally he glares at Nickel, the back of his head, the ridiculous red hair, as he continues packing cans. Johnson and Rumson and Nickel. They come and they go, Danny thinks, punching the nails into the dried wood. Somehow, Danny is still here.

Sometime later Danny looks up the floor and sees a man with the tie showing a woman around the plant. In nine weeks he has never seen a woman in this space. She is short and wide shouldered, and her hair shimmers in a black bun under the fluorescent lights, like the girl in the bar. She follows the man with the tie up the stairs into the office, and they close the door.

Everybody in this vast, cavernous plant hates each other, Danny thinks. Machinists and sorters and cutters and canners, the people responsible for unloading boats full of dead slimy fish and those at the loading zone responsible for filling other boats with labeled, odorless cans. It is this universal loathing that pulls things in through the receiving dock door and pushes things out through the loading zone door. Everyone makes somewhere between four-fifty and five dollars an hour. Floor people get incentives and bonuses that might add up to an extra twenty to twenty-five dollars a week. Everyone lives in debt. Everyone waited four to five hours in line to fill out a two-page application for this job, and everybody had to go stand by a pay phone in town and hope it would ring. Everyone now knows they are lucky it rang. And everyone knows somebody who got injured or fired since they've been here, who was no better or worse a worker than they are.

It's Wednesday morning. When Danny punches in, he sees the woman across the floor, using an electric knife to slice pink strips of fish parts and stack them on a belt. She wears boots and jeans, a flannel shirt, safety glasses, and a respirator mask. The knife is attached to a red spiral hose running down from the roof. It's her, Danny thinks. It's the girl in the bar. He moves away from her quickly.

At three o'clock Danny is loading a new boat with four hundred stacks. The boat is tied off at a bad angle, exposing a two-foot gap on the right side between the boat and the dock. Rumson pulls the forklift to the dock and leaves rows of stacks on the edge, requiring Danny and Nickel to carry the heaviest stacks into the dark hollow of the boat with a hand truck and stack them by hand.

"So you see," Nickel snorts, lazily half-pushing a stack up just as Danny is about to cord the row, "I hear that a chick got herself a plum job working over there on the floor."

"That doesn't go there yet," Danny says, stepping into Nickel's path. Danny pulls his stack out. "You've got to start a new stack with the fours."

Deep inside the well of the boat, it is dark and damp and cold. Outside, through the plywood and steel walls, Danny hears the ferry blowing its horn, heading down land. He peaks between the boat and the plant, hoping to catch a glimpse of the ferry, to see if there are still hippies camped up on the sundeck, staring out at the distant mountains. But he can't see the ferry; a huge rusting processing boat, tied to the next pier, blocks the view. It is unmarked and has been parked there for three weeks. Nobody knows where it came from or what it's doing here. Fast-food wrappers and plastic bags have begun collecting in the water around its stern. Danny slides a new stack on the hand truck and steers it back into the cavernous boat. He can make out Nickel's luminous red hair in the interior. He has dropped his latest stack by the wall, where it is unraveling; cans drop into a puddle on the steel floor.

"See, I applied for machinist," he says, holding his arms out as if to ask why. "I sure as hell didn't want to do no pick-ass loading. That's for sure. I mean, no offense or nothing. But I worked on pipeline for eighteen months before I came down here. I'm certified."

"You need to pick those up," Danny says, putting his stack in place and gesturing toward Nickel's. "We need to start a new row." Nickel lights a Winston with a square silver lighter. The flames reveal that the stacks he is loading are off-center. If he doesn't hide the last sloppy stack with a neat new stack quickly, Rumson might show up, and he will have to restack the whole boat.

"Thing is," Nickel continues, "the floor is all about overtime. Them suckers produce, they get paid. This here is chicken shit. That girl over there, she don't know it; maybe she got hired because they got a quota thing or something, I don't know what. But when she starts slowing things down, there's gonna be shit all over the place. Like the kind that hits a fan or something."

"We get lots of overtime," Danny says. He starts picking up Nickel's loose cans. "Thing is, we have to do things right. If we don't get it right, Rumson isn't gonna give us a chance to get it right the second time."

"I was a welder, a certified welder," Nickel says, pressing the back of his wet shirt to the boat's icy wall. Then he leans forward, leaving a pressed stain, like a little mushroom cloud. "I welded quarter-ton pipes onto mounts." He stares up toward the floor. "I'd like to see that little girl over there do that."

The hollow thuds and shuffles from the work in the well of the boat are broken by the snap of something exploding on the floor, followed by yells.

"I told you so," Nickel says, walking down the floor to stare at what happened. "This is going to be good."

Danny feels relief. This weird new tension is over. People get hurt here, and they simply get let go; they never come back. Then Danny starts worrying about her. The thought that she got hurt—that somebody might have hurt her—makes his ears burn.

Nickel comes back disappointed. "It weren't her fault," he says. "It were the canners, not the cutters. Some little bastard done sliced up his hand bad. He tried to save the sheet from falling, and for what? But she'll git somebody hurt sooner or later. You wait and see."

It's Thursday morning. One of the floor workers nods to Danny as he walks past after punching in. Through his breathing mask, he asks if Danny wants to play some hoop with the floor guys during the three o'clock break. "Sure," he says. He guesses that "hoop" means somebody has a ball they chuck up at a hoop tacked onto the wall of one of dozens of buildings surrounding them. This must be a peace offering, Danny thinks. Maybe they'll have some smoke. Maybe we'll hang out, smoke a doob, and throw a ball up at a hoop.

When the break buzzer sounds, the floor guy waves Danny frantically out the door. He is with another guy everyone calls "the Samoan." The nickname makes no sense, really; the Samoan has a blond perm, wears a company T-shirt and a tool belt. Danny follows Floor Guy and the Samoan to a paved area that is shoveled clear of the industrial garbage—planks, packing materials, cans. Someone long ago marked out a half-court and nailed a net and backboard up over a steel door that was welded shut. Waiting there are two other floor guys and Nickel, who looks angrier than usual.

"Check, ball!" the Samoan screams, throwing a ball into Danny's stomach.

Danny's hands have no grip. He drops the ball just as Nickel tries to slap it out of his hands. He fakes a two-handed shot, dribbles once with both hands, then pushes the ball hard to Floor Guy. "To the net, dippass!" the Samoan screams while he dribbles left and right on the court's perimeter. Danny runs toward the net. The ball smashes into his nose. A white flash of light blasts before him, accompanied by a smell like burnt rubber. Nickel scoops up the ball and passes it to one of his teammates, then sets a pick, pressing an elbow against Danny's kidney. Nickel's teammate glides past him for an easy layup.

"I thought you said he could play," the Samoan says to Floor Guy.

"I said I thought he could play."

"I never said I could play," Danny adds.

"Just check the goddamn ball," Floor Guy says. "Then get me the ball. And don't be a pussy."

Danny bounces the ball to Floor Guy, who starts dribbling wildly again. "Now do something!" Floor Guy yells. "Move!"

Somewhere in the maze of surrounding warehouses and outbuildings, a truck horn echoes mournfully. Danny's nostrils sting and smell like blood. He charges again for the base of the net. This time Nickel sees him coming and sticks a leg out. His elbow and the ball skid together across the pavement. He hears the slap of hands between Nickel's teammates. He limps back toward the plant. He sits on the concrete curb by the front door. He holds his bleeding left elbow in the cupped palm of his right hand and waits for the shift bell to buzz inside the plant, calling him back into work. He has only a few minutes to stop the bleeding. If he's bleeding, Rumson might send him home early; he'll miss some hours, and they may replace him.

He can barely make out the players behind a dumpster. He can hear the squeaking sneakers of the game continuing on the ruptured tar surface, the dull bang of the rim when the ball bounces free. Soon the bleeding seems to stop. He removes his bloodstained hand to look at neat slices etched into his forearm. Little gravel stones cling to scraps of white skin. He picks one out. Someone sits next to him on the curb. He looks up; it's the new girl from the floor. She is staring at his elbow, wincing sympathetically. She grips a home-rolled smoke between startling white teeth.

"You want a hand with that?" she asks.

"Yes, that is, I mean, no," Danny says. "It's not so bad. It just looks bad. It looks badder than it is, I think. It's better than it looks."

"I know they got a first-aid kit in there," she says. She has an odd, low voice, a thick accent from somewhere else. "You want me to go get it?"

"No, thanks. I mean, they sort of get pissed. If it's not work related, I think. I was playing basketball."

"They're not very good," she says, looking at the distant players, puffing smoke out between her teeth.

"I'm not very good either," Danny says. "I don't know how to play."

"No, not the basketball," she says. "The management. They make so much money, but they are not very good about taking care of their people. You get hurt, they should help you. There's no medical plan, no nothing. You guys bust yourselves for them. They should help you. If they help you, you're happy. You're happy, they'll be happy."

She looks away toward the sea, which is surprisingly clear and luminous this morning—waves and waves, all pouring endlessly away from here, in the other direction, down land, down land. to the other sea. "I just think they should pay us fair wages, that's all," she says. "And some benefits. We work so hard. Don't you think we work hard?"

"Yeah."

"You know," she continues. "Me and some friends of mine are having a little gathering tonight in town, at that church out past the graveyard. We're just going to have a little gathering to talk about all this. To talk about how maybe we can change things. You're welcome to come. There will be food and stuff."

"Okay."

She gets up, then pulls a folded blue paper from her pocket. "Here's a little something about the meeting." Danny takes it hesitantly. Without reading it, he puts it in a pocket. "You don't have to come," she says. "But if you're angry about this, about the way things are, you may want to come and talk about it."

The buzzer echoes across the parking lot. "Will I have to say anything?" Danny asks.

She flicks the end of her cigarette into the lot. "Not if you don't want to, I guess," she says. "I guess nobody has to say anything if they don't want to."

In a second she disappears. Later, when Danny gets in line for his paycheck at the office, he decides to tell her he's definitely coming. But when he reaches the parking lot, she is gone.

Danny reads the flyer while he walks back toward town. He doesn't really understand it; it's about dock workers and boat workers and cannery workers all coming together, and fair wages and health care. It's in Spanish on one side and English on the other. There's a fist shooting out of a star and quotes, something about a fight.

Danny cashes his paycheck at a bank. Hurrying up the hill to his trailer, he leaves ninety dollars for rent under his pillow—forty-five dollars for this week, forty-five for last week. This leaves him forty-four dollars.

Danny splashes cold water from the sink around his face and neck. He has no clean shirts, but it doesn't matter. What will he say at the meeting? What will she want to talk about? It is very confusing to him. He walks down the hill, trying to think of something.

He approaches the old man's cottage. There are no fresh footprints in the mud. He imagines knocking on the old man's door. He will hand him thirty-eight dollars. "I think I found something of yours," he'll say. The old man's face will light up. "Of course, of course," he will say. "Please come in." Danny will sit with him in a dust-filled parlor. The old man will sit in his trench coat and slippers and tell Danny a story of what it was like working the docks in the old days. Danny will relay this story, compare it with life on the docs today. This is a very solid plan, he tells himself. This is it. Everything comes together.

But in front of the cottage, Danny thinks he sees a light through the old man's curtains, and he panics. He keeps walking. I have to think this out a little more carefully, Danny thinks. He walks all the way to the Foghorn. Sitting with a longneck, all of his confidence drains slowly from his body. Then the door bursts open, and Danny's two shuffler friends from Monday night explode into the bar.

"There he is!" they yell. "We got jobs! *We're* buying *you* a beer now."

"Hey, guys," Danny says. "That's great. But I got to go meet some friends."

They are already quite drunk, and they seem hurt. "Hey, man," one says. "I thought we were your friends."

He's right, Danny thinks. And one more beer can't hurt.

It's Friday morning. Danny opens his eyes. He tries to jump out of bed, but his legs don't seem to work. He looks at his elbow, which seems to have reopened itself and is sticking to the sleeping bag liner; there is dried blood all over the pillow. He reaches underneath, and the rent money is gone. Now Danny remembers; he came back for it in the middle of the night. He looks for his wind-up alarm clock on the floor. Work started an hour ago.

On the walk down the hill, Danny thinks of what he's going to say—not to Rumson, but to her. He starts to imagine his story from the night before, only he adds some layers to it. "There's this old man I help out sometimes," he pictures himself telling her as she walks with him away from the plant. "He used to work on the docks here for forty years, and now his hands are so screwed up he can't reach down and clutch things." In Danny's mind she's smoking her rolled smoke thoughtfully, listening. They've walked to the beach and are watching the waves. "We're meeting again next week," she'll say. "I'd really like you to come." "I'll be there," Danny tells her. "I'll definitely come."

On his way in, Danny passes production; she is not there. The Samoan looks up at Danny and mutters from behind his mask. Danny walks straight into Rumson's office. Rumson does not look up from the stack of invoices.

"There, it is him now," he says. "You smell like a rum cake."

"I'm sorry I'm late," Danny says. "I was sick. I tried to call." Danny licks his cracked lips. "It won't happen again."

"No, it won't," Rumson says. He keeps staring at the schedule. "You have some catching up to do. Two boats coming in at once. Here are the work orders. We need eighty-eight stacks by four o'clock. You can go join your friend there. He will leave at five, and we will all leave at five. But you, my friend, will stay until finished."

Danny walks back to the dock where Nickel sits on a crate smoking; a stack of wooden planks and the nail gun lay scattered on the floor in front of him.

"Somebody told me you're the palette expert," he says.

Danny picks up the nail gun and plugs it into the compressor. Stepping around Nickel, he lays out the planks, two on the floor, eight across. "You missed quite a little scene here this morning," Nickel says, snickering. "It appears that everybody's favorite lady over there was some kind of commie. She came here to try some kind of labor agitator crap, invited some of the floor staff to some kind of commie meeting. They ratted her out though. She came in, and they were waiting for her, the man with the tie and everybody. She was lucky to get out of here in one piece."

The air pressure gauge reads ready. Danny punches nails into a board, which cracks and splits. He picks up a second board and places it down on the first.

"Stupid commie bitch," Nickel says.

Danny turns to look at Nickel. Danny is going to hit him. Danny is going to lose his job. But then, everything changes. Nickel looks at Danny, and the cigarette drops from his lip.

"Hey," he says, "watch what you're doing!"

Danny has just punched a nail through the side of his boot into the board. He tries to pull it free, but it's stuck. So he kneels there, watching a little pool of purple blood form around it. Rumson comes out and joins Nickel, and they start laughing. Danny starts laughing too, while he pries the nail out. He wraps his foot, boot and all, in a Styrofoam sheet and some shrink wrap, just enough to stop the bleeding through the boot. Still chuckling at himself, at his foot, and at everything else, Danny hobbles toward the loading zone where the next boat starts roping itself in.

DOWN LAND

Danny is sitting in the back seat of a dark car. Wipers smear mud back and forth across the windshield. In the front seat, a giant with a huge mane of hair hunches over the wheel.

"Thanks for picking me up," Danny says.

"Yeah," the driver says.

The driver squints at Danny in the rearview mirror. Next to him, in the passenger seat, is the back of a woman's head. It's a large head matted with patches of blue hair.

"I came out on a trail, back there a bit," Danny says, trying to brush some of the wet ash off his backpack sitting between his legs. "There aren't any cars. I thought I was walking all the way back out to the highway."

"That's a pretty tough spot to get stuck at," the driver says.

"Especially this time of year," the woman's head says. "This is a park road. They closed the Denali park road this morning. I heard it on the news. They had eight inches of snow."

"That's the interior. That's a long ways up from here," the driver says.

"Well, you're lucky we came along," she says. "Aaron always picks people up."

"Yeah, been stuck out there a few times," the driver says.

"I really appreciate it."

"Yeah," he says.

"We can get you back out to the highway anyhow," the passenger says. "Maybe there's still some trucks coming up the peninsula. Most of the summer traffic left long ago."

"The highway's a big help." Danny pulls a clump of mud from his hair.

"How far you going?" she asks.

"Back up to Anchorage tonight."

"You live in Anchorage?"

"I don't think so."

"You don't think so?"

"I'll know when I get there. I'm either going to stay or make a run for the down-land ferry."

"You know it's another eight hundred miles to the ferry," she says.

"Yeah."

"Well, you'll get to Anchorage by nightfall," she says. "This is Aaron. I'm Peggy."

"Thanks for picking me up," Danny says again.

The light changes. Sunlight tries to break through the leaves. Aaron and Peggy lean forward, looking for something ahead.

"Do you live around here?" he asks.

"Oh, no," Peggy says. "We're just up from Kenai for the day. It's down the peninsula a ways. We're looking for a spot down here on this road, just around the bend here. It was in the paper this week. We just wanted to come up here and see this spot."

"You were walking?" Aaron asks.

"Yeah."

"How long were you up there?"

"Five days."

"This time of year?" Peggy asks. "Alone?"

"Yeah," Danny says, dusting ash off his sleeve. "I think I bit off a little more than I could chew."

"So you were up there when Mount Spurr blew the other night?" Peggy asks.

"Yeah, I guess," Danny says. "Something blew somewhere. Ash came raining down. The sky lit up like it was on fire."

"Spurr's across the inlet, down about thirty miles," Aaron says.

"Sent a big black cloud rolling up the inlet, right into town," Peggy says. "I was sitting by my picture window at about six o'clock, staring at the sky lighting up, and I thought the world was ending. It dropped an inch of ash on town, didn't it, Aaron? We thought we had it, didn't we?"

"Yeah," Aaron says.

"Me too," Danny says.

The branches open up. A short wooden guardrail separates the car from the sea. Low green clouds blur the edges between shore, sky, and sea.

"Should be right up here someplace," Peggy says.

She grabs Aaron's arm very tightly. She points out to the sea.

"Here it is!" she says. "Oh, Lord, pull over!"

They stop on the shoulder and point out to Cook Inlet. A hand-painted sign reads "No swimming, fishing, or wading."

"This is where she was! Oh, good Lord in heaven." Peggy gasps. She tries to turn to Danny. "The saddest story in the paper this week. A young woman walked out into the marsh at low tide. Looking for shells. She was from Japan or someplace, and she couldn't read the warning signs. When the tide turns here, the marsh sucks you down. Isn't that right, Aaron? You can't pull your legs out, and then the riptide comes rushing back in. They sent a boat out for her, but they couldn't pull her out in time. She drowned when the tide rose over her head. Poor little thing."

"Jesus," Aaron says. They stare out at the water.

"Well, what do you say?" Peggy asks, trying to turn again. "Do you think we can get lunch someplace up ahead?"

They're moving again, under a canopy of leaves.

"I came up here five years ago," Peggy says. "Me and my husband, Roger, we were teachers in Portland. At least I was, before I went on disability. I came up here so my sister could take care of me while Roger's away. Then she passed. At first I thought, Oh great, I'm stuck up here. But then I came under the spell of the place. Aaron's only been up here three years, but he's got the spell too, don't you, Aaron?"

"Sure." Aaron shrugs.

"That's what happens to people up here, they get under the spell of the place," she says. "It's the end of the summer, and you're still here. I'd say maybe you got it too."

"Yeah, maybe."

"I'm guessing you won't get past Anchorage. If you're still here, you're probably here for good."

"Maybe. I guess I'll know soon enough."

"You'll know. Won't he, Aaron?"

Aaron shrugs.

Peggy smiles at Aaron. "Since I met Aaron, he's just become my little helper, driving me places all the time, aren't you, Aaron?"

Aaron is slow to respond. "Yeah, I guess so."

"And while Roger's been gone, we just take off every Sunday, and we just travel all over Alaska. And we have an awful lot of fun together, don't we, Aaron?"

Aaron looks at Danny in the mirror, smiles, and rolls his eyes. "Yeah. I guess we do."

The first outbuildings of a small village appear through the windshield. Twelve cabins line a street ending at a pier, then the sea.

Overgrown weeds stick out of split log fences. An old school bus stands parked on cinderblocks beside a wooden diner.

"Don't blink or you might miss it," Peggy says.

As they pull up in front of the diner, a column of motorcycles comes up from the dock.

"Oh, look," Peggy says excitedly. "That there's a Norton, isn't it, Aaron?"

"Oh yeah, a 'sixty-eight," Aaron says.

"Aaron knows his bikes." Peggy beams. "Used to have a Harley."

"In a past life," Aaron adds. "I sold it when I came up here."

Danny climbs from the back seat. He tries to brush the remaining streaks of ash from his arms and legs. Peggy opens her door and swings her legs onto the ground. She pulls a pair of orthopedic crutches out and lifts herself to her feet. Danny opens the screen door and holds it for her. Breathing heavily, Peggy maneuvers herself up the steps.

The diner has four counter stools and two tables. A waitress in a checkered apron stands behind the counter, hands on her hips. Two fishermen sit at the counter, picking at heaps of food. Each holds a bottle of Budweiser. The waitress points to a table at the far end of the room by a window.

Peggy struggles to work her way through the narrow passage between the stools and booths. The fishermen turn and watch her move through the room. She chuckles and points a thumb at the door.

"That's an awful narrow door!" she says. "I almost got stuck!"

The fishermen turn back to their lunch.

"I thought they were going to have to just leave me up there!" she says.

The fishermen shake their heads and snort.

"They'll just have to make a new door somewhere to get me outta here!" she says.

"Aw, now," one of the fishermen says.

"They'll just have to take off the roof and airlift me!"

The fishermen laugh. Aaron rubs his eyes with the heels of his hands. A cook pokes her head out from the back, a cigarette dangling from the corner of her mouth.

"Keep it down now, kids!" the cook yells. "Y'all are having way too much fun out here!" Peggy roars. Her eyes roll deep into their sockets. As she positions herself to sit, the waitress brings out a pot of coffee, pours three mugs, and leaves the pot.

Sitting across from him, Danny has his first full view of Aaron. He's a head taller than Danny. A handlebar mustache hangs limply under a long, crooked nose. Huge fingers tap heavy brass rings on the table.

Peggy picks up a menu. "Well, men, lunch is on me," she says.

They order lunch. Peggy talks excitedly about her first winter and their favorite bars and the herd of caribou that cross through town each spring and the paragliders who drop from the cliffs in the summer. Lunch comes, huge sandwiches and crocks of hot soup.

"You won't get past Anchorage, I'll bet. You're gonna stay up here. You'll see," Peggy repeats.

"Yeah, I'll see."

"It just pulls you in. The longer you stay up here, the more it pulls you in."

Danny remembers being up on the mountain, just before the volcano. Right after the cannery closed, he decided to try to quit drinking, sober up, quit smoking. Somebody told him about this trail through a pass; he bought some gear and food in town and hitched out to the trailhead, where he had his last cigarette and his last beer. "So long, old buddy," he said to the cigarette butt, stomping it out with his new boot. He walked up a trail in rain and fog. The third night the rain broke, and the clouds blew over. He looked up at the ledges he'd climbed to, huge blue stone cliffs laced with streaks of red and green tundra. He felt the alcohol flooding out of his system, leaving his body like a ghost. I don't have to work anything out with anybody, Danny thought then. He never had to go back down land. He could stay up here forever.

 "Yeah," Danny says to Peggy. "But I've got things. People. Back down land."

Peggy chuckles to Aaron. "We got plenty of those up here too."

Danny watches drops of water slide down the Budweiser labels to the counter. He remembers how he was up there and the ash came over the ridge—a billowing black cloud reaching for him. He thinks of the black clumps settling on the surface of his tent, of the darkness, of the choking smell of sulfur. He repositions himself in his seat.

"So where did you two meet?" Danny asks.

"Well," Peggy answers, "we met through my church. When I fell ill, I left my job, and I needed somebody to help me get around while my husband's away. And I got lucky, and Aaron showed up."

"Community service." Aaron chuckles, flashing yellow buck teeth. "Five hundred hours."

"Aaron helps me with my errands and takes me places on Sundays. And we've just become the best of friends, haven't we, Aaron? We just have so much fun together, don't we?"

Aaron makes a face. "Oh yeah," he says. "Barrel of laughs."

"Where's your husband?" Danny asks her.

The light leaves Peggy's face. She turns to Aaron, who stares down into his coffee.

"Well, actually, Roger's down land, down in Oregon, in the state penitentiary."

"Oh," Danny says. "Sorry."

"Well, he did something wrong, and what's important is now he knows it, that's the important thing. He knows it, and now he's paying for it, he's learning a hard lesson. But he had to learn it. And I still love him. And I still call him all the time, don't I, Aaron? And don't we have fun? We just laugh and laugh. And Roger's going to be just crazy about Aaron, they're just going to hit it right off. And you're going to be crazy about him too, aren't you, Aaron?"

Aaron glances over at the empty beer bottles. "Yeah, sure I am," he says.

"Roger's getting out next year," Peggy continues. "And when he does, we're going to get him up here. And he's going to catch the spell, I'm just sure of it. And we're going to do nothing but have fun, all of us, aren't we, Aaron? Aren't we going to have fun and explore and go on adventures? Because life's just one big adventure. I'd forgotten that for a while, but Aaron's brought me back to it. An adventure. You know it. Roger's got to learn that too."

They all turn to look out the window. Outside four wild-looking children, barefoot with long blond hair, climb into the bus and stare back at them through the broken windshield.

At four o'clock, the diner closes. They return to the wagon. The rain has passed back out onto the inlet, washing another layer of silt from the trees. As the wagon climbs a hill, they pass under huge pine trees. A splash of sunlight sends gold beams spiraling down through the branches to the dark forest floor. Peggy gasps.

"Isn't it beautiful back here," she exclaims. "After it rains, the woods are so beautiful. And if it wasn't for you, we would never have come back here and seen this. If Aaron hadn't pulled over and picked you up, we never would have even known this beautiful place existed. You know, we never would have seen these woods, and we never would have met you, and now we're just like old friends. That's part of the spell. It's always like that up here, isn't it, Aaron?"

She smiles over at Aaron, who looks ahead, focused on the road. The highway overpass comes into view. Aaron pulls over at the base of the ramp.

"That's the Anchorage Road, that way. We're headed back over this way," he says.

"Thanks," Danny says. "Thanks so much."

"You keep moving, don't hang out in Anchorage, you'll be okay," Aaron says. "You'll beat the snow. There's still plenty of logging trucks headed down land this time of year."

"You get yourself settled up in Anchorage, then you come down and see us in Kenai," Peggy says, but she's adrift now, like she's hypnotized.

"Yeah," says Aaron, "we'll see you around."

Neither turns as Danny climbs out of the wagon. He can barely make them out through the windows as they lean over the dashboard, look up at the trees, make a U-turn, and drive back down the peninsula.

DRAGONFLIES

Danny is sitting at a picnic table at the Fairbanks Municipal Campground across from Cashtown Annie, who is no longer Cashtown Annie, but just Annie. Danny can't imagine exactly how she tracked him down all the way up here; they traded letters when he was in Bend last spring, and they joked about meeting up in Alaska and how they'd meet up in front of a post office at noon on Labor Day. Danny decided to walk past that post office at noon on Labor Day, and there she was. She was driving up to Fairbanks, she told Danny, to interview for a job with a chiropractor. She'd always dreamed of moving to Fairbanks, and now, here at this picnic table with all her worldly belongings packed into a beat-up little Datsun, here she was.

Annie sits quietly, telling Danny all about her life after they parted ways. "Yeah, so, I went into rehab, and then they sent me to a halfway house, and then I went back to the Burg, and you know, things were still bad, like I missed Vlad, you know? And then I messed up, and then I went back to rehab and then another halfway house, and then my sister called me, and it was like, oh my gosh." Annie is wearing a hooded baja shirt and wool mittens. Without the red hunting cap, she looks frail, Danny thinks; her hair is short and spikey, and her big brown eyes still don't register anything. "I spent the fall and winter in Flagstaff with my sister, and she taught me things. She's learned so much, things out there in Flagstaff, and it's like, now I know things. Like, man. I found my spirit, you know? And my people? And now I'm way up here in Fairbanks interviewing for a job. It's deep."

"Yeah," Danny says. "Deep."

"Yeah, man, like it's really deep. And you. Finding you up here. Boy, you sure pulled yourself together up here."

Danny blushes when she says this, but it isn't a proud blush. He only quit drinking a week before when he walked off into the woods. He doesn't think he's going to last long.

They sit up drinking herbal tea and talking late into the night, Annie going on about her sister and her practice and the spirit circle she joined in Flagstaff. Annie has changed, Danny thinks. She is all new age-y and outdoorsy and positive, saying nice things about everything and everybody; but she's a lot shakier than she was back then.

The next morning Annie drops Danny off downtown and drives off to her interview. Danny is free for the day. He walks around for a while. This place is surprisingly blue and green, he thinks. There are bright yellow daisies exploding into the air along the riverbank. There are millions and millions of them, breaking out of the brackish muck alongside the river. There are dreamy blue mountains drifting in the distance. Up against the river, there is a row of boarded-up hotels and a couple of department stores and a lot of bars. Yukon Jack's. Klondike Billy's. Drunks shuffle along the riverfront, hands stuffed in their pockets, into one bar, out of another. It is nine in the morning, and they are everywhere. The riverfront plaza has banners hanging from lampposts—Welcome to Fairbanks! Extremely Alaska!

Danny sits down on a bench. Then he lies down on the bench. Then he falls asleep. When he wakes up, two men are sitting on a bench across from him. Their faces are bright orange, and their tongues, hanging out of their toothless mouths, are the color of ivory.

"Hey," Danny says. Neither blinks. They are dressed in ragged double-pocket flannel shirts over T-shirts stained beyond recognition. Flies circle their heads. An empty bottle of something lies on its side on the bench between them.

"Well, I suppose I'd better be moving along," Danny says. He gets up as if he has somewhere to go and starts walking.

Fifty steps down the pavilion, he turns, and they are still there. Their heads have turned as if they are watching him, but their tongues are still hanging out. This is it for Danny. He starts walking faster. He is going to try to find the road back to the campsite. She'll find me soon enough, he thinks. He passes another gauntlet of bars, a little more roadhouse-y, with trucks parked out front. Danny wants to go in—he could say screw it and walk right in—but he told Annie he quit drinking. It isn't going good. He has to stop thinking about it. He decides what he really needs, right here and now, is coffee. And then he sees it—across a parking lot is a red, double-decker bus with more daisies planted all around it and little white tables and chairs. It's next to a huge pile of rusting machine parts. A delicately painted sign says "Chena Cafe."

Danny climbs into the bus. A guy behind a little counter stares at Danny. He has on a black beret and one of those funny little beard-things under his lower lip. Is this the guy, Danny thinks? The guy from the Old Mill Mall? Danny only lasted a day there, but he is pretty sure this is the same guy.

"How you doing?" Danny asks.

"Yes," Beret Guy says.

"I'll just have a cup of coffee, I guess."

Beret Guy clears his throat. "We don't have 'just' a cup of coffee. We serve expresso, cappuccino, and lattes."

"You have anything else?"

"We also serve fruit drinks and protein shakes."

"Can you tell me where I can just get a regular cup of coffee?"

"Anyplace. You can probably get a regular cup of coffee just about anyplace," Beret Guy says, turning away to wipe down an immaculate cappuccino machine.

"All I asked for was a cup of coffee," Danny says. He heads out and starts walking. Fairbanks fades away behind him. The road passes a long strip of hunting stores and used auto part stores and then a beautiful roadside bar, its doors swung wide open, man-laughter and the click of pool balls. But Danny keeps walking; he doesn't stop until he gets all the way back to the campsite.

Annie's interview went pretty badly; crying over the macaroni and cheese they share at their campsite, she reveals that she is totally broke. Danny has a few hundred dollars—enough to drive back to the ferry, get to Sitka, and maybe get back down to the lower forty-eight, if they stretch it. But before he left the cannery, Danny tells Annie, somebody told Danny to head down to Homer; there is always a two-week rush on the Spit this time of year, and they are always looking for workers, and you can make six hundred bucks in two weeks. You just have to buckle up and work in a cannery for two weeks. Annie says she'll do it; they'll both just buckle up and do it. So they load up her car and drive down to the Spit.

On the way down, Annie tells Danny that her sister was up here and said Homer is the most beautiful place in the world. When they get to the edge of the Spit, Annie leans forward and squints over the steering wheel. "This isn't what I pictured," she says.

A single two-lane road stretches two miles in front of them, out into the bay, with little side roads like stitches leading to docks or warehouses or straight into the water. They are surrounded by the most beautiful glacial bay you'll ever see, circled by snow-capped volcanoes and glowing, splashy water. But Annie can't stop looking at the Spit itself, which, Danny agrees, looks pretty bleak this day. On the seaward side is a long, unprotected beach with all sorts of nets and logs and boat parts and cans and Styrofoam buoys covered in green-and-black algae and sea sludge. Every hundred yards or so is a mini village of blue-tarp-and-plywood shacks circled around a big firepit, always smoldering, piled with driftwood. On the other side are rows and rows of halibut boats and crab boats and floating fish processing boats. Bars and outfitter stores stack up on the piers between windowless corrugated tin industrial buildings.

They drive out to the end of the Spit, where the marina and a bar and a two-story motel tilt on one of two docks; the other has collapsed into the sea. A stiff wind blows straight up from the sea and encases the Spit in a cold, fishy, smoky smell, like burning tires. Telephone poles lean away from the sea, wires hanging everywhere. Big green flies run the place. Transients and out-of-work cannery workers and off-boat fishermen shuffle single-file along the road, back and forth from the mainland, or lean against the telephone poles, staring vacantly at nothing.

They drive back down the Spit and find a vacant stretch of beach; Annie pulls over, and Danny starts pulling out the tent.

"Why, exactly, do you want to camp in this particular place?"

"Because this is free," Danny tells her, "and the state campground costs ten dollars."

Danny reminds her of what the guy told him up in the cannery—there is work down here, but no place to live, so you have to sleep on the beach with the rest of the cannery workers. Danny sets up the tent in the middle of the beach, at the farthest distance from two plywood camps. Annie sits in the car and closes her eyes. A shrouded figure in a wet poncho stands watching them from one of the camps. Danny goes up and talks to the shroud. Then he returns to the car.

"Well, it looks like the canneries down here closed, sort of, last week. Something about the fleet or something. I guess there's something up with the fleet."

"So," Annie says, not looking at Danny; she is staring out at the sea, a beam of sunlight breaking free under a blue cloud and spreading itself, soft gold, over a clump of pine trees on an island. "So what do we do now?"

"I guess we spend the night, then head down for Sitka. The guy said there was probably work in Sitka."

Annie keeps looking out to sea, waiting, Danny guesses, for another sunbeam to appear. But the clouds seal up, and it starts raining again. Danny pulls up a bunch of driftwood, and they get a fire going as darkness falls, holding their rain ponchos over their heads, watching the fires fade at the plywood camps, not a sign of people, not a sign of life.

"There's gonna be work down in Sitka," Danny says. "I just know it. I got a good feeling about Sitka."

In the center of Sitka, there is a miniature, perfectly symmetrical Russian Orthodox church painted bright white and surrounded by wooden crosses of the departed, all hemmed in with a whitewashed picket fence. Danny can see the church perfectly through the large picture window of the Suds and Duds combination bar-laundromat-bookstore where they are drying themselves and their clothes before heading back out to find a place to sleep because they don't have money for the town campground. The ferry ticket from Haines to Sitka cost more than they thought.

Danny has walked around Sitka all day in the rain, asking about work; there is no work. "Him and the hundred other shufflers stranded in Sitka looking for work," a guy on the dock yells to a guy on a boat as Danny walks away. "But I never seen none of them working."

They still have just enough money for the ferry from Sitka down to Bellingham and a couple tanks of gas. Annie has friends in Reno, she says, good friends who can set her up with a couple hundred bucks once they get there. In Reno, Annie says, they can talk. In Reno they can "recalculate things."

Sitting at the Suds and Duds, Danny wants a drink real bad. A big guy in waders and a Johnny Reb Confederate baseball cap is standing red faced by the little bar, drinking shots like he just survived the sinking of the *Andrea Doria* or something. The guy has a rifle propped up next to him. He stands there, drinks a shot, wipes his mouth with the back of his hand, says, "Well, ain't that something?", stares out at the cathedral, sighs, then waves at the tiny woman with the huge hoop earrings behind the bar to set up another shot. This happens about twelve times while Danny sits next to the dryer praying, praying that it will stop soon, and smiling at Annie, sitting there next to him. Annie is pretending she is reading the *People* magazine she found on top of the dryer, but she is clearly just filling with dread of everything and hating all of this, of that, of him, Danny thinks. In this two weeks, she has gone into a total transformation. She hates being stranded, Danny thinks. She hates being out of luck, and Danny is luckless. She convinced herself this journey was going to save her, and where is she? In the Suds and Duds in Sitka, Alaska, scraping quarters out of the ashtray in her old Datsun to run a dryer.

"Well, I suppose by now they're missing me plenty," the mighty fisherman says, knocking down half of one last shot before placing his red mustached face into a beefy forearm and falling asleep, standing up, in the Suds and Duds.

The sun breaks out, lighting up the church in a luminous burst of whiteness. The dryer rattles and groans to a halt. Danny is just getting up when the mighty fisherman wakes up and looks him over.

"You ain't so big," he says.

"You got no idea how small I am," Danny says.

"Funny. Huh. You two looking for a place to crash?"

"No, we're all set, thank you."

"Well, if I was you, I'd head up the mountain right there and find the forest service road and take a right and follow it up three miles, and there's a forest ranger cabin up there. It's abandoned, and the forest service don't never use it."

"Thanks," Danny says. "We're all set, but thanks."

"Beats hell out of sleeping in your car," the mighty fisherman says, "and you sure don't want to pay twenty bucks to sleep in a tent with all them bears poking around."

"Thanks for the tip," Danny says.

Annie has already gone out to the car with the laundry. "What did he want?" she says.

"He told me about a great place to camp, a cabin up in the woods. It's a forest service cabin. It sounds really nice."

"Does it cost anything?" Annie asks.

They drive up to the end of a little gravel road, park, pack some things into their packs, and start up a trail that climbs steeply through giant fir trees. Sitka peeks through the branches—the cathedral, the little stores and houses, the boats bobbing in a sea of boats—then the branches close around them. "Here, bear," Danny repeats over and over, searching the dark pockets of brush. "Yo, bear."

It starts raining, but it is always raining. By the time they climb to the top of the ridge, the rain has soaked through their ponchos, their boots, their clothes. They are standing in a thick cloud. They are above the tree line, a strip of rocks wedged into another strip of rocks. The rain and wind push them up onto a little dirt road winding into the fog. Another mile up, they enter what appears to be an open ridge.

Something emerges in the fog, barely at first, then a little more clearly—a little one-room cabin. It is empty. Danny spreads out his sleeping bag on one side of the floor, and Annie spreads hers out on the other. They switch into dry clothes. Danny is hungry—he knows Annie is hungry too—but they aren't about to start cooking something with the bears, all the bears. Something is crazy with the bears this year. It's all over the news; it's all anybody up here talks about.

Annie sits out on the little porch, her poncho wrapped around her. Danny sits down next to her. They stare out at the tips of the trees just below the ridge, swaying in a crosswind, barely there in the darkening mist.

"You think that guy knows we're up here?" Annie asks.

"What guy?"

"That guy in the laundromat. You think he told us to come up here? So he could come up and kill us?"

"That guy? No. He's harmless."

"But he had a gun," she says.

"It's bear season. Everybody up here's got a gun."

Something bright orange splashes into their sights, fighting its way upwind. It lands on Annie's arm. Then another and another. A flock of blue, orange, neon green dragonflies, fighting their way south through the rain, landing on the rocks and branches, on the roof, and all around Annie and Danny.

Danny sits still, thinking, This is so beautiful, so amazing, so meaningful.

"So, we really got to talk," Annie says, brushing the dragonfly off her arm. "I've really got to recalculate things."

DAISY

Annie tries to drop Danny off at the Reno Trailways station, but they are building a new bus station. So she takes him to a temporary station behind a huge industrial building and waits with him there for the bus.

Annie is fidgety. She clearly cannot wait for the bus to come. She keeps staring in the wrong direction, and then she starts whistling. Danny never, never heard Annie whistle. And there she is, whistling away.

Thankfully, the big red-and-silver bus appears from around the corner. They do that sort of awkward half-hug that might as well be a handshake.

"Well, see you around, I guess," Danny says.

Danny stuffs his backpack under the bus and climbs the stairs. He looks back to wave, but Annie is squinting in the other direction. The driver pulls the door shut, and the bus starts clacking up the road. There is only one seat open, toward the back of the bus. Danny sits down in the aisle seat next to a young woman curled up in her seat. She seems very angry that he is there. She has to move her backpack. Danny offers to put it up for her, but she stuffs it under her seat. He looks out the window behind him, thinking he'll try the wave again, but Annie is already gone, car and all. Annie is going back to Flagstaff to be with her people, to do her thing. This is now this, Danny thinks, and that was that.

Danny pulls out a book and tries to read it. It's some Russian crap, way over his head. The tension from the woman in the adjoining window seat is too thick, like maple syrup. She is pretending to be asleep, but Danny knows she isn't sleeping. The bus gets on the highway, and after some time, it climbs up into a mountain pass. It passes a sparkling lake, the sun setting against a wall of trees, the water sparkling sapphire blue, like emeralds. Danny wants to climb out and swim in the lake, forget the book, forget Annie. Then the driver makes an announcement about the Donner Party, who were stuck by that lake in the winter of the Gold Rush, ate each other, and then ate themselves. Danny forgets all about the swim. The history lesson ends, and the highway crawls back down the other side of the mountain. The sun sets. The aluminum tube pitches itself into the darkness.

The bus pulls off the highway and stops at a Quick Mart. A bunch of people get off. The girl next to Danny yells, "EXCUSE ME!" She jumps out of her seat and runs toward the Quick Mart. He settles back, closing his eyes, thinking she is gone. But a moment later, he hears, "EXCUSE ME!" He jumps out of his seat again and lets her climb in. She has six cans of beer in a cardboard container, all popped open, like she tried to drink them all in the parking lot. She flips the snack table down and puts the container on top of it. She arranges each can so the popped-open mouth of the can is pointed toward her mouth. She takes a can and holds it to her mouth, shaky, sipping it very slowly, staring out the window at the passing lights—a streetlamp here, a distant house out there. She doesn't put the can down. She holds it to her lips until she's done, crumples the can in her hand, and picks up another. This goes on for four beers. Danny keeps pretending to read in the dark—he doesn't want to turn his lamp on if she doesn't—but then she goes for can number five.

"Oh, what the hell," she says. "It's my birthday for Christ sake. You wanna beeping beer?"

In the dim cabin light, Danny looks at her for the first time. She is older than he thought she was. Her hair is matted, stringy around her face. Her nose is crooked, her teeth are crooked. Her whole face is set at an odd angle to her head. She is wearing a yellow baseball cap that says "LIFE AS IT SHOULD BE" in big blue letters and "Stockton, USA" in little letters. There is a crumpled fake leather jacket and a black concert T-shirt. Her eyes are what get Danny though; even in the dark cabin light, her eyes are the same cobalt blue as that lake back there.

"Thanks," Danny says, "but I can't. I don't drink anymore. I drink quitting. I mean, drinking. Quit. But thanks."

"Oh, that's okay, man, that's cool, me too," she says. "I quit drinking too." She drains the fifth beer can and reaches for her last.

"Happy birthday," Danny says, but she's already turned away, sucking on that last can. Danny goes back to pretending he's reading his book. "I am poor, and naked, and an atom in the vortex of man," some Russian guy says to some other Russian guy. Danny likes that line. He reads the same line over a couple of times, committing it to memory.

"So how far you going?" she asks Danny.

Danny tells her how far he's going.

"Wow, all the way to the city? I want to go out there sometime, see all those lights. I hear somebody can walk up to you and say screw you, and you can turn around and say screw you, and nobody gives a rat's ass."

She crumples the last can and drops it on the carpet.

"There," she says. "Yeah, I'm only going back to Stockton. Yeah, I'm going back to my momma's house, if she'll take me. She don't give a flying beep about me, man. She's got five other kids; she likes them all better. Yeah, I left three months ago, and I bet she don't even notice I'm gone. She didn't like my old man. But she was right, she was right. He just threw my ass out, back there in Reno. She was so right about him, yeah. So, yeah, I called her, I told her I'm coming home, but I got the answering machine. I don't know if she even got the message."

She bites her finger. The bus passes a huge overpass, a tangle of serpents lit by headlights and streetlamps, then darkness.

"Yeah, the thing is, I don't even know what I done wrong this time. I just woked up, and he was staring down at me, and he says, 'Daisy, what are you doing?' and I says, 'What do you mean, what am I doing?' and he says, 'Daisy, how long you been sleeping?' and I says, 'I ain't sleeping, I'm watching *Saved by the Bell*,' and he says, 'Daisy, *Saved by the Bell* is on at eight o'clock, and it's three in the morning, and what are you doing?' And that's when I looked around and I seen that the stove is all burned black and the curtains are all roasted, and he had his Molly Hatchett poster tacked up over the dinette and that was all roasted too, and the whole trailer, I figured it out, was all filled with black smoke, and then I guess there were some little flames or something still burning on the stove, and the ceiling was a little, you know, black in spots. And he says, 'What are you doing?' and I say, 'Why do you keep saying that? I'm cooking a birthday cake for me and myself because it's my birthday tomorrow and happy birthday to me'—mind you, tomorrow being today—'and what are *you* doing?' I went on, because sometimes I start talking and I just can't stop, 'What are *you* doing coming home again at three in the morning?'"

She reaches down, picks up one of the crumpled cans, and starts chewing on the rim, just below the opening. "Yeah, I said it."

The bus runs down another ramp, then starts slowing down. "Stockton," comes the bus driver's voice over the intercom. "Next stop is Stockton."

"Yeah, anyhow, I know Momma won't even let me in the door," she says as Danny climbs out of his seat to let her out of hers. "I run out on her and the kids, for this beep, of all reasons." She pulls her pack behind her—a little blue backpack with all her belongings—and rushes up the aisle. The bus brakes shush in an island of light, an empty parking lot surrounded by shadows.

"Happy birthday," Danny says to her backpack.

She stops and turns. That crooked face. Those cobalt eyes. She looks at Danny like they haven't been in a conversation— Who is this weird old shuffler talking to me? How does he know it's my birthday? And then she turns away.

"Happy birthday to you, Happy birthday to you." She sings this quietly to the back of each seat on her way to the exit, tapping each seat cushion gently on the back, not missing one. Then the steel door hisses open, and then it slides shut. Danny sees her standing alone in the parking lot's blackness under that lone streetlamp, looking around, her head jerking back and forth, stringy hair swinging wildly in her face, and then her shoulders fall. She drops her backpack to the ground and stares at her feet.

Danny looks out the other side of the bus. There is a cluster of people there, an old woman and five younger people, teens and young adults, holding a hand-painted banner that says 'Happy Birthday Daisy," all crooked faces, all cobalt eyes, peering into the bus, hoping, hoping to see her when the bus pulls out. Danny watches them as the bus moves, and they suddenly jump up and down, shouting and waving and running across the parking lot.

The red-and-silver bus snakes out into the desert darkness, and Danny has the two seats to himself. He wants to sleep, but he can't stop thinking. Not about Annie and not about Daisy. It is those beer cans, glistening, rattling around at his feet. He can almost taste that metal. He can almost smell those bubbles.

The Trailways bus snakes its way into San Francisco as shadows cast themselves from rows of office buildings out into a lavender harbor. Danny climbs off and faces waves of faceless bodies pushing, pushing into buses and revolving doors. Danny walks and walks and walks. There is a blinking red light outside an office—*Hotel, Hotel, Hotel*—and a dark little courtyard filled with stacks of damp boxes. An old lady sits at an old desk. The rooms are forty bucks a week. Danny has to pay up front. He hands the lady two twenty-dollar bills, his last twenties. She doesn't look at him. She doesn't say anything. She looks at the bills very closely, holding them up against a light bulb. Then she pulls keys out of a drawer and leads Danny upstairs to his room. The room is very clean. The bed looks like a hospital bed. There's a sink and a mirror and a little chest of drawers. A window with dark yellow curtains peeks straight out at another little window with dark yellow curtains. The bathroom is down the hall. The bathroom has a shower.

"No bath!" the lady yells , like Danny startles her. "Only shower!" she adds. She pulls the door shut behind her.

"Thank you, ma'am," Danny says to the door.

He drops his pack in the corner and lies down on the bed. It dips in the middle. The pillowcase is clean. The case smells like detergent, but the pillow itself smells like cheap wine. Danny tries to picture the shuffler who lay there before him. Probably one of those winos he passed on the block. The wino probably got kicked out the day before, empty wine bottles and all. The boxes in the courtyard are probably his. They are probably filled with his huge collection of empty wine bottles.

Danny stares up at the light bulb. He tries to think of Annie. He tries to remember what it is like to be next to her. He tries to remember what she looks like. It is impossible. She is impossible.

He gets up and stuffs the keys, still in his hand, in his pants pocket. The door clicks behind him. Somebody coughs down the hallway. It's a long, deep, dry cough. Danny coughs back at the cough. Then he goes down the stairs and out to the street. Darkness has fallen. A cold, dense fog shrouds everything. A bus stop sign on the corner winks at him, promising someplace else. Danny wraps his coat around himself, stuffs his hands in his pockets, and stands there a minute, like he has someplace to go.

Back down the street, Danny sees the hotel lady watching him through her yellow curtains. She is wearing a green sari, backlit by the office light bulb and front-lit by the red neon sign.

A bus comes, and Danny climbs into it. The bus is super-heated and super-lit. Rush hour commuters stand hanging from bars or sit squashed in plastic seats. The riders are very busy with themselves. They all wear sports-Walkman yellow headphones and white sneakers. They all hold a magazine folded in one hand and stare at it intently. They all appear to be reading *The New Yorker*. Why *The New Yorker*? Why not the San Franciscan? Why not the San Franciscer? Danny really cracks himself up with that one. He barks out a quick laugh. That clears some space for him.

The bus goes up a hill, then down a hill, then up and down six more hills. Commuters keep getting off, but nobody gets on. Soon Danny has a seat. He wants a *New Yorker*. He wants to know what the big deal is. But they all take their *New Yorkers* with them. So he sits there, watching the streaks of wet traffic lights, reds and yellows, filter past the foggy windows. The bus passes rows of little restaurants filled with couples staring deeply into each other's salads. Then it passes some bars—horsey-looking people pumping their fists at a football game on the TV.

Danny thinks about beer—all the different kinds of beers sitting in those taps, waiting. Then he tries, again, to think of Annie and to imagine what she is doing back in Flagstaff, back with her sister, with other people. Just impossible.

"End of the line there, bud," the bus driver says, opening the front door slowly.

The bus hisses and then falls silent. The bus driver sits silently, staring straight ahead. Beyond him, through the dripping windshield water, there is only darkness.

"Thank you, sir," Danny says.

He climbs out of the bus and is shrouded in a blowing void of deep, wet blackness. The sea is crashing into rocks somewhere below him. He thinks of Annie for real this time—not Danny seeing Annie, but her seeing him, out here alone, for real. He looks down over the rocks, looking for the sea, waiting for the dragonflies. He sees himself sitting in one of those fancy bars, drinking beer after beer, telling a group of laughing strangers all about the dragonflies. But the dragonflies don't come up from the cliff, they don't settle on his arms, they don't rest all around him. Danny knows they aren't coming, but he waits there anyhow. Then he turns around, and he walks straight back, all the way back to that hotel.

THE MAKER OF RICE

Danny lucks out; he gets a long-term temp job, watching the front desk at a senior center nicknamed "the Glock." All day he checks visitors' IDs and makes sure none of the residents gets out. Visitors come very rarely. At least once a day he chases a resident down the block and gently guides them back into the residence.

Late this Saturday afternoon, the Governor comes to get Danny at the Glock. He sits in the dayroom on a couch next to one of the residents while Danny finishes his shift. The Governor lights a cigarette. He squints intently over Danny's shoulder through the barred windows as the sky slowly turns orange, then purple, then black above the harbor. Danny looks over his shoulder at the game he's pretending to watch on the television's green screen. "So the game I'm watching here,"

Danny says to the Governor, "there's this kid playing running back from West Texas who, according to the announcer, ran for three thousand yards in high school last fall."

"Is that so," the Governor says without moving.

"Yeah, I believe they said he played in Lubbock or in Amarillo." Danny waits for a response; there is none. "Which I imagine," he adds, "would be a pretty tough place to play ball."

"Yeah," the Governor says. "Ready?"

They walk together up the avenue to the Associated. They purchase a five-pound bag of rice, lentils in little plastic sacks like pillows, bags of brown onions, cloves of yellow garlic, Styrofoam cups, plastic spoons, aluminum trays, tomatoes, tinfoil, and a bag of charcoal briquettes. They split the bill, which always comes out to twenty-two dollars. Shouldering the bags, they climb a hill together up to the Governor's. Danny stops in a deli to purchase a big cup of watery coffee while the Governor waits outside. They then climb three flights of stairs up to the Governor's rented room. The utensils are in place, hanging in the Governor's little galley kitchen. They sit down on milk crates at a huge oak table, stacked with religion books and newspapers, which Danny moves to the floor. They start the stove to boil water for the rice. The Governor chops onions and garlic.

They never reverse roles. The Governor is the maker of soup. Danny is the maker of rice. After an hour, Danny fills long trays with fluffy white rice. He covers them in tinfoil and puts them in the oven. The Governor sits reclined, somehow comfortably, on a milk crate at the far end of the table, crushing garlic cloves with the flat blade of a big knife with one hand. With the other hand, he holds up to his face a yellowed paperback book. The Governor is farsighted, he once admitted, but he does not believe in glasses. With both hands busy, somehow he deftly lights, smokes, and puts out a chain of long white cigarettes.

"So what are you reading?" Danny asks him. "Saint Augustine," he replies. "Is it a good book?" "Pretty good," he says. Danny drinks the last of his coffee from the big Styrofoam cup. "I am the rice-maker," he announces, wired on caffeine, toasting himself, trying to get a laugh. The Governor does not look up from his book. "I am the maker of rice." A huge vat of soup simmers on top the stove, and the rice, in the broiler below, settles in for the night. Danny gets up to go. "Night," he says, rattling down three flights of rickety stairs. Before popping out into the lamplit street, a voice comes down the stairs. It is the Governor's.

"Yeah, night," he says. "See you in the morning."

Danny calls him the Governor, but only to himself. In broken, very limited conversation, he never learns much about him. From his accent, Danny knows he is from the Southwest, but for all Danny's hints and questions, he never tells Danny where he is from. Danny knows he spends weekday mornings doing a needle exchange in the Mission; afternoons, he does some kind of street outreach for sex workers in San Jose. Weekends he does this.

One night, while he pulls pebbles out of the lentils over the sink, Danny asks him why he does all this. He shrugs, his back turned. He tries to tell Danny something about penance, about how he is an assigned, un-ordained-street-mission-something-in-transition back where he comes from. He was sort of sent here, he mumbles. It is a question of governance. "Yeah, it's kind of hard to explain," he says. Then he stops trying to explain it.

There is one other thing he tells Danny; recently he's picked up handball. He plays for five or six hours on Saturdays, before he comes to get Danny, with some people he met in the housing project someplace. The Governor learned by watching, he says. When he stopped watching, he stepped into their games. He is getting pretty good now, the Governor says. At handball, he can hold his own.

This morning Danny wakes up to the hotel lady banging on his door. "Visitor!" she yells.

The Governor waits on the stoop, a cigarette in his mouth, staring up at the sky. "Yeah," he says. "It looks like it might rain." The Governor's rust-brown Nissan Sentra is running at the hydrant. The soup and rice are laid out evenly across a plywood board across the torn-out rear seats. Danny climbs through the window on the passenger side. The door is rusted, but it never quite shuts completely; it is strapped to the headrest with a bungee cord. The Governor pops the car into gear. Danny closes his eyes. But as always on Sunday mornings, the Governor wants to talk.

"Yeah, so it appears that there is a situation growing now in Ethiopia," he says.

Even though he hasn't had a drop of alcohol since he quit up in Alaska, Danny feels hungover and remorseful. "I am the maker of rice," he says to himself.

"Yeah, it appears to be emerging as some form of massive hunger crisis."

"What are you talking about?"

The Governor lights another cigarette effortlessly; he blows the smoke out the cracked corner of the driver's side window and stares ahead.

"I'm talking about Ethiopia, man. It's getting bad over there. I sat up last night reading about it in the paper."

They are now on the ramp to the bridge. Beneath them, the brittle roadway gives way to corrugated steel. Danny can see the surface of the road through the cracks in the car's floorboards. The bay appears, white clips of foam above brown swirling silt. The lentil soup splashes behind him in its sealed vat.

"Yeah, it's going to be Ethiopia," the Governor says. "The next big situation. It's coming. You'll see."

The Governor parks on the side of the park, across from a row of burned-out shells of old apartment buildings that stare down like hollow skulls. The first-floor windows of each building are cinder-blocked shut. Steps with broken, ornate pedestals climb steeply to windowless steel doors with chains and padlocks. Danny feels hidden beneath the canopy of dead tree branches reaching out from the park. The Governor hurdles over the bent steel park fence effortlessly, landing without a sound next to an empty bench. Danny hands him the soup vat, the rice trays, the charcoal bricks, the lighter fluid, and the tin pans. Then Danny climbs over. He checks both ways for police. The Governor lights the little makeshift grill on the cracked concrete sidewalk. It is still early; the ramshackle tarp-and-plywood shelters to the left are silent; the blankets and coats and plastic sheets huddled on the stage of the bandshell to the right have not yet moved.

Danny sits next to the Governor on the bench and waits. The proximity of warm coals and the smell of warming soup make him sleepy. He jerks his head up and checks quickly over his shoulder. The windows of the abandoned buildings are still empty. They wave meek little flutters of torn curtains and tarp. There is a tangle of black branches. The park smells like burning things.

The Governor sits still, his hood up, an unlit cigarette dangling from his beard, paging through a long letter someone has sent him from somewhere else. It is handwritten in long, neat script on beige unlined paper with a crest on the top of each page. The Governor chuckles to himself for a moment. He leans forward and fans the coals with the letter. It looks like poetry, Danny notices, as he waves it; the words are laid out neatly in patterns across each page. The Governor leans back again, staring more intently at the letter. He lights his smoke, takes a deep drag, leans forward, and deposits the letter onto the coals under the bubbling soup. The letter flames and browns instantly.

Something stirs beneath the blue construction tarp, the portal to a series of plywood constructs built under what was once a playground. A head pops out. "Hey, man," the head says to the sleeping bodies behind it. "It's those soup guys. It's the guys with the soup." He brushes himself off and rises to his full height, which is daunting. A single-file line of eight bodies crawls out behind him. Danny calls them the Snorkels, but only to himself. Somewhere they all acquired fur-lined navy blue parkas. None of the parkas matches the size of its owner, and none of the zippers works.

"We were the first ones in here after the riots," Big Snorkel told Danny once. "As to the rest of these bums," he went on, waving one free arm out at the smoldering tangle of wreckage, the bodies lying wrapped in blankets and tarp, "I don't know where they all came from. I just woke up one morning, and they were here. I don't give a crap. They're cool. Except for the Bandshellers. You want to stay clear of them."

The Snorkels warm their hands over the coal fire for ten or fifteen minutes. They bum a few cigarettes off of the Governor, who sits detached, scooping rice into little Styrofoam cups, then pouring the steaming lentil soup over the rice. Big Snorkel asks Danny what day it is, who are the Raiders playing today, whether he saw any cops circling the park on his way in. "It doesn't matter if you did or you didn't," Big Snorkel says. "They are always here. They're circling the perimeter. They'll come back with their horses and crap. But this time we'll be ready for them." Each Snorkel takes another bowl, glances over his shoulder at the bandshell, and climbs back under the blue tarp.

The Bandshellers come next. Cut up from random skirmishes, they never speak. They take their soup and walk away. They're followed by the Permanents, the junkies and alcoholics who congregate at old crumbled chess tables; then by Stragglers who've come to the park only recently, many with no memory of how they got there. There's a woman who screams unthinkable obscenities at the Governor, then thanks him very politely for the soup. There's the old man who takes out his dentures and puts them on the end of the bench next to Danny before eating, then pops them back in and walks away.

There's a steady stream of people, a gathering. Then there's a silent pause, like the air shifts. Danny looks up through the branches at the thickening clouds.

"Rain's coming in now," Danny says.

The Governor says nothing. Danny wants to ask him about the letter, but he has to wait because, , as if appearing out of nowhere, the Duke appears in front of him.

"You fellows have certainly been in business this morning, that's for sure," the Duke says. "I couldn't help but notice from my offices." He points to his shopping cart filled with plastic bags, next to a bench covered in cardboard. "A brisk business you gentlemen are running." The Duke sits between Danny and the Governor, holding a Styrofoam cup between his hands and warming his feet, which stick out from gaping holes in the front of his boots, next to the coals. "Sadly, I have some bad news for you gentlemen."

"What's the news?" Danny asks the Duke. But he's staring up at the sky now, where a piercing blue hole has appeared between the low-hanging clouds.

"Rain," the Duke says.

Danny watches the Duke absently scratch the white stubble clinging to his bony throat. The Duke looks back at Danny, stops scratching, and clears his throat.

"But what's the news?" Danny asks again.

Just before the Duke speaks, a clattering noise, a metallic stampede, a sea of cascading marbles advances quickly through the center of the park. A man in a long purple cape emerges from the overgrown weeds, a homemade yellow rope harness strapped around his chest. His legs are bare except for homemade boots made of bright silver duct tape, attached directly to his feet. He pulls three shopping carts, one after the other, each filled to capacity with canned food. In his right hand, the man holds a large wooden staff, which may have once been a fencepost. The Duke stares at him wide-eyed. He is an old man with the face of a child, and he is small and round, his feet swinging excitedly under the bench. "Orangeman," the Duke whispers.

Orangeman reaches into a cart and rummages through the cans. He pulls a tin can of pineapple out and hands it to the Duke. The Duke stares at the can for a moment, then at the Governor. "Would you mind?" he says, pointing at the red coals. "Not at all," the Governor says. "Help yourself." The Duke pulls a metal instrument from his coat pocket and begins deftly cutting open the can's lid, bending it back into a sort of handle. All the while he smiles up at Orangeman, who sits down beside him and hangs his head, exhausted. He waves a weary arm at his carts full of canned food.

"They will never starve us out," he says. "They will have to burn us out. "

Danny and the Governor quietly pack the pots and tins and cups and load them over the fence and back into the car. They leave the coals burning in the tins on the sidewalk between the Duke and Orangeman.

*

The Governor pulls up at the fire hydrant in front of Danny's building. "Yeah," he says. "So this is the end of the line for me."

"What do you mean?" Danny asks. He stops jiggling the car door handle. He pictures the letter, turning brown in the coals.

"Yeah, well, it appears I've been reinstated. I'll have to report back, and they'll give me a mission."

"Oh," Danny says. "Here in the city?"

"I'm thinking not so," the Governor says. "I'm thinking maybe Ethiopia."

"Oh. So you won't be headed out for some time then."

"No, actually," the Governor says. "Actually it looks like I'll be headed out tomorrow."

"Oh," Danny says again. "What about the soup?"

The Governor restarts the engine. "All it takes is a pot and some soup."

"Huh. So what are you going to do now?"

"Head out and get in a couple last games of handball."

"Okay, then," Danny says. "I guess I'll see you around."

"Yeah," the Governor says, concentrating on the rearview mirror, popping the brake. "I'll see you."

Danny has the late shift back at the Glock; the same resident sits alone on the couch, in his robe, staring up at the TV. The Raiders lost, the 49ers won, and the resident doesn't register any of it. At midnight Danny punches out and walks out to the street. I really should say goodbye to the Governor, Danny thinks. I should give him a proper farewell, in a "job well done" sort of way. I should at least shake his hand or something.

Danny walks all the way up to the Governor's hill and leans on his buzzer. There is no sign of his car. Danny wants to yell up at the dark, empty windows, but he doesn't really know his name. "It's me," Danny says, but quietly this time. "The maker of rice." There's no response; he must have missed him. Oh, well, Danny thinks. That's that. He crosses the avenue and walks down the hill, back to his apartment building. Danny has a vision—maybe the Governor assigned *him*; maybe he'll get home and find the steel pot and ladle and two long trays and the oak table stacked in front of his room or at the front door. Danny runs home, turns the key, and opens the door. But there's nothing there.

LENNY AND TRIA

Alice waits until Danny hands her a check for the entire three months rent, with a one-month security deposit, before explaining to him how the building functions. She begins with the neighbors.

"Remember that you're in Oakland now, not San Francisco," Alice tells Danny, as if he didn't know this. "Now, on the first floor, there is a man who never leaves, who has lived in a small room under the stairs for thirty years. He was a bohemian poet or something, and sometimes recites his poems out loud to himself, which travel up the sealed chimney late at night. It doesn't sound like words; it sounds like bursts of small arms fire or something." Alice tells Danny to not let these voices disturb him. "There's not actually somebody bricked up in the fireplace." She says this with great anger.

They are standing in the middle of her tiny, narrow living room, surrounded by her half-finished landscape canvases, which are splashy, but otherwise not bad. One looks like a tree trunk or a close-up of a flower stem tangled in dirty vines. Danny wants to tell her he thinks they are quite good. He wants to ask if she ever finishes any of her paintings. But it occurs to him that if she feels they are finished, that might make her angrier.

She holds the apartment keys in the palm of her right hand, rattling them occasionally but not handing them over. For twenty minutes she prattles off a list of things—how she intends to come back for her paintings and her bookcase, how the hot water turns off sometimes. "And the poet," she says, "but I already told you about him.

"And Lenny and Tria?" Alice asks. "I told you about them, right? They're next door, and Lenny's, um, troubled, and Tria's deaf and screams a lot. And they hate me. A lot. They spy on me. I swear. At least he does. She's deaf. But he's listening. I know he is." Alice bursts into laughter. "So they might be a little, you know, I don't know. Threatened by you. Or angry or something. But you know. Don't bother calling 911, and don't get involved if you hear them yelling. Because no one ever comes and, you know. I gave up long ago. Let's see," Alice asks herself. "Did I forget anything?"

"Do you ever finish any of your paintings?" Danny asks.

"What did you just ask me?"

"The keys," he says. "Can I have the keys?"

"Oh, sure," she says. She looks out the two front windows at the draining light of day. "Well, I better get going," she says. "It's going to get dark soon, and it's a long drive to Portland. Well, goodbye, apartment. Goodbye, old home. See you around." Danny follows her to the door. She turns the bolt lock. "Oh, and one more thing," she says. "I think it's good to tell you, just so you know. Nobody owns the building. There's no landlord, no super. Nobody."

"Nobody?" Danny asks.

"Yeah, nobody. So we've been, you know, on rent strike, I guess, for a couple of years now."

"Oh," Danny says. He looks up at the lone light bulb in the empty kitchen.

"We think the former landlord's in court with the city or something. So if you see somebody wandering around like a marshal or something, and you don't know who it is, don't let them in."

Danny hears her tramp down the crooked stairs. There is a noise in the darkened hollows of the stairwell, like a long yawn, then the door slams shut behind her. Danny is alone with the keys, his box of belongings, and Alice's half-finished paintings.

After a week Danny convinces himself there is nobody else in the building. There is no sign of Lenny and Tria or the man under the stairs. Each night, as he sits typing into his typewriter, he hears shuffling and whispers and creaks, nothing definitively human. It is insufferably hot and damp in the apartment. He buys a fan and sleeps in his underpants on a sheet over his sleeping bag in the middle of the hard living room floor. He dreams of voices in the sealed-up fireplace, but when he wakes up, lying on the floor, dripping with sweat in his underpants, there is nothing but silence.

One evening as darkness is falling, as Danny is pushing through the half-broken front door, he is surprised by a voice beneath the stairs. He has to lift the door with his shoulder, he's discovered, while turning the key to get the key to turn. Alice failed to tell him this. As he pushes it open, there is a voice in the darkness. "Well, hello there!" A ghostly form appears waving a pale white arm. Danny can make out a bearded man, as tall as he is. As the man steps into the pale light created by the open door, Danny sees that he is wearing a robe, falling open; he is covered in thick gray hair.

"Fear not!" he says, holding up one shaking palm and clutching his robe to his chest with the other. "I am indigenous."

"That's great," Danny says.

"Are you the marshal?" he asks.

"No," Danny says. "I'm a subletter. Alice?"

"Oh," he says. "Another subletter. Well, I hope you're happy." He turns and disappears under the stairs.

It has the potential to become a real job, he is told. But Danny is working for very little money for someone who, in the end, will probably never pay him at all. His assignment: to write a proposal for the senior day center located in the basement of an old church, across the street from the Glock. The senior day center is located at the bottom of a steep, winding staircase, which the residents can't get down or up. The senior day center received a renovation grant the year before that helped them fix the basement up quite nicely. It has a nice little dining room, an activity center, and a little library. It has administrative offices and a neat little kitchen. But because of the staircase, it has no seniors. Danny's job is to write a phase two renovation grant proposal to install an elevator. He tries again and again. Each Monday, he drops off a new draft; each Friday he goes in to receive his revisions.

The senior day center director sits stuffed behind a tiny desk in a tiny corner office, rubbing her face repeatedly with huge, rubbery hands. It is rumored that, because of the stairs, she never leaves the building. Each Friday morning Danny sits in a small folding chair outside her office door for forty-five minutes beyond the appointed hour. She sits on the other side of a thin plaster divider. He can hear her rubbing her cheeks, the squeaking of her palms against soft flesh. Then she telecoms her receptionist, sitting out by the front door. "Send him in," she says.

When Danny turns the corner, she sits holding her head, with a pencil, pretending to be deep in thought about this week's draft. She clearly hasn't read it yet. She sucks air in through her lower teeth in quick sucking sounds. She is making little checkmarks next to each paragraph. "We're a senior day center," she corrects him. "Not a senior day *care* center. We don't give them snacks and naps."

"I'm sorry," Danny says.

Farther down she stops again. "This paragraph is, I don't know. Ugh. I mean, it's okay. I'd just like you to breathe a little excitement into it."

When he is finally released, she switches into creepy-little-girl voice. "We really need this elevator, please?" she says. That really freaks Danny out, like someone is hidden under her desk. Danny rushes home and tries to breathe some life into a next draft, but quickly grows bored and heads off to sit in the park or down to the waterfront to watch the boats.

Five weeks in, late at night, Danny sits alone typing a new draft of the senior center elevator proposal that he knows is far worse than the last. Then he stops, staring into Alice's tree trunk. Danny does this often when he sits here. He hears a clear, piercing scream come from the sealed fireplace. Although he's never heard a definitive noise out of Lenny and Tria's apartment, they'd been there all along.

"What are you?" the woman's voice yells. "Are you dead or something? Are you dead? You ain't moving. You ain't talking. You ain't hardly breathing! You're just laying there! Laying there! You're driving me crazy!"

"Keep it down, will you!" a muffled man's voice responds, closer, like it is directly against the kitchen wall, inches away from Danny, listening to him typing.

"Why don't you just move!" the woman yells. "Just move or something! What are you! Are you dead or something?"

"Oh, for crying out loud, will you?" the man yells. The floorboards start creaking, a door pulls open, and huge, heavy steps clomp down the stairs. "Don't leave!" the man yells. "Don't leave me! Where are you going to go?" A door slams; now Danny can hear sobbing, very clearly, against the wall.

But while Lenny sobs, Danny is a little bit happier. Finally! he thinks. It's like he's a part of something. He goes to bed on the floor smiling at the thought. He wakes up in the morning, still smiling, lying there on the wood floor, staring up at Alice's half-finished painting, staring back down at him from the wall.

But then the marshals bang on the front door, and Danny has to start all over again.

THAT THING YOU BURIED

So Annie writes, and she really, really wants Danny to come visit her in Flagstaff. This is important. She really wants him to come out to the desert and come for a hike. Just a hike. The desert makes everything right, she says. The desert cleanses people. Danny has run out of places to go, so he gets on a bus and rides way out to the desert. Annie picks him up in her car. And in Annie's car he becomes drunk from the sun of the desert. It's so clear and so hot here. It rims his eyes in a burning silver.

"So we'll head out tomorrow. I can't wait," she says.

Danny hasn't seen her in months, and she's already somewhere else.

"I got the tent and everything in the trunk. We can sort it all out later." She squints over the steering wheel. "I'm so fired to get up there. The late autumn wildflowers."

From this stretch of road, Danny can see the great range and beyond it, the high peaks, a stretched white line through that sunbaked filter.

"There's only one thing," she adds. "We have to be really, really quiet at my house. My sister isn't sleeping well. All her energy has left her."

"Your sister?"

"Yes, you remember. I have a sister."

"Her energy?"

"Oh, she's just, it's just this thing. She had this friend visit from Santa Fe, and they had this, like, thing."

"A thing?"

"Yeah, they had this serious thing."

Now the heat starts to bake Danny's forehead.

"Yeah, what happened is this: The friend and my sister had all this bad energy. The friend said, 'Hey, this bad energy. Why don't we just bury it?' And they took it into the forest, and they...they just buried it."

"But what was it?"

"What was what?"

"What did they bury?"

"It was this thing, man. Aren't you listening?"

The mountains disappear under finger clouds, stuffing them into a gray sack.

"I thought I was."

"Maybe I'll explain it someday." She sighs.

*

In her little house, Danny puts his backpack down quietly by a closed door, by a couch. Music creeps from under a door, something about "a soul being on fire" or something. A voice deep-breathes to the beat: "muh, muh, muh." Danny enters a little galley kitchen. There's a dream catcher and a spaghetti-headed Garfield calendar. "I hate Mondays," the calendar says. Tomorrow is circled on the calendar with an arrow through Danny's name. In the lower right-hand corner is a drawing of a snake.

"No beer," she whispers, entering the kitchen behind him. "Sorry."

"I don't drink anymore," Danny says. "I quit drinking, remember?"

"Oh. Cool. You want a cup of tea?"

"Hey, what's this?" Danny says, pointing.

"Oh, that? That's a snake."

"Why a snake?"

"I don't know why." She puts a pot on the stove. "I hate snakes."

"Me too," Danny says. "Man, snakes give me the willies."

Early the next morning they head up to those mountains.

They drive up and up and up this canyon. The sun rises behind them and paints everything red and orange. The road climbs up into an emerald green forest. Then everything turns crystal white, like it just snowed this morning.

"I thought we were going to see wildflowers," Danny says in the shoveled park service lot. Annie rummages through her trunk and pulls out a tent, a mess kit, a stove, a bag of food. They stuff these things into their packs and go.

The trail is wet, snow sinking into puddles of mud under stark clumps of trees.

As they climb, Danny tries to remember if he dreamed all this or if he really woke to her sister on the edge of the couch last night. She looked like Annie's sister, only older, though she was younger.

"Oh look," the sister said, "here he is again! If it isn't the return of Glenn Campbell."

"I'm not Glenn Campbell."

"Oh, that's right. So why'd you come back out here?"

"She invited me. We're just going hiking tomorrow."

"Are you going to mess her head up again?" She made that "muh" sound again.

"I didn't mess her head up. She messed her head up. But we're all straight now, we're cool."

"Whatever," she muh-ed. "We'll just see about that. I'm going to make a grilled cheese. Do you want a grilled cheese?"

"No, thanks," Danny said, and he fell back asleep. Unless he dreamed the whole thing, in which case he was asleep the whole time.

Now the trail's muddy path climbs deeper into the snowpack. The air up here is cold and sweet and stinks, that menthol piney smell. Something is happening to the air as Danny climbs, his lungs, this altitude. It's like oxygen is sucking itself in and out of his trachea, pulled through an old sock.

Danny has to stop. He stops. She's up ahead of him, ten paces. She stops in place without turning.

"Takes some getting used to," she says.

Her voice hasn't changed. She is immune to this altitude. Danny looks around at the bowl of darkening air around them. The snow fans out like flower petals toward surrounding cliffs, like the yellowed teeth of a drunk. There's a cluster of stunted pine trees, far below him now, the tree line. Water pushes down from above: the trail a creek, the snowpack a pond. A cold blast of wind blows up the valley from where they left her car. It cuts through the seams of Danny's cheap parka; it presses his sweat-soaked undershirt to his ribs. Danny adjusts his shoulder straps; this only makes him colder.

"How much farther?" he asks.

"Right over that pass."

"Was there this much snow when you were here before?"

"I've never been here before."

"Oh. So how do you know about the wildflowers?"

"I just know," she says. "That's all."

"Seems like a funny time of year for wildflowers," Danny mutters to himself, but only when she's beyond earshot. They are moving again. Danny focuses on Annie's blue backpack. It's very small. We don't have enough, Danny thinks, enough tent, enough sleeping bag, enough dry clothes. We'll never get a fire. Everything will soak through.

But they keep climbing. The sun slips under the range; the snow turns blue around them.

"What do you think?" Danny says when he catches up with her, carefully pressing words through chattering teeth.

They stand in a black patch of earth, a little cut between the snowbanks. The ground is damp here but not soaked, and there's a dried tangled branch of dead tree sticking out of the snow. Danny guesses they might be able to turn it into a little fire. She turns to look at him. In the fading light, she looks crazy, like her sister in the dream. Clumps of ice dangle from her hair, her eyes are wide open, and her cheeks are burned red.

"This looks okay, I guess." Annie drops her pack. "I was going to press on, but I guess this is okay."

Danny unravels and sets up the tent as quickly as he can. He climbs out over the snowbank to break branches off the tree to build a fire. His hands are numb, and his ears burn in the wind. He comes back to the campsite, and he finds her in the middle of the clearing. She is digging a large black hole into the earth with a rock.

"Oh, great! Is that for a fire?"

"No," she says.

And she keeps on digging.

THE RAPTURE

Danny wakes up in a seat on a train that is moving very quickly. He pulls his cheek away from the cold glass, and a twist of condensation pours down his face, his neck, and his arm. His arm is dead asleep, pinned beneath his weight, folded on the armrest. Danny shakes his arm out instinctively. The cloud of steam where his face was pressed against the glass shrinks and disappears. Feelings trickle painfully down into his fingers like sparks.

Danny rubs his newfound hand against the glass and looks out at red terra cotta, black slate, blue sky. It is all bathed in a strange silver light, like a filter. A green Quonset hut passes by. All of its windows are boarded up. The train snakes up some kind of wide desert gulley. He checks his pocket; the envelope with thirty-five dollars, his ticket stub, and the note with Big Brother's address is still there. A strap from Danny's backpack hangs over the rail.

Danny pulls himself up over the empty aisle seat and looks up and down the train car. Very few seats are occupied, and the occupants are all asleep. Danny climbs out of the seat. He follows signs to the food service/observation car, which is entirely empty. In the food service area, the attendant rises slowly from behind the bar, as if he is also just waking.

"May I help you, son?" the attendant asks.

"Good morning."

The attendant yawns, then reaches for a Danish in a box. He absentmindedly shuffles the box.

"May I help you, son?" he repeats.

"Can you tell me where we are?"

"We're in the food service car, son."

"Yes," Danny says, resting both hands on the counter. "Some morning, huh? It's really something out here, isn't it?" He smiles at the attendant, who doesn't smile back. So he looks up at the menu. "I'll have a coffee, please. Black."

"Milk and sugar are over there."

"I'll have a black coffee, thank you."

The attendant yawns, wider this time, straight at Danny.

"One dollar and eighty-five cents."

Danny counts out the change. "Thanks," he says and starts walking away.

"And you get a free refill," the attendant says.

"That's great, sir. Thank you so much."

Danny walks deeper into the hurtling, snaking tube and up some stairs to the observation deck. He sits in a revolving chair surrounded by a glass dome. The train is now passing through a town. Each neat little house has a hedge and an outbuilding. Bicycles lie untended on lawns. A bone-thin man in a suit, with a hat and briefcase, stares at the train as he closes his gate behind him. Danny waves instinctively. The man stares up at the sky above the train.

Danny searches for something—a road sign, a water tower, a state license plate—that can tell him where he is. After a few prim blocks, the town disappears behind a barn.

A conductor enters the observation deck. "I'll need to see your ticket," he says.

Danny reaches into the envelope and finds the crumpled ticket. He looks at the smudged letters. Where is he going? He cannot find a destination.

"I'll need to see it," the conductor repeats.

"Where am I going?" Danny asks the conductor.

"To the end of the line," he says.

"Where am I now?"

"You're in the desert." The conductor shrugs, waving an arm at the observation deck windows. "Where do you think you are?"

The coffee is sour and bitter, but it is warm. This is going to be all right, Danny thinks. I'll figure this all out. He takes another sip. He senses someone else in the car, moving toward him. It is a tiny elderly man in a knit cap and a trench coat. He has a long knife in one hand, which he is using to clean the black fingernails of the other.

"Morning," the old man says.

"Good morning."

"Yeah," the old man says distractedly, like he's talking to his knife. "I don't lick nobody's boots." Then he walks away, rocking back and forth in the aisle, still cleaning his fingernails with the knife.

"Me neither," Danny says when the door slides shut.

At some point in the observation deck, having finished the coffee and bracing himself for more conversation with the attendant in order to acquire a refill, Danny remembers that not so very long ago a person dropped him off at a train station, gave him forty dollars and a train ticket and a handwritten note about where he could find Big Brother, and helped him pull his backpack out of a trunk. That person apologized for dropping him off, then drove away, in a car, in one direction. Danny sat for some time in the station, trying to remember who that person was who dropped him off and why. A friend of Big Brother or a friend of a friend of Big Brother.

Then Danny loaded himself onto the train, found his seat, and fell into the deepest possible sleep. But just before he did, Danny remembered that person telling him something on the drive to the station. "The way I see it, I'm not, and I never was, the problem." That person looked clean and scrubbed and pressed but had those hollow eyes that held the depths of the sad sea behind them. "The problem's the little man. There's a tiny little man in the back of my head, whispering to me, trying to get me to mess up my life—and when I did, I reached for the drink. I'm not thirsty, mind you—if I'm thirsty, I'll drink lemonade—but that little man is thirsty. He has to feed his thirst. So he gets me to screw things up, and he gets me to drink. It's a cycle, man," that person said, staring up at a red light hanging from a cable in a downtown crossing. "I just got to ignore that little man, buddy. I won't ever let him pull me down again."

Danny wakes up from another deep sleep. A thin strip of neon beams streams through steel grate windows high above him, slowly illuminating a faded mural where an Indian chief holds an olive branch out to a Western settler, who is holding a rifle. This time it is late at night. Danny is no longer on the train. He is lying across a hard bench in a station, half-propped up on his backpack. His feet itch mercilessly, and his back aches, and now his other arm is asleep. He starts to doze off again.

The neon beams stream into a more direct white beam, blinding Danny. Covering his eyes, he realizes it is a flashlight, shined straight in his eyes by somebody with a badge and a gun belt. Danny can barely make out mirror sunglasses; a row of silver teeth; a baseball cap; a badge.

The night watchman stares down at Danny.

"Hell," the silver teeth whisper. "Ain't it?"

Without answering, Danny gets up, pulls the backpack on, and follows the direction the flashlight has made toward a door. It opens out when he presses on the bar, then clicks shut behind him.

A deep blue fog blows across a city street in front of Danny. The street's surface is a confused blend of bent brown trolley rails, cobblestones, cement, and tar road surfacing. Running like rivers between these are large manhole covers, displaced gravel, and sand. In front of him is a large, lake-sized black puddle. Without thinking, he steps in it. The cold water jars him awake, quickly soaking through the soles of his old boots. I better get new boots, Danny thinks. And they better be good boots. He reaches into his pocket and is reassured to find the envelope with the ticket stub and his last thirty dollars.

Danny stands for a minute in the puddle. The fog's cool mist sprays the back of his neck. A young woman appears upside down in front of him, out of the mist, in the gentle ripples on the far side of the puddle. He jumps back, startled. His boots make a loud, sort of reverse splash, sending an arc of water onto his backpack, which he dropped just a moment ago on the sidewalk.

"Hey," she says from across the puddle. She is shivering; her arms folded, soaking wet. Streaks of mascara run down her cheeks, and her bleached hair is matted to her head.

"Hey," Danny says back.

"Some puddle," she says.

"Yeah."

"Hey, um. Can you spare a loonie?"

"I'm sorry, I don't understand."

"A loonie," she says. "Can you spare one?"

"I'm not sure what one is."

"Okay, then. Thanks anyway."

She turns and slips back into the gray mist.

"Can you tell me where I am?" Danny asks.

"You're at the train station," her voice rings from the fog.

"Can you tell me what city I'm in?"

There is no answer. By the time Danny picks up his bag and works his way to her side of the puddle, her steps have faded. His boots squish so loudly they echo. Danny pulls the backpack onto his shoulder and starts walking. It must be, like, six o'clock, he thinks. Too early to wake up Big Brother. Big Brother's working up here. Big Brother's a jazz musician now. Big Brother works nights, Danny thinks. If I'm where I'm supposed to be, I suppose I'll find him later.

As he walks, Danny tries to remember something—anything—about the train ride, the time before the train ride, why he went there, and why he came here. It comes back to him. He remembers Annie digging the hole. She whispered things into the hole. Then she got him to whisper things into the hole. Then they filled in the hole. Then they realized how cold it was and walked all the way back down to her car by moonlight. Danny was freaked out by the hole. Something about Annie. Something about him. They didn't talk all the way down. She got into the car, and he started walking. He walked for days and nights, north, a little dirt road through a pass. The cops picked him up for vagrancy on the Utah border and threw him in a cell. He had it all to himself—three meals, a hot shower. He was there eight days. Then one day, Big Brother's friend or friend-of-a-friend showed up. Then the train. Then this place.

Then there are loud clanging bells: a road crossing or fishing boats? This place here, Danny thinks, smells like the sea. The blue light is growing, brightening, pulsing. The fog will lift, Danny is certain of it. He will find his way.

Danny squishes along quickly, trying to follow the path of the looney girl, long gone in the fog. He vaguely senses closed storefronts, steel gates, shuttered windows passing on his left and right. A window box of flowers appears—gray in the mist, then pink as he approaches, then bright red as he passes. It feels so good, he thinks, good to be off the train, good to walk and clear his head. I was on that train a long time, Danny thinks. He remembers the two coffees, then a warm can of soda and a bag of potato chips. He remembers recycled air exhaled from little knobs, rain and snow and dead little towns drifting slowly by. His spine had begun curving to the train seat. His arms conformed to the armrests. He slept in short intervals, then got up and walked between the observation car and his assigned seat, swaying back and forth with the rolling, clicking train.

Danny remembers at one point, in the darkness of night, standing in the silver door space connecting two cars, bending down to get a better look outside the windows. There was nothing but blackness and the blinking stars of distant homes.

Now Danny takes a deep breath. Then, a white delivery truck comes roaring out of the fog with its high beams on, honks, swerves to miss him, then barrels down the street he'd been walking up. On the truck's back gate is a large painted fish.

Then a police car passes, slowing down; the officer, in a checkered hat that makes him look like a parking attendant, takes a close look at Danny. He drives away, but Danny's spirits sink. I definitely screwed something up somewhere, he thinks. Someplace between here and there. A major life screw-up. It's not good to go into details right now though. There will be plenty of time to settle up later.

The road opens up to some kind of an open market with rows of plywood booths. The market is just beginning to spring to life. A few people mill around in hooded parkas, setting up their wares. One booth reveals curtains of beads—ruby red, sparkling blue, sea green, bright orange—hanging from strings. Little buckets of beads rest inside bigger bins of beads. Hypnotized by the color, Danny moves slowly until he is standing directly in front of the booth. An old man with a scarf tied around his head nods and continues bringing out beads.

One cloud moves left, and another moves right, and the sun bursts from the sky. Dazzling streaks of color spark from the hanging beads and glow in little colored pools of light in the buckets.

"What is this?" Danny says, splashed in the colors.

As a siren wails somewhere behind him, louder and louder, the old man looks up into the sky, spreads his arms to the sunlight, and beams in the same glow of glass beads.

"This!" the old man says. "This is the rapture!"

"The rapture!" Danny says, spreading his arms as well. But then the sirens wail away, and the sun tucks itself back into the clouds. The old man turns to unloading his booth, and Danny keeps moving.

CITY OF VAPORS

At dawn Danny opens his eyes. Light is filtering into the park. For a moment he feels he is shrouded in a veil or a mist. He is sitting where he sat down some hours before, late into the night, on a park bench under a streetlamp.

When Danny got here, it was pitch black, and he could see nothing beyond the lamp's modest reach. Now a smudge of blue sky streaks diagonally across layers and layers of ripped gray clouds. One of those big boats, all loaded up with red and yellow cargo bins, slogs across the harbor toward a big bridge. Big pine trees lean out over the shoreline.

An empty beer can sits on the sidewalk in front of Danny. The can must have slipped out of his cold hand in the night and rolled to its present position. I really should pick that up before someone comes along, Danny thinks. Then he closes his eyes and falls back asleep.

"Is that your beer can?"

Danny opens his eyes. A little girl is sitting on a stingray, about six feet from the bench. She is wearing an oversized Canucks rain parka with the hood tied tightly around her head. The parka hangs down to her knees. Her sneaker toes suspend her above the cracked sidewalk. Puddles of black water spread around her in all directions.

Danny rubs his face. "Did you say something?"

"Is that your beer can?" the little girl repeats in a sing-song voice, rocking back and forth on her toes.

"No," Danny says. "No. That is not my beer can."

"Can you move your *beer* can, please?" she sings.

"But it's not mine."

"Can you move your *beer* can, please?"

Danny stares at the can. Its open pop-top stares back at him. Danny starts untangling himself. Sometime in the night he pulled his rain poncho out of his duffel bag and tucked himself into it. The poncho is an army-surplus number and smells like surplus cheese. This weather, Danny thinks to himself. This damp, damp weather.

"Sure," Danny says, reaching down. "Sure, I'll move it."

He stands up, stretches, and yawns. He picks up the can, crumples it, sits back down, and closes his eyes. The little girl pushes off and peddles past the bench. She makes a whispering sound as she passes, like the wind or the little waves lapping on the rocks or the dew dripping from the surrounding trees—hiss, hiss, hiss.

Danny balances the crumpled can in the palm of his hand. The big cargo boat is still there, but it is under the bridge. It doesn't appear to be moving. Why, then, is it already under the bridge?

Danny closes his eyes again. He starts remembering things—recent things. The train station at night, a telephone booth, and a cop. Last night or the night before. Nothing is clear, and none of it matters.

"Okay, bud," Danny says aloud. "What now?"

"Did you sleep here?"

Danny opens his eyes, startled. The little girl is on her second lap.

"Did I sleep here? No," Danny says, incredulous. "I didn't sleep here."

"You don't have to sleep in the park, you know," the little girl says. "You don't have to be a shuffler if you don't want to be."

Danny looks out toward the bridge. The boat is moving. Then he turns to the girl. The Canucks logo is shimmering metallic green and blue, a hockey stick, and a puck against the slate gray parka. Her hood is pulled tight with a drawstring, revealing only her two sparkling eyes.

"Thank you," Danny says.

"You're welcome."

The little girl pushes off with her toes again, then gets her feet on the pedals just in time—she veers left, then right, then straightens out. She makes that whispering sound again— hiss, hiss. As she rides past, Danny looks down at the thin wake she creates in the puddles. He looks back at the harbor, but the boat has disappeared; then he looks back at the girl, but she has already pedaled into the woods.

Danny stuffs the rain poncho back into his pack. He walks out of the park, sticking to the waterfront, shielded by trees. He crosses a big road and sees a bus stop. He stares at a map. He tries to memorize names of roads branching off the bus route, but there are so many.

Danny remembers looking at the name and address of the hotel where Big Brother is living. In his mind he can still see the yellow piece of paper. He doesn't remember the name now, but he remembers the sound of it. The Senator Hotel or the Senate Hotel or Center Street or Central Avenue. Danny checks his pockets one more time, but he definitely lost the piece of paper. "I'll just have to look for it," he says out loud. "I'll just have to find it." He walks ten blocks into the beautiful glass-and-steel city. The apartment buildings and the office buildings all look the same. The sidewalks are lined with tree beds filled with short, squat, I've-been-here-all-the-time trees. Every corner has a cop, glaring at anyone who looks like Danny.

Danny catches his reflection in a plate-glass window, stops for a second, and tries to brush his bushy hair from the left side of his head to the right. Startled by the result, he hurries back toward the park—making sure to stop first at a little grocery store for another six-pack. There's one last bill in the envelope. It says it's a twenty, but it has a picture of the queen of England where Andrew Jackson's supposed to be. He hands it to the teller anyway, who smiles, hands him back a handful of odd-looking bills and coins, and puts the beer in a bag for him.

The bench Danny previously occupied is being slept on— so many shufflers in this city!—so he moves farther down the path, finding a new bench. It faces the harbor, but even better, it is across from a softball field and a parking lot. Watching the game means that maybe Danny isn't a shuffler. He sits down and pops open a beer can. It's late afternoon now, with shadows creeping from the big evergreen trees out into the lapping water. I really should be eating something, Danny thinks as the first slug of beer hits his empty stomach.

He turns his attention to the game. He tries to figure out how many outs there are, what inning it is. The players aren't very good. They are fat, middle-aged guys in tight softball jerseys. The jerseys are beautiful, dark red on one team and sky blue on the other. Guys tap grounders and pop out softly to the infield. They switch sides a couple of times. One guy strikes out, slams the aluminum bat down on home plate, and marches back to his dugout. His teammates open an Igloo cooler filled with iced beer and clap him on the back.

*

Daylight dims. The softball guys stand around drinking Molson and Labatt's from dripping blue cans pulled from the ice chest. They stand there, stretching, drinking, acting like ex-ballplayers. But they are not ex-ballplayers. Danny knows this because, in addition to dropping critical passes on his high school football team, he also dropped his share of important fly balls for the baseball team. Danny knows where the dirt sticks to your pants. He knows why parts of his knees still don't bend right. I should go over there and tell them a few things, Danny thinks, cracking his second beer, which is semi-cold, then his third, which is close to warm. I should tell them a couple things about ball.

Danny notices a particular guy on the red team. He is not dressed for softball. He is sitting on the bench, his legs crossed. He has long, stringy hair, and his teeth are all messed up. He is moving his hands a lot. Danny can just barely make out what the guy is saying to the softball guys, who stand around him listening attentively. "Like you, for instance," he says to the fat guy who struck out. "You had it, man! But you were too far off the bag." Then he hits the next guy, gently, with the back of his hand. "And you, man! Your swing is too tight." The softball guys are handing this guy beers—those icy Canadian lager beers that burn the back of your throat and shoot up your sinuses. "Man, you know the game," one of the softball guys says. This guy shakes his head. "Yeah, I played a little," Danny hears him say. The park goes a few shades darker, and the streetlamps turn on above the little group of men crowded together in the softening light. This guy starts telling them some totally made-up story about a semipro recruiter or a double-A manager. They stand there, spellbound, fat and hunched in their softball uniforms with towels draped around their necks.

But then something funny happens; this guy says something stupid or his story doesn't add up. Danny can't make it out. But the softball guys all become very quiet, and they unhunch themselves, looking off toward their cars in the parking lot. A cold mist starts filtering down from the fluorescent streetlamps, and the first shiny lights are sparkling across the parking lot, out across the bay. And one of the softball guys says, "Well, I suppose we oughta pack it in." They start packing stuff into the back of their trucks and vans. This guy offers to help them carry their stuff, but they all tighten up.

Then a park ranger shows up in the parking lot. "Time to get home, boys," he says to the softball guys. "I got to pull the gates shut." And this guy instantly disappears. Danny's never seen anything like it. This guy, Danny thinks, totally played those guys for four or five beers, and then he just disappeared. Wow, Danny thinks. What a shuffler. Danny pulls his cheesy-smelling poncho out of his pack and wraps himself in it tightly, making a little hood to keep the rain off his face. He drinks the last beer—warm now, like the rain—and then he falls asleep.

Well, one night I woke up in the shell of a car
Snowflakes drifting past that long-closed bar
And it don't not matter; cause I never got so far
I couldn't not still dream about you…

Somebody is singing. Danny opens his eyes, then jumps up with a start. Sitting at the far end of the bench, in the dark, is the silhouette of a man, back-lit by a streetlamp, trying to strum a note on a broken guitar. He plays the same note over and over, like he is trying to figure out how the thing works.

Well, them neon lights still glowed through the glass
Schlitz and Shaefer, Guinness and Bass
Now me sitting there, with my frozen drunk ass
Outta beer, outta bucks, outta smokes…

It takes Danny a minute to remember where he is. He was only asleep for a few minutes. Two huge tankers, top heavy with cargo bins, are tugging themselves under the bridge and back into the harbor. The sun just finished going down over there, and the moon is just starting to come up over here. The bridge changes color, from blue to silver. Across the bay a million strangers are absentmindedly flicking a switch or pulling a string, and a million little light bulbs stretch out for miles up into the foothills.

"Hey, man," the silhouette says. "Are you familiar with that song?"

"I'm not familiar with that song, no," Danny says, realizing that this guy is the guy who was shuffling the softball guys.

"That's because I myself wrote that song. That there song is a Hot Dog original. But I can't remember how it goes. Do you know how it goes?"

"I think if you wrote it, I probably don't, no." Danny scratches his head and then starts scratching all over. It has been a couple of days now. "But it reminds me of a Kris Kristofferson song or maybe a Marshall Tucker song."

The silhouette starts plucking again. The guitar is broken at the neck, and he is holding it together with one hand.

"Oh, so it's like one of those country-collaboration-song things."

"No, man," Danny says. "It's your song. You wrote it. I am just telling you who it reminds me of. Because you asked."

"Well, I certainly appreciate that you appreciate my song, but I'm not sure you know what you are saying."

"Yeah, well," Danny says.

"Because first of all, I happen to know that Kris Kristofferson is a movie actor. And second of all, Marshall Tucker was the guy who got killed in that plane crash. Anyhow, I found this guitar in that dumpster over there, and I think if I can fix it, and if I can remember a couple of my songs, I'm going to go play in front of that college bar over there on the other side, and get some free beer, and make me some money, and maybe get discovered. Only I think I need some duct tape. You got any duct tape?"

"No, buddy," Danny says. "Sorry. I don't have any duct tape."

"Oh. You got any beer?"

"No."

"Oh. Well, you want to come along anyhow? Mooch some beers off the college kids? Get out of big park before the vapors come looking for you?"

"What are you talking about, vapors? I'm not a shuffler. I'm just sitting here watching the boats go by."

"Oh, yeah, sure, buddy. I don't mean nothing personally or nothing. I just thought, you know, this is not a good place to, you know, be out late. Because, you know, this is the City of Vapors. And there are some real bad vapors in this park. You know. Real, real bad vapors. Like some seriously evil crap, man. All these bad vapors come out at night, and they look for people. They're looking for someplace to go, man."

Danny pulls his pack onto his shoulder and collects his beer cans. There is moonlight and streetlamp light and little blinking lights around the harbor, and then there is only misty darkness.

"The vapors are not happy, man," this guy says. "Those people walk the park by day. But the vapors roam the park by night."

"Thanks, man," Danny says. "Hey, I got to go meet somebody. It was nice talking."

"I'm serious about the vapors, man," this guy says as Danny walks away. "Later, man! Just holler if you need me. You ask around. Everybody in this town knows me, man. They call me Hot Dog." He hears the guitar string again, fading, muted now in the woods—brum, brum, brum. "Everybody," Hot Dog says one more time, and then he starts singing again:

Outta beer, outta bucks, outta smokes, outta luck,
Outta beer, outta bucks, outta smokes, outta luck....

Then the park's little noises are washed away by the roar
of the city's traffic.

Senator, Senate, Central, Center. Centennial? A hotel or a
street or a district? Danny tries a new route, cutting to the west
this time. Walking around the strange city of modern glass
buildings, perfectly laid-out sidewalks dotted with little
planters and bus stops, the hopelessness of his situation starts
settling in. He stops into a Quick Mart, buys a bag of pretzels
and a can of beer. In the new money, that's another three
dollars. Canadian dollars go a lot faster than American dollars.
The guy behind the counter looks at him funny as he pulls the
crumpled bills out of his pocket. A lady with a boy in a stroller
looks at him funny when he holds the door for her on his way
out.

Danny remembers how excited he was to get here. He was
almost there. He almost made it. Big Brother was going to help
him get on his feet. Big Brother was going to set him up until
things got squared away. Danny was on the up and up until
yesterday, when he lost the piece of paper with the hotel on
it—in the train station, at the open-air market. He retraced his
steps, and then he got lost. And then he gave up, and he just
wanted a beer more than anything in the world. Just one beer
to take the edge off, just one beer to smooth it all out.

The glass buildings give way to a strip of brick row houses.
At the top of a short hill, Danny finds a little neighborhood
park—big fluorescent lights, a playground, benches, and not a

body in sight. Danny sits on a bench overlooking the strange city curved around the harbor like a bowl of twinkling lights. The big park spreads out directly below him. A bank of fog drifts across the harbor and wraps its fingers around the row of trees where his bench is. A sense of panic fills Danny's lungs. I'm never going to find him, he thinks. This was so stupid. This was such a bad idea. Wow. The horror of his predicament immediately travels to his empty stomach. I better try to eat something, he thinks. The pretzels are hard to eat, but Danny makes himself eat them. He washes them down with the beer. He brushes the crumbs from his crumpled shirt. The fog spreads deeper into the park below, moving across the ballfields. The vapors, he thinks. Holy Christ. I can't spend another night in that park. I better get another beer.

A flashlight hits Danny directly in the face.

"Park closes at dusk," the voice says. "Time to move along."

A walkie-talkie clicks once, then twice. But nobody says anything.

"Oh, officer," Danny says. "Maybe you can help me. I'm looking for a hotel. It's the Senator or the Senate or the Centennial something. Either that's the name of the hotel or the street or the district. I'm supposed to meet someone there, only I lost the directions."

"Yeah, I'm going to need you to gather your things and get moving. I'm going to need you to do that right away."

"Officer, I'm not a shuffler or nothing. My Big Brother's a musician. He just got a big record deal. I'm serious! He's up here making a record. They put him up in a real nice hotel. I just talked to him last week. I just came up here to visit him. But I can't find the hotel."

"Yeah, well, look. We got a lot of people out here with problems." The officer flashes his light around the park. "This city's all filled up with people who got problems. And now I got a problem. Because it's after dusk and I'm supposed to clear this park of shufflers. I'm supposed to keep you all moving. You are all supposed to keep moving until you move away. So why don't you keep moving? You can go sleep down in the big park. Ain't nobody gonna bother you down in the big park."

"Okay," Danny says, pulling his backpack onto his shoulder. "I'm just looking for a hotel, that's all. I just can't seem to remember the name."

"Yeah, yeah, go take your problems to the big park," the voice from behind the flashlight says. "And don't let the vapors get you!"

Danny walks down the far side of the hill into a wood-clap neighborhood. Restaurants are closing, but bars are still open. Old gas lanterns hang from poles. For a few blocks, there is a wave of people on the street digging through garbage cans or panhandling or, in one case, standing in an intersection stopping all the honking cars and yelling something about the government. They disappear when Danny reaches a tree-lined avenue with young people milling around on the sidewalks. In a block he hears the familiar plucking of a guitar string: brum, brum, brum.

Now the snow on the windshield is tugging the reins,
I should probably climb out and heat up my veins,
The sun will rise up soon, the heat dulls the pain
And a new world will spread out before me;
Outta beer, outta bucks, outta smokes, outta luck
Outta beer, outta bucks, outta smokes, outta luck

Sitting on a milk carton with an empty beer mug in front of him, Hot Dog holds the broken guitar across his lap. He stops singing when he sees Danny. "Hey, it's you, guy, isn't it?

Guy on the bench. I knew it, man. I knew you'd show up. Here," he says, handing Danny a half-empty pitcher of beer. "Drink up. Nobody gave me any money, but some college kid was bringing me pitchers for a while. I drank, like, four of them. But I ain't drunk. Because there ain't no drinking on this job."

Danny drinks straight from the side of the pitcher, only taking half the remaining beer. He looks into the bar. A group of young women in mismatched college sweatshirts and flip-flops stares out at this guy, silent, a full pitcher and four little mugs floating between them. Hot Dog takes the broken guitar and the pitcher and stuffs them into a garbage can.

"Well, thanks for the beer," Danny says. "I got to get moving."

"Hey, man! Where are you going?"

"I got to find Big Brother's hotel. It's got to be around here someplace."

"Yeah, well, you ain't never gonna find a hotel that doesn't probably even exist."

"Yeah, well, again, thanks for the beer."

"Hey, man! You need a place to crash? Like, I'm thinking of heading out to my place, checking in with the old lady." Danny thinks of the cops, of the park, of the vapors. "You can sleep on the couch. It's safe there, it ain't so bad."

"Couch, great, thanks. But I'm sleeping in a king-size bed tonight with clean sheets and pillows."

"There's supposed to be a Nor'wester moving in tonight," Hot Dog says. "You don't want to be out here when the cold air blows in."

"Clean sheets and pillows and room service," Danny says over his shoulder. "I'm not sleeping on your couch. I'm not a shuffler."

A van pulls up in front of Danny as he tries to cross the intersection. A cop rolls down a window. He has a hairy forearm and a wristwatch.

"Good evening," he says.

"Good evening, sir," Danny says.

"Reason why you're loitering in this district right now? You know there's a midnight curfew in this district."

"He's with me, sir! I do know about the curfew, and I'd like to apologize," Hot Dog says, coming up behind Danny. "To be honest, my wife just left me today, and I'm a little out of sorts. My friend and I were in a conversation about it, and we were walking around, and I think we just lost track of the time."

The cop shines his flashlight up and down the two men.

"One of you got proof of residence?"

Hot Dog pulls a card out of his pocket and gives it to the cop, who examines it carefully. "It's been sort of crazy, you know," Hot Dog says. "My wife, she took a job about a year ago with one of those art galleries downtown as a receptionist, and she met one of those art guys, a sculptor or something, and he's one of those rich guys, you know, and he makes giant steel naked lady windmills and puts them on I-beams all over the place, and the next thing I know she takes off to go live with him on some island somewhere. Can you believe it?"

"Okay, well, like I said." The cop hands the card back to Hot Dog. "There's a curfew."

"Yes, sir. We'll leave immediately."

"Sorry about the wife. Hope you're okay."

"Thank you, sir. I guess I'm the first guy in history to have his wife leave him for a guy who makes naked lady windmills."

"Amen to that." The cop chuckles and rolls up his window.

Danny and Hot Dog walk down the sidewalk toward the park. The cop follows them in the van but stops at the next corner and turns away. Danny and Hot Dog cross two wooden barricades. A mist hangs low in the grass. The moon throws wild shadows.

"Wow," Danny says. "Hey, I'm really sorry to hear that story about your wife."

"What, are you kidding me? That was about, I don't know, like, one hundred percent made up on the spot." Hot Dog starts laughing, slapping himself on the sides. In the dim light, he really doesn't look good. He looks faded. His face is all beat up, and his clothes are in tatters.

"I am good, man. I'll tell you this—old Hot Dog's the best. Naked lady windmills. I mean, that's good stuff, man, you got to admit. But seriously, you got to keep an eye out for that cop with the van, man. They wear you down, and when you're all worn down, they find a reason to get you in that van, and they drive you sixty miles out of town with the lights out. Then they drop you in the middle of nowhere. That's how they keep the shuffler population down."

Hot Dog clears his throat. "Not that you're a shuffler. And me neither, of course. I screwed some things up for sure. But I got to keep my feet firm in both worlds, man. I got to take care of my people over here and my people over there. And of course, my ancestors." Hot Dog sweeps his arms around at the park, the mist. "The vapors won't harm you if you're walking with me. Come on, man. I am the dispeller of vapors." Hot Dog pulls out a bottle of Wild Irish Rose, half-empty, takes a swig, and hands it to Danny. "Hot Dog, the dispeller of vapors. I'll drink to that! We'll go out to my family place right over there." He points across the harbor at the strings of lights, half-blurred in the lifting fog. Danny recognizes the same bench by the water where he met the little girl a million years ago. "And we'll get us some hot food, a good night's sleep, and we'll get you up in the morning, and you'll go find your big brother."

"How do we get all the way over there?"

"Well, you know, there's a ferry, but the ferry costs money, and the last one left at midnight. So we gotta just walk over that little bridge."

Danny looks up above the trees at the ribbon of steel, sparking lights, and cables.

"That bridge?"

"Yep, that's the one. I go over it all the time. There's a walkway. You'll see."

The pedestrian walkway is under construction, so Danny follows Hot Dog, who climbs over the concrete divider and onto the roadway. A fierce, cold wind blows straight at them as they walk single file along the edge of roadway. Danny looks over the side, but only once. Chopped rebar slats poke out where the walkway used to be, and white foam waves churn around in the coming wind and tangled currents far below. He focuses his eyes on Hot Dog's back as he strides with great purpose. Danny flinches when a truck roars past, its horn blasting, but it doesn't hit him. They pass over the great arch and descend the other side. They slide down the concrete arch at the base of the bridge to avoid the toll booth collectors and crash into the woods.

In the woods, at first, it is shockingly dark; Danny follows Hot Dog only by listening for the occasional click of glass from the old wine bottle. When they climb down to the waterfront, there is a trail along the little clumps of rocks, now glowing from the giant bridge high above. Danny watches the sparkling white and red lights and the headlights of trucks and cars gliding over the bridge.

"I can't believe we walked over that bridge," Danny says.

"Me neither," Hot Dog says over his shoulder.

"I thought you said you walk over that bridge all the time?"

"I said I go over that bridge all the time. Usually I take the city bus."

The woods open up to another ballfield. They cross the outfield and hop over a chicken-wire fence. They walk through a parking lot behind a strip mall. All the parking spaces are empty. On the other side of the mall is a street. Hot Dog turns up the street. They zigzag between some little houses, climbing the hill under a canopy of trees. Dogs bark at them. Televisions mutter things and send streams of glowing colors onto lawns cluttered with old mattresses and stripped cars. Somebody yells at somebody, but nobody yells back. The little houses turn into double-wides and then little single-wide trailers, divided by rusting old steel fences, some with razor wire. Hot Dog stops in front of one such house, staring through the fence, half-masked in vines.

"That there's my house," he says.

Danny looks through the fence and sees a sea of flowers. He knows nothing about flowers, but even in the dim moonlight, he can make out every color in the world, a mad tangle of flowers and vines and leaves all fighting to rise above and reach the light of the moon, the air, the bees. Beyond the flowers is a picture window. A woman is asleep on the couch in front of a TV. Three kids—maybe nine, seven, and five— sleep in different positions, draped over the woman and the couch.

"They look so peaceful," Danny says.

"Just look at this garden, man. You ever see anything so beautiful in your whole life? You ever smell anything so beautiful as this garden?" Hot Dog pulls the bottle out and takes a long, last pull. He hands it to Danny. It's empty.

They stand there for a minute.

"Hey, man," Hot Dog says. "What do you say we go get a drink someplace?"

"But it's three in the morning. Aren't you going to go in?"

"I don't know, man. Now that I'm here, I just don't know. I screwed up pretty bad, man. I just don't know. Come on, man," Hot Dog says. "I know some places we can still get a drink. We'll come back later."

"But you walked all this way to see them. You walked over the bridge."

"I don't know. I don't want them to see me like this. I don't want them to think the old man's a shuffler or nothing." Hot Dog scratches his chin. "Yeah, you know, you're right. It's the vapors, man. They get into your head. They make you think negative thoughts. Even me. Even me. I got to dispel those vapors, man. I just got to go in there."

"But I thought you said..."

"What, that the vapors won't come get me? The vapors don't care, man. The vapors hate everybody." Hot Dog tries to brush his hair straight with his fingers. "So listen, man. I'll go in there and settle them down, then I'll come get you, and we'll cook up a big dinner, all right? My old lady cooks up all sorts of crazy foods. Only, you got to wait out here, okay? I got to explain to them that I brought somebody. I got to explain that you're not a shuffler. Plus, they haven't seen me in a while."

"Sure, man," Danny says, "I'll wait right here."

Danny watches Hot Dog walk, very slowly, up to the door, stopping to smell the flowers. He jiggles the front door and walks in. Through the picture window, Danny sees one child, and then a second, and then a third raise their heads, then their arms. "Daddy's home," they cry out in unison. He walks over and touches their heads, then falls to his knees. "Daddy's home! Daddy's home!" They curl up next to him. The woman never opens her eyes. With a strained look on her face, she pulls him over to her shoulder, where he buries his head, shuddering like he's crying. They all appear to fall asleep together again, all together on the couch in front of the TV. Danny starts walking downhill, downhill, back to the waterfront.

*

Danny wakes up on a bench next to a pier, the city across the water now, wrapped in a curtain of hard blue sky. It is much colder. He wraps himself more tightly in his poncho. He watches a line of commuters in raincoats stand in line to board a little ferry. Every time the ticket checker looks away, Danny sees a shuffler jump out from behind a pier and run onto the ferry. Danny packs up and moves toward the ferry. A sign says that a ticket costs three dollars. He stands behind a pier, watching the ticket checker. When the checker looks away, Danny makes a run for it.

As the ferry approaches the waterfront in a new part of the city, Danny is seized with panic. On a clear day, the glass towers seem to go on forever. I'm never going to find this hotel, Danny thinks. I'm never going to find Big Brother. He wonders if Big Brother is even here. Maybe he blew off the trip up here. Maybe something fell through.

Or maybe Danny has the whole thing wrong? Maybe he came to the wrong city? Danny the Shuffler. Danny the Shuffler. Everybody he knew along the way—Stickman and his sister, Gina the hairdresser, Booch and Beano and Lapper, Spotley and Darrell, Sir Henry, Vlad the Impala, Beret Guy, the Governor, Daisy, and Annie—especially Annie—they all know that Danny is a shuffler. They all see right through him. They are going to tell stories about Danny the Shuffler— Danny who couldn't hold a job, Danny who couldn't hold his beer. Danny who shuffled from beat job to beat job, going nowhere fast. Danny the Shuffler blew any chance anybody ever gave him. Danny the Shuffler was a loser who was trying to drag everybody down with him. Now wait until they hear this one, boy. Not that they ever will, but what if they did? What if they heard that, eventually, Danny the Shuffler's Big Brother tried to help him out, and he blew that one too?

Danny climbs off the ferry. He takes a look at the big park jutting out into the harbor. In the sunlight it glitters a luminous green. He remembers the little girl on the bike. He can almost see her out there, in his head, riding around on the sidewalk. Then he starts walking along the waterfront, in the other direction this time. "I still got a few dollars left," he says out loud. He feels people moving away from him. "I'm not a shuffler," he says to himself or to the people or maybe to the little girl. But he is a little less certain this time.

Five minutes later, Danny passes in front of a large glass hotel. Across the street, he sees a man climbing into a van. Two other men stand behind the van loading guitars in cases and amplifiers and other equipment into the back. The man looks familiar.

Danny stands there, hesitant. The panic clutches his throat. He is a mess. He should come back later. He should clean himself up. He should have himself a beer.

But before he can turn away, Big Brother looks up and sees him.

"Danny!" Big Brother yells. "Danny!"

Big Brother comes across the street, his arms stretched out wide. He is laughing. "Little Brother, you made it!"

Danny looks down at his shoes. For many years afterward, he swore that, at that moment, he saw a veil or a mist or a cloud drain itself from his body, pour itself into a sidewalk drain, and disappear. Then he looks up at Big Brother.

"Yeah, Big Brother," Danny says. "I made it."

CREDITS

Parts of this story have been published in thirteen literary journals: "Stickman" (*Stockholm Literary Review* and *The Other Stories* podcast); "T-Shirt Lady" (*21 Stars Review*); "Chucktown" (*Vagabond Journal*); "Red Tide" (*Nomadic Journal*); "Yellow Pages" (*Inwood Indiana*); "Shipping" (*Monadnock Journal*); "Downland" (*Taj Mahal Review*); "Everything Comes Together" (*Willesden Herald* and *fresh.ink*); "Rosie" (*El Portal Review*); "Firewood" (*Other Voices* podcast); "Something to Show You" (*L Magazine*); "Daisy" (*Freshwater Review*) ; "Lenny and Tria" (*Seltzer*).

The author would also like to thank Flexible Press's Bill Burleson (Publisher) and Vicki Adang (Editor) and mission-driven organizations that provide support and inspiration: Pen Parentis, Sustainable Arts Foundation, NY Writers Coalition, Creative Center at University Settlement and BronxLoaf.

ABOUT THE AUTHOR

Frank Haberle's short stories have won awards from *Pen Parentis* (2011), *Beautiful Loser Magazine* (2017), the Sustainable Arts Foundation (2013), and the Freshwater Review (2021). They have appeared in more than thirty magazines including the *Stockholm Literary Review*, *Inwood Indiana*, *Necessary Fiction*, *The Adirondack Review*, *Smokelong Quarterly*, *Wilderness House Literary Review*, *Cantaraville*, and *Hot Metal Press*. Frank was selected for *The Other Stories* August 2018 podcast (www.theotherstories.org/stickman-by-frank-haberle), the October 2018 Story of the Month at the *Willesden* (UK) *Herald*, and the Fall 2018 *Baltimore Review*.

Frank has worked for three decades for New York City community-based organizations. Currently he works with New Settlement in the Bronx and volunteers as a writing workshop leader with the NY Writers Coalition and the Creative Center at University Settlement on the Lower East Side. He lives in Brooklyn with his wife and three children.

Made in United States
North Haven, CT
18 February 2023